May 2019

D1523042

SUNKEN SHADOWS

SHADOWS LANDING #2

KATHLEEN BROOKS

DISCARDED

GREEN COUNTY
PUBLIC LIBRARY
112 West Court Street
Greensburg Kentucky 42743
932-7081

All Rights Reserved. No part of this book may be used or reproduced in any manner whatsoever without written permission, except in the case of brief quotations embodied in critical articles and reviews.

This book is a work of fiction. The names, characters, places, and incidents are products of the writer's imagination or have been used fictitiously and are not to be construed as real. Any resemblance to persons living or dead, actual events, locale, or organizations is entirely coincidental.

An original work of Kathleen Brooks. *Sunken Shadows* copyright @ 2019 by Kathleen Brooks.

❀ Created with Vellum

Bluegrass Series

Bluegrass State of Mind

Risky Shot

Dead Heat

Bluegrass Brothers

Bluegrass Undercover

Rising Storm

Secret Santa: A Bluegrass Series Novella

Acquiring Trouble

Relentless Pursuit

Secrets Collide

Final Vow

Bluegrass Singles

All Hung Up

Bluegrass Dawn

The Perfect Gift

The Keeneston Roses

Forever Bluegrass Series

Forever Entangled

Forever Hidden

Forever Betrayed

Forever Driven

Forever Secret

Forever Surprised

Forever Concealed

Forever Devoted

Forever Hunted

Forever Guarded

Forever Notorious

Forever Ventured (coming later in 2019)

Shadows Landing Series

Saving Shadows

Sunken Shadows

Lasting Shadows (coming later in 2019)

Women of Power Series

Chosen for Power

Built for Power

Fashioned for Power

Destined for Power

Web of Lies Series

Whispered Lies

Rogue Lies

Shattered Lies

Moonshine Hollow Series

Moonshine & Murder

Moonshine & Malice

Moonshine & Mayhem

PROLOGUE

CHARLES TOWN, *South Carolina, 1719 . . .*

TIMOTHY LONGWORTH CAST out a net from his small fishing boat. His home, Charles Town, was no longer in sight. He and his friends moved around the boat with an ease born from growing up on the ocean. They'd been boating and fishing since they were old enough to walk. At fifteen they helped provide dinner for their families while their parents worked.

Timothy's father was a bookkeeper and his mother one of the most sought-after seamstresses in all of Charles Town. They lived on a farm north of the town, right on the river. Timothy had gone to school to learn his letters and numbers. But it had always been the ocean that called to him. He would soon turn sixteen and begin an apprenticeship. His father was pressuring him to enter the business, and he would, but he wasn't going to start early. He was determined to spend the last few months of his childhood on the water.

"Samuel," Timothy called before tossing an apple to his friend. Samuel caught it and bit into it, holding it in his teeth as he tossed out his own net.

"Thank you," Samuel called around a mouthful of apple.

"I'll take one," William yelled from the other side of the boat. Timothy reached into his canvas bag and threw the apple to his cousin.

"Did you see Hanna at the town dance?" Samuel asked as he chewed his apple.

"I think we all saw Hanna at the dance. I'm surprised her parents let her out of the house looking like that. Not that I'm complaining." William smirked. Hanna was a woman of ample . . . apples.

Timothy grinned as they teased each other relentlessly over girls. "You just wish Hanna would notice you," he shot to his cousin before throwing a flopping fish at him.

"Hey!" William screamed before picking up the fish. His arm was pulled back, ready to send the fish flying when he stopped. "What's that?"

"Nice try," Timothy laughed as he prepared to dodge the fish.

"No, really. It's a ship." William squinted and dropped the fish.

Timothy turned and raised his hand to shield his eyes from the sun. Oh no. His heart raced, his stomach pitched. "Pirates!" he yelled as they instantly began yanking the nets from the water. He could see a black flag flying atop the mast. The black flag meant the pirates would give quarter if Timothy, Samuel, and William would surrender without resistance. If a red flag was raised . . . Timothy shivered at the thought.

"Why are they bothering with us? We don't have

anything of value," Samuel said as if trying to calm everyone.

"They're gaining and quickly," Timothy called out as they tossed their nets on the deck and raced to hoist the sail.

"Where's the wind?" William yelled frantically as he helped to pull the rope as their sail lifted up the small mast of their boat.

"I don't feel even a breath of air," Samuel said with a slight panic.

"There has to be something," Timothy said between deep breaths as he pulled the sail all the way open and began to tie it off. "After all, their ship is moving and moving quickly." Too quickly. They were closing fast.

Finally, the air caught in the sail, but Timothy knew it was too late. They'd never make it to safety.

THE PIRATE SHIP loomed large and menacing as the three boys huddled together. They were armed only with fishing knives. Timothy looked up into the grinning face of the famous pirate Captain Lawrence Stringer, or Black Law as he was known by the men and women who whispered about his dastardly deeds in the pubs. He was both revered and feared in equal measure.

He was known for being fair, but harsh, to anyone who crossed him. He smiled down on them with his brown beard flitting in the wind as he whipped off his hat. He didn't look so fearsome.

"Boys, what a happy coincidence we ran across you. We just so happen to be in need of some young boys to help us with our shipment. See, we recently took on a large cargo, and I am in need of assistance. Grab your jackets and come aboard," Black Law called to them as a rope ladder was tossed over the side of the ship. It might have sounded like he was requesting assistance, but the boys knew it was an order.

"What do we do?" Samuel whispered.

"We do what he says or he'll kill us," Timothy answered as he slipped the small fish knife into the band of his pants and reached for the rope ladder.

Once on board, Black Law and his gang quickly surrounded them. Timothy wanted to be brave, but he held tightly to his friend and cousin for security.

"Do any of you know your letters and numbers?" Black Law asked as if they were meeting at a gathering instead of a kidnapping.

"I-I do," Timothy stuttered.

"Good. You're with me. You two, get to work. Do what the men tell you, and you'll fit in fine. Disobey and die. Understand?"

The boys nodded as two pirates who looked and smelled as if they hadn't bathed in months reached for William and Samuel. With no choice, Timothy followed Black Law from the deck to the captain's quarters. Black Law stood tall, well over Timothy's still growing height. It also looked as if he bathed weekly and trimmed his long beard. His clothes were mostly clean, and he smelled of rich perfume Timothy had smelled on some of the toffs who strolled around Charles Town as if they owned it. Well, they owned the fancy mansions anyhow.

"What's your name, boy?" Black Law asked as he dropped into a chair and stretched his long legs out straight in front of him. He reached for a bottle of liquor and drank directly from it.

"Timothy, sir."

"Well, Timothy. I've got an important job for you. Do it well and I'll give you this."

Black Law reached onto his desk and opened a rectangular polished wooden box. From its depths, he pulled an emerald the size of his fist from it.

Timothy had never seen anything like it before. "Will I also get my freedom?"

"You're free, boy."

"I'm free to go home?" Timothy asked, confused.

"You are home. Now, follow me and I'll show you what I need. Paper and ink are in the desk there."

Black Law stood and slipped the giant emerald into his pocket. He strode from the room, expecting Timothy to follow. Timothy didn't follow. But as he was coming to terms with the reality that he was never going home again, a sharp slap cracked across his face. "When I give an order, you follow it. Understood?"

"Yes, sir. Sorry, sir."

Timothy grabbed the paper, quill, sand, and ink and stuck to Black Law's heels as he strode through the bowels of the ship. Timothy caught a glimpse of William scrubbing pots and Samuel peeling potatoes nearby. They walked until they reached the hold and Timothy gasped. Chests filled the hold from wall to wall, stacked higher than Timothy stood. There had to be fifty chests in the hold.

Black Law reached up for a chest. "Help me with these, boy."

Timothy reached for the other handle and together they pulled down six chests. Black Law flipped the lid of a small casket and Timothy went mute with shock. It was filled with gold. Chest after chest was opened and pearls, gold, silver, and jewels were revealed. "We took this off a ship going to Mexico.

Some rich lord or something. I need you to record everything in these chests. By the time you're done, we'll have reached our destination in the north, and it will all be sold. For your help, you get the emerald and a permanent job as my bookkeeper.

His father would be happy. Timothy finally had a bookkeeping job.

Black Law hung the lantern on a nail and then walked away. Before climbing up to the top deck, he turned to Timothy. "Steal anything and I'll cut off the hand you don't use to write with. I'm fair and reward obedience but cross me and you'll live to regret it. If I let you live at all."

And then Timothy was alone. He knew exactly where he was, and from the brief time he was on deck, he knew the direction they traveled. They were heading north. Probably to Boston or maybe they'd travel to London. What Timothy knew, though, was that his best chance to live was to escape —and soon. He knew these waters and knew how to get home. What he needed was a diversion.

He grabbed the paper and quill. Dunking the tip into the ink, he wrote: *If I shall perish, it was Black Law who captured Samuel, William, and me. His ship rides low, and lower shall it ride. No amount of gold, silver, or gems will save me. To my family, I shall miss thee, but I leave one last gift. As the snake's tail sounds, you spin me like a dancing master. He Loves Me So. As I love you. Goodbye and Godspeed. Timothy Longworth.*

Timothy wrapped the note in oilcloth and looked around. Inside one of the chests was a solid silver box. He used the key in the hanging lock to open it. He pulled the lock through the clasp and opened the box. He dumped the necklace and earbobs from inside and stuffed the oilcloth with his note inside it. Before closing and locking it, he rested one gold coin on top of the oilcloth. He shoved it into the pocket of his jacket and looked around. If his memory was right, the rowboat was tied on the opposite side of the wall from where he stood.

Tiptoeing out of the hold, he sought his friends. "*Psst.*" The boys' eyes shot up as Timothy motioned for them to follow. They looked around and then scrambled to follow Timothy back into the hold. "Help me move these to barricade the door."

"Bloody hell, look at all this," William whispered.

"Look at it later. Help me!" Timothy whispered urgently. Together they stacked chest after chest in front of the door.

"What now?" Samuel asked.

"We escape."

Handing jewel-encrusted daggers and swords to each of them, Timothy went to the wall and began prying boards from the wall. It took all his strength but finally, a nail popped free.

"We'll drown!" William hissed.

"That's the plan," Timothy called over his shoulder. "But if we move fast enough, we'll be able to get out and swim to the rowboat before they realize what's happening. I have a note to my parents here," he said, patting his pocket. "If I don't make it, be sure it gets to them. Now let's move!"

William and Samuel didn't hesitate. It was their only option, and they knew it. They'd need to remove three boards to be able to fit through the gap, but time was not on their side. The second the first board was free, water began to rush in. They worked quietly except for their grunts of force as they pried nails and boards free. Water gushed in as they struggled to work against the water as well as against the strong build of the ship.

They had gotten two boards off when they heard shouts from the deck. The room was filling with water and

Timothy's heart was pounding. His arms were shaking and there was no telling his sweat from the ocean water quickly filling the hold. There was banging on the door as the pirates tried to break their way in.

"Hurry, lads!" Timothy yelled a second before there was the sound of wood cracking. The pressure of the water was going to help them out.

"It's going to blow!" William yelled as they swam quickly back and wrapped their arms tightly around a post. The hold cracked open to the right of the rudder as the ocean rushed in. The force of the water tried to pull them from the post, but then it evened out and that's when they moved. They took a deep breath and swam for their lives.

It seemed as if time slowed. Timothy's lungs and eyes burned as he pushed against the current and slowly pulled himself from the sinking boat and up toward the dimming light of the setting sun. Finally, his nose and then mouth broke the surface of the ocean. He dragged in a breath that was half air, half ocean, but he had made it.

Samuel was the first to pull himself into the boat and used his knife to slice the rope attaching it to the ship.

"Stop!"

Timothy was pulling himself up when Black Law yelled down at them from his lodgings. There was a second rowboat, but there was no time to cut it loose as pirates began to jump into the water to catch them.

"You're all dead!"

"And so are you," Timothy yelled back as he grabbed the oars while Samuel hauled William onto the rowboat. They moved into position and even though they were exhausted, waterlogged, and shaking, they rowed for their life.

. . .

"WE'RE GOING TO MAKE IT," Samuel panted. It was dark and they'd rowed nonstop into the city of Charles Town. But they hadn't stopped at the first chance they got. Home was just north of Charles Town and the fastest way there was by the river. They would be safer there.

Suddenly, in the darkness, there was a cracking sound. Timothy was slammed forward and then there was shouting as the night lit up with muzzle fire and filled with the smell of gunpowder. Timothy put his hand on his chest and felt something warm and wet.

"Swim for your lives," Timothy muttered as he dropped the oars.

"I told ye you were a dead man," Black Law shouted as the water began to fill the rowboat. They weren't going to make it after all.

1

PRESENT DAY, Shadows Landing, South Carolina ...

WADE FAULKNER YANKED the tie from his neck as he pushed his cousin Ryker's speedboat faster down Shadows River, heading toward Charleston Harbor. He wasn't glad to be called in for a rescue, but he was glad for an excuse to leave his cousin Gavin's wedding as both his Shadows Landing and Keeneston cousins were ganging up on him for his desire to find love.

"How many people on board?" Wade asked Coast Guard dispatch from Ryker's radio.

"Unknown. We received a Mayday and then heard the explosion a second before the connection went dead. I'm sending you the coordinates for the EPIRB." A second later the coordinates from the boat's emergency position-indicating radio beacon, or EPIRB, pinged onto his phone.

Wade was a rescue swimmer for the Coast Guard. He was stationed in nearby Charleston, South Carolina, and with the location of the emergency call, he'd arrive a good ten minutes before a boat from the base.

The night was clear. Gavin and Ellery's wedding had been perfect in their small town of Shadows Landing. The clear night also allowed him to see the smoke rising up into the moonlit sky. "ETA three minutes," Wade said calmly as he scanned the area, taking in the river's depth and turns. He pushed Ryker's boat to dangerous speeds for amateur boaters, but he'd grown up on this river and he knew every bend, twist, and turn.

"Damn," he said to himself as he came around a wide bend and saw a boat fully engulfed in flames. "Dispatch, I'm on scene. I have one boat on fire, looks to be a fifty-footer. I don't see anyone yet." Wade took in the scene. "There's a second smaller boat nearby. It's anchored. I don't see anyone on it."

Wade slowed as he approached the fire. He could feel the heat from it even though he was still a good distance away. He carefully scanned the area as he shed his tux jacket, kicked off his shoes, pulled his shirt off, and found what he was hoping he wouldn't. There was someone floating face down.

Wade dropped anchor and was already diving into the water. The warm water covered his head before he moved his arms in strong and sure strokes toward the body. It only took him seconds to reach the man. Wade wrapped an arm around him and hauled him quickly to the boat. Wade pulled himself up and over before reaching down and dragging the waterlogged man onto the boat.

"I need a medic," Wade said into the radio before putting his finger to the man's neck. No pulse. The man was in his fifties and wearing swim trunks and a polo shirt. *Fortune's Mine* was embroidered on the pocket. Wade pressed his hands to the man's chest and began CPR, even though by the evidence of the knife wound to his gut, CPR was unlikely to help.

DARCY DELMAR TOOK slow breaths on her oxygen as she dove under the dark waters of the Cooper River. She had a lead, and she didn't want anyone to know it. That was why she had snuck out in the nighttime to go diving—something that wasn't advised when she didn't have a partner. But nothing was going to stop her. She'd found a clue that could lead to the biggest treasure recovery in history.

The Cooper River was deep, up to forty feet in the middle, and she hoped she didn't have to go that far down. She was armed with a knife in case she ran across a shark and a metal detector with a flashlight attached. She looked at her depth. She was twenty-seven feet down as she slowly scanned the thick mud and sand of the river's bottom.

The bottom of the river could only be described as spooky. She had very limited vision. The water had a chill to it that made her a little jumpy. And she'd watched way too many horror movies when she was a teenager not to envision a killer shark or giant squid lurking just outside the light of her flashlight, ready to eat her.

Darcy felt the fear, but she embraced it instead of letting it rule her. She'd done night dives before. She was prepared for anything. Instead of worrying about sea creatures set to attack, Darcy focused on the clue she found and slowly scanned the area with her metal detector. So far she had a bag full of cans, tools, and junk, but nothing from the year 1719.

Looking once more at her depth, she went deeper still. Thirty feet was nothing new to her. She was trained as a deep diver and felt comfortable diving to one hundred feet before needing advanced equipment. And luckily for her, the part of the Cooper River she was diving in wasn't even half that depth.

Darcy scanned the bottom of the river with her metal detector but then froze as she raised her flashlight. The metal detector hadn't gone off, she didn't need it to. She'd found it.

THE MAN WAS DEAD. Wade sat back on his heels and looked out across the water. A boat burned and a boat anchored. Which one belonged to the dead man?

"Dispatch, I'm getting a closer look at the boat anchored near the fire."

"What's the name on it?"

Wade pulled up the anchor and slowly cruised to the surviving boat. "*Sea Runes*," Wade said to dispatch before reading off the registration number.

"The boat's owner is Ms. Darcy Delmar of Key West, Florida."

"I'm boarding," Wade said as he tied off his boat to the *Sea Runes* and climbed aboard. "Hello? Coast Guard. Is anyone on board?" Wade yelled.

He waited but heard nothing in response. The boat was older, well used, and well loved. It was in great condition, which also meant that unfortunately the door was solidly locked. He wasn't able to get inside without breaking in. Wade looked through the windows and when he was sure no one was around, he used his cell phone's flashlight to peer through the wheelhouse window. A large map of the Cooper River hung, and next to it a large map of Charleston Harbor and beyond. There was red marking all over both maps, but it was the X on the Cooper River that caught his attention.

Leaning closer, Wade confirmed what he thought he'd seen. X marked the spot and the spot was exactly where he was now. So the question was, where was Darcy Delmar?

"Wade, backup is arriving in two minutes," Wade heard the dispatcher's voice crackle over the radio.

Wade moved to the back of the boat and looked at the large tub of water set up close to the motor. Wade looked to the right of the motor and cursed. He knew where Darcy Delmar was.

The small ladder that allowed boarding from the back of the boat was in the water, and when he looked closely he saw a glow stick was attached to the base of the ladder. The glow stick alerted the diver of the boat's location.

Wade leaped back onto Ryker's boat and picked up the radio. "Diver in water, repeat, diver in water. I'm going in after her."

"I'll alert the rescue crew," dispatch replied as Wade lifted up the bench seat and pulled out Ryker's gear. He didn't need much as he didn't plan on staying under long, so he grabbed fins, a mask, and a small oxygen tank that attached to a mouthpiece so that he didn't have to strap tanks onto his back. The small independent bottle of oxygen wouldn't give him long, but enough to make a quick dive to find Ms. Delmar and bring her to the surface. The question was, once he had her, what would he do with her? Thinking that she could be the killer, Wade strapped a knife to his thigh before turning on the flashlight and getting into the water. The muddy waters of the Cooper River closed over his head and he began to search.

2

DARCY REACHED out with her gloved hand and brushed the thick mud and sand from the object jutting five feet up from the bottom of the river. Her heart beat rapidly as she felt the solid object under her hand. She'd done it. She'd found it.

She was so excited her hand shook as she continued to clean the object enough to determine it was in fact a small rowboat. Taking a deep breath of air on her tank, she pulled up her swim bag and reached inside. Before she could excavate the rowboat further, she needed to claim it. Darcy pulled out a GPS tracker and attached a small flag with her name, address, and phone number on it. She dove down and stuck the flag into the bottom of the riverbed and made sure it was secure before turning her attention back to the rowboat.

Darcy was reaching for the small brush she carried in her bag when a light caught her attention. It was just a blink of a light. So small she could barely see it through the murky waters. One would think that meant it was far away, but because the water was murky, the source of the light was likely much closer.

Dammit, he'd found her. That bastard! Well, she wasn't going to let him steal another discovery from her. Darcy turned off her light and began swimming straight for him. She'd teach him to stop poaching her hard-earned discoveries once and for all.

WADE HAD SEEN A LIGHT. He knew he had. But then it was gone. Did Ms. Delmar think to hide from him until he ran out of air? There was no hiding from the dead body on the surface or the fact that numerous Coast Guard swimmers would be descending on the area shortly. As for a plan of escape, it was a bad one.

Wade kept his gaze on the last area he'd seen the light and swam straight for it. A ripple in the water that shouldn't be there was the only hint Wade got before a person shot into the light from the shadows and tackled him—as much as someone could tackle someone underwater. But the person wrapped their arms around his waist and he felt them searching for his tanks. They were going to pull his oxygen. Too bad he was using independent oxygen for this dive.

The long hair and breasts pushed against his stomach gave it away that his attacker was female. He'd found Darcy Delmar, or more accurately, she'd found him. And she was fighting him with all she had.

Wade tried to dislodge her as she moved to attack his face. He felt her trying to rip the oxygen from his mouth before giving up and reaching for his mask. He decided he'd had enough. He'd wrestled in the water with his cousins and this little hellion, while doing an admirable job, had nothing on his cousins.

Instead of swimming away, Wade wrapped his arms

around her. He fisted a diving strap in one hand and pinned her neck with his other hand before kicking hard for the surface. His oxygen was running out. He needed to get to the surface. The little hellion didn't give up, though. She was struggling to reach for something when he suddenly felt the poke of a knife against his side right as they broke the surface.

"You bastard! I'll kill you!" she sputtered as she spit out her oxygen.

"I think you already did," Wade responded as he held tight despite the knife to his side. He saw the moment she realized she was caught. Her eyes went wide, and she took in the boat on fire and the Coast Guard who had arrived.

"You're not Leon Snife," she sputtered. "What the hell is going on?"

"I'm with the Coast Guard and you, Darcy Delmar, are wanted for questioning."

"For what? Whose boat is on fire? Why are there people on my boat?"

"For murder."

"MURDER!" Darcy shouted and suddenly flashlights were turned onto them.

"Put down the weapon and lift your hands in the air!" someone yelled at her.

"Look at me, Ms. Delmar," the man holding onto her said as she looked around in surprise.

Darcy dragged her eyes back to the man she should have never mistaken to be Leon, even underwater in the dark. This man had quiet confidence written all over him. His body was lean and muscled. His shoulders were so wide she couldn't see around them without leaning. And how did he smell good? This was the Cooper River, nothing should smell good in it.

"Ms. Delmar," he said again as she drew her gaze from the top of his shoulders that were visible above water to his face.

"I didn't kill anyone."

"Why don't you hand me the knife and then we can get out of the water and talk."

"Oh," Darcy said, looking at the knife she had a death grip on. "I wasn't going to hurt you. I thought you were someone else, and I just meant to cut his oxygen hose."

The man held out his hand and Darcy handed over the knife.

"Put away the guns. She's cooperating. Aren't you, Ms. Delmar?"

Darcy nodded. She'd never been in trouble her whole life, and now there were guns aimed at her and they all thought she killed someone. "Who do you think I killed?"

Hands reached down from her boat and grabbed her. Darcy shrieked and instinctively tried to fight them off.

"Ms. Delmar," the commanding voice of the man in the water said, cutting through the panicked haze. "Let my men help you onto your boat. They need to make sure you are not armed. Help them out and allow them to search you, okay?"

"Okay," Darcy said, going limp as they sat her on her own boat. Her equipment was peeled from her body and she was patted down as she watched the man climb from the water.

First, his head appeared. His wet hair was dark as night and she wondered what color it was when it was dry. Next came forest-green eyes, a smooth angled face, a strong neck, and those shoulders.

"Hey, watch it," Darcy snapped as a pair of hands ran down the sides of her breasts as they checked for weapons.

She heard the man from the water chuckle and turned her attention back to him in time to see his bare sculpted chest and rippled stomach appear. No wetsuit? That was strange. Stranger still was when he climbed all the way up. He was wearing . . . tuxedo pants?

"Who are you?"

"Wade Faulkner," he said with a happy-go-lucky smile that seemed out of place from the stern and serious man he'd been just minutes ago in the water.

"Did the Coast Guard get a new uniform?" God, those pants were riding low on his hips. If they just fell a little more . . .

Wade chuckled as he sat next to her and pulled off his flippers. "I was at a wedding. Okay, guys, let me talk to Ms. Delmar for a moment. I don't think she's going to attack me with all of you around."

Darcy was so grateful when the men backed up. "We need to finish searching the vessel," one of the guys stated.

Wade nodded and then turned toward her. "Can we have the key to unlock your boat? We need to have a look around."

Darcy pulled the rubber bracelet from her wrist and handed it to Wade. There was something about him that made her trust him. "Would you please tell me what's going on?"

"Do you know whose that is?" Wade asked, gesturing with his chin to the burning boat as he handed the key to another member of the Coast Guard.

Darcy squinted, but it was too burnt for her to tell. "I'm sorry. I can't tell."

"You thought I was someone named Leon Snife. Who is he, and why did you think I was him?"

Darcy sighed as she wrung her hands. She noticed her knee was bouncing and she tried to calm herself. "He's one of my rivals."

"For what?"

"I'm an underwater archeologist."

"You mean a treasure hunter," Wade said.

"Yes. And no. I have studied the best ways to have minimal impact on the ecosystem when I make a discovery. And I also want my discoveries to end up in museums, not sold to the highest bidder on the black market," Darcy explained.

Everyone thought she was crazy. She'd spent years working to find this one treasure. She'd been labeled a kook. Her friends called her eccentric. The few remaining members of her family didn't understand her. And she was almost out of money. If she didn't find this treasure soon, she was going to have to give up her dream.

"So, who is Leon?"

"He owns Fortune's Mine Treasure Hunting, and he's despicable. He's the worst of the worst. He follows me and other hunters and swoops in under the cover of night and steals what we've discovered. He only likes the action. Not the years of research and history that goes into finding a sunken ship or treasure."

"And he's stolen from you before?" Wade asked, looking interested.

"Yes. I found a handmade canoe from over a thousand years ago and I marked it with my own small buoy and headed to make a formal claim on it. When I got back with the state's representative and a representative from the museum, my buoy was still there, but the canoe was gone. A massive hole was left in the riverbed where the canoe had been. Three weeks later, a thousand-year-old canoe was put up for auction in a country that doesn't really care about U.S. law regarding salvage and finds. Can you guess who the seller was?"

"Leon Snife," Wade said, and Darcy felt as if she'd finally found someone who understood. "I bet you'd like to kill him for what he did."

Darcy was taken aback a little. "Not *kill* him. But ruin him, sure. I'm not the only one who's tried either. He's as slippery as an eel."

"Who else has he pissed off?"

Darcy almost laughed. "The better question is: who hasn't he pissed off?"

"How many hunters are in Charleston now?" Wade asked.

"I don't know about the amateurs, but Leon is here and a couple professionals. Between the amateurs and the professionals, there's always someone around. The amateurs come and go so I don't know them well, but Leon uses them just as he uses us."

Wade stood up and held out his hand for her. "Can I show you something?"

"Of course, what is it?"

"I need you to tell me if you recognize someone."

"Here?" Darcy asked, looking around.

"On my boat."

Darcy glanced at the boat tied up to hers but didn't see anyone. "Um, okay."

"You can just kneel here and lean over. I've got you."

Wade put his hands on her waist and Darcy felt the heat seeping in through her wetsuit. She wasn't going to kid herself. Wade's large strong hands felt glorious. What she did for a living could be quite solitary and having a man touch her . . . "Oh no!"

Darcy's stomach heaved at the sight of the dead and bloody man on Wade's boat. She promptly spun around, trying to get away from the body, but Wade had her in his arms. She tried to push away, but he tightened his grip. And that's when she threw up all down his gloriously warm and strong chest.

3

DARN, he didn't want it to be Darcy, but the second she saw the body Wade was starting to believe was Leon Snife, Darcy tried to bolt. Innocent people didn't run. Darcy, her sinfully curvy body he was sure she got from hours of swimming each day, was pressed against his chest. He tightened his grip and held her face to his chest. Diving into the water for a nighttime chase wasn't on the top of his list of things to do.

"Oh no," Darcy groaned. And here was her confession. It was so sad when someone as obviously intelligent as Darcy turned to crime. She'd spend the rest of her life in jail now.

"What the hell?" he asked. Wade felt the warm liquid slide down his chest and pulled back so he was still holding Darcy but at arm's length.

Tears and snot ran down her face as she wiped her mouth with the back of her hand. "Sorry. I was trying to get to the rail."

"Are you okay?" Wade asked, feeling like an ass for misreading her reaction as guilt.

Darcy took a deep breath while one hand went to her

stomach and the other over her mouth. Wade saw the second her eyes widened as he helped propel her to the railing. He held back her hair and softly rubbed her back until the convulsions stopped.

"I am so embarrassed. I've just never seen a dead body before. I didn't think I'd be so grossed out, but there was a lot of blood."

Wade saw her face blanch even whiter and knew he had to get her mind off the body if she were going to calm down. "Tell me about yourself, Darcy. Where are you from?"

"Key West," she said as she closed her eyes and breathed deeply.

"I don't know many people actually from Key West. I know some who have moved there later in life. My parents moved to Florida after they retired."

"My father was in the Navy. He was stationed in Key West my whole life. It's how I became interested in treasure hunting. There's a big museum there dedicated to it."

"When did you decide to do this for a living?" Wade asked as he continued to soothingly rub her back.

"Always knew it. I love history and I love the water. It was the perfect combination, so I got a bachelor's degree in history and I minored in marine science. Then I went on to get my master's degree in underwater archaeology."

Darcy was beginning to sound calmer now, and Wade knew he'd have to ask her about the body soon. "How long have you been hunting?"

"Since I graduated. I've found just enough to pay for my next hunt. I'm twenty-eight, and while I looked for these smaller discoveries, I've been studying the one I'm working on now since I was sixteen." Darcy opened her eyes and took a deep breath. Color was beginning to return to her face.

"What are you working on now?" Wade asked, drawn into the mystery of it all.

"Now?" Darcy looked back toward his boat, then snapped her head back. Nothing."

"You've been working on nothing for twelve years?"

"That's right."

And just like that, all the suspicion went straight back to Darcy. She was hiding something, something so big she instantly clammed up. "Was that Leon Snife?"

Darcy looked off at the Coast Guard workers putting out the fire and nodded.

"When the knife you held on me gets tested, will it have Leon's blood on it?" Wade asked quietly.

"No!" Darcy spun around to face him with wide eyes. "You think *I* killed Leon? Oh my God, are you arresting me? Wait, can you even arrest me? It doesn't matter," she said, shaking her head. "I didn't kill him. Search the boat. Take all my clothing. Fingerprint me. Give me a lie detector test. I don't care. Do it all so you don't think I actually killed someone!"

"Wade."

Wade turned to see one of his friends gesture to the police boat on its way over to them. He turned back to Darcy and saw the moment she noticed the police arriving.

"I didn't do it!" she cried as she grabbed his arms. Her hands were strong as she clung to him. "You have to believe me."

"Do you have something on under your wetsuit?" Wade asked instead of comforting her.

"Yes, why?" she asked, her face filled with confusion and fear.

"Because they're going to take you in. They will place you on a hold until they can get your knife and clothes checked out overnight. If there's no blood found, then they will probably let you go with restrictions to not leave town. You're going to have to take off your wetsuit and put it into an evidence bag."

"Charleston PD," a man in a wrinkled suit who looked slightly green called out a second before the boat came to a stop. He was probably in his early forties and his light brown hair was cut short, but it still looked shaggy. He was also very fit, which made his clumsiness on the boat somewhat surprising.

"Wade Faulkner, U.S. Coast Guard and first to the scene," Wade said, identifying himself.

"Faulkner . . . any relation to the doctor that got some of the force fired?"

Well, crap. Wade's cousin, Gavin, had saved a woman from a storm only to find out someone had tried to kill her. That person ended up having a lot of connections, some of whom had reached into the police department.

"That's my cousin. You have a problem with corrupt cops being fired?" Wade asked, pulling himself up to his full height and staring down at the detective who was trying to climb on board.

"Hell no. I wanted to shake that man's hand, but you'll do for now. Detective Willie Chambers. And you are, ma'am?"

Wade wanted to put his arm around her and give Darcy his support. He couldn't. He couldn't interfere with an investigation, especially when he wasn't sure if that investigation would show the woman next to him was a murderer or not.

"I think I'd like a lawyer, please," Darcy squeaked out. "I can do that, right?" she asked, looking up at Wade. Wade felt with his whole being that he wanted to protect her.

"Yes, you can," Wade answered instead of wrapping her up in his arms.

"Is that okay, detective?" Darcy asked as her body began to shake.

"Yes, ma'am. Would you mind at least giving me your name?" he asked kindly, and Wade relaxed his breath, realizing Detective Chambers wasn't going to push Darcy.

"Darcy Delmar, sir. And I didn't kill Leon."

"So noted. The nice officer over there is going to hold up a blanket for you to undress behind. I'm sorry, but we're going to have to take your wetsuit."

Darcy looked to the female officer and nodded. "Can I get something to wear from below deck?"

"I'm sorry," the detective said. "We'll be taking all your clothes with us to make sure there are no blood particles on them. You can have the blanket, though."

Darcy looked ready to cry, but she simply nodded and stepped away with the female officer. Detective Chambers looked back to Wade and pulled out his notepad. "Tell me everything you know."

Wade hated to tell him that Darcy pulled a knife on him underwater. He did anyway as he relayed the complete story from beginning to end. By the time he was done, Darcy was sitting next to the female officer wrapped in nothing but a blanket as her boat was being secured to a police boat. It would be hauled into the police marina and impounded. It would be searched along with Leon's boat now that the fire was out.

"So, this is Leon Snife," Detective Chambers said as he examined the body. "And Ms. Delmar thought she was alone when she went into the water?"

"Yes," Wade answered.

"And she identified the body?"

"Yes, sir," Wade answered for the second time.

"I'm sorry," Detective Chambers said, standing up and wrinkling his nose. "What is that smell? Is it the body?"

"Oh. Um. No, sir. That's me. Ms. Delmar threw up on me after seeing the body."

"Hmm, that's a strange reaction for a supposed murderer." Wade saw the detective glance at Darcy and tighten his lips. "What do you think, Faulkner?"

"Me, sir?" Wade asked. He'd never been asked what his opinion of a case was before. He was the one who risked his life and saved people and then handed them off. He was never involved beyond that.

"You were the first person to see the body and to see Ms. Delmar. You can tell me what you think of her reactions. Do you think she did it?" Chambers asked him.

"No, I don't. But I do think she has to be cleared beyond a shadow of a doubt so that any case made against the real killer won't use her as reasonable doubt."

Chambers grunted as if he'd been there, done that, before. "I couldn't agree more. But I won't know for sure until I treat her as a suspect and gather the evidence. She'll be in jail for a couple days. By then I hope the tests come back conclusive."

"I know she can't wear her own clothes, but what about one of my shirts?" Wade asked, reaching around Chambers for his discarded tux shirt and jacket he'd pulled off before jumping into the water to try to save Leon.

"Go ahead," Chambers said as he watched the newly arrived coroner begin to work. "But quickly. I'm having them take her in for booking in just a minute."

Wade grabbed the clothes and climbed over to where the officer sat with Darcy. "Here, the detective said you could put these on."

"Thank you," Darcy cried as tears slowly rolled down her face. She pulled the shirt over her head and blanket and buttoned it up to her neck before standing up and pulling the blanket out from under the shirt. She then slipped on the jacket and stood looking like something out of a wet dream. Her hair was drying and looked tousled. The shirt and jacket hit her at mid-thigh, which left plenty of leg to give him a tantalizing peek. It didn't matter that he'd seen her in a wet suit. Seeing her and knowing she was naked under his clothes was a turn-on.

"I hate to ask you, but I don't know who else to ask," Darcy said as the officer gave them only a couple feet of privacy.

"What is it?"

"Do you know a lawyer?"

"Okay, Ms. Delmar," the officer said, reaching for her upper arm. "You need to come with us."

Wade watched as she was escorted onto the police boat and handcuffed. Darcy looked back at him frantically as they headed for the marina. She watched him until she was out of sight and then Wade practically shoved crime-scene tech from his boat as he scrambled for his cell phone.

"Where the hell is my boat?"

"It's the middle of the night. What do you need your boat for?" Wade asked his cousin Ryker when he answered.

"I was going to sneak into my Charleston home, but someone took my boat."

"Why would you need to sneak there?"

"Because I have a houseful of Keeneston relatives who want nothing more than to fix me up with women. Aunt Paige suggested Maggie. Aunt Annie said she knew someone in Keeneston who would be perfect for me. I don't want to hear any of it."

Wade laughed. "You're trying to run away from our sweet aunts."

"They aren't sweet. Have you seen how they shoot a gun? And I found Aunt Annie using my thousand-dollar set of knives for throwing practice out back yesterday."

"I have your boat, and you might not get it back for a little while. I need your help," Wade said, putting aside talks of his relatives.

"What do you mean, I can't have my boat back?"

"It was official Coast Guard business," Wade said vaguely.

"And?"

Ugh. There was a reason Ryker was so powerful. He didn't miss the details. And he was ruthless. It was why he owned and operated a very profitable shipping company.

"And, I had to pull a murdered body out of the water so the coroner and the police just need to borrow the boat for a bit."

"Dammit! I liked that boat and now I need to get rid of it," Ryker cursed.

"You don't have to get rid of it. You'll have it back in a week."

"I don't want it back. It had a dead person in it."

"Are you afraid of cooties?" Wade asked, shaking his head. He knew Chambers could hear him when Wade heard the detective smother a laugh.

"We have enough problems with ghosts. I don't need one on my boat. Now, what did you want?" Ryker asked, clearly unhappy.

"A girl needs a lawyer."

"What kind of lawyer?" Ryker asked as he instantly switched back into business mode.

"A criminal one."

"Did she do it?" Ryker asked.

"Does it matter?"

"No. Unless she's to blame for the death cooties on my boat."

Wade smiled. Everyone thought Ryker was so tough. He was, but hidden underneath his cool and commanding exterior was a kind and funny man.

"For what it's worth, I don't think it was her."

"Good enough for me. Where is she?" Ryker asked.

"She'll be arriving at the police marina in fifteen minutes, and then they'll take her to the station."

The line was quiet for a moment and Wade thought Ryker might have hung up. "One of my attorneys will meet her at the marina. She'll be in good hands. Does this have anything to do with your wanting a serious relationship?"

"What?" Wade asked. He was so regretting telling his cousins he wished he had what Gavin and Ellery had found —love.

"I mean, some people send flowers when they like someone. Although lawyers are much more expensive than flowers. If this girl is a murder suspect, then the lawyer will equal a diamond necklace and earrings. Hope she's worth it."

And then Ryker was gone. He was probably gleefully waking up their cousins to tell them all about the murderer Wade had fallen for. But he hadn't fallen for her. He was just helping her out, right? And it wasn't as if she were really a murderer, right? Hopefully.

4

DARCY COULDN'T STOP SHAKING as the police boat neared the marina. They thought she killed Leon. When Darcy dove into the water earlier that night, she was the only one around. Damn him. He would try to sneak in and steal her discovery. But what had happened to him? All Darcy knew was that she wasn't the one who killed him.

The boat pulled up to the dock and was tied. When Darcy was helped from the boat, she looked up and saw a woman in a freshly pressed pinstriped skirt suit with a briefcase in hand, waiting for them at the locked gate.

"Gosh almighty. What is Olivia Townsend doing here?" Darcy heard the female officer whisper to the other officer.

"Ms. Townsend, can I help you?" the male officer asked, stepping forward to unlock the gate that would lead Darcy to who knows where. Jail probably.

"I am Ms. Delmar's attorney. I will be accompanying you to the interrogation room where you will be turning off all video and audio surveillance. You will allow my client a hot drink and some food as well as a fresh change of clothes." The woman was in her early thirties with blonde hair in a perfect updo that matched her barely-there nude makeup, both flawless for two o'clock in the morning.

"Oh, I don't have any clothes," Darcy said.

Olivia gave her a little smile. "You do now. Now, please, not one word until we are settled. Okay?"

Darcy nodded, then looked down at Olivia's designer pumps. There was no way she'd be able to afford her. What was she going to do? She was about to ask, but remembered Olivia's firm command to not say a single word and kept her mouth shut. They were escorted into the police station and settled in an interrogation room. Her attorney left the room momentarily but soon returned with a bag from a very upscale Charleston boutique.

"Here we go. No eyes or ears. See how these fit."

"Thank you," Darcy said, taking the bag and looking inside to find a pair of slacks, a cute top, underwear, and strappy sandals . . . all in her size. "How did you—?"

"I'm very good at my job, Ms. Delmar."

"Darcy, please. But I'm afraid I am not able to afford this, or you," she said, handing the bag back to Olivia.

"It's been taken care of." Olivia smiled and gently pushed the bag back toward her. The idea of having underwear on again after dreading having to sit on the gross chairs in the police station won out and she dressed quickly.

"Here you go," Olivia said, handing her a little bag with a brush, hair band, and some basic makeup in it. "A picture is worth a thousand words. You get walked out of here looking a wreck in nothing but a man's shirt and opinions will fly— and not good ones. But put on your armor, hold your head high while showing a little of that vulnerability in your eyes, and the public will love you."

"Public? I don't care what the public thinks of me."

Olivia laughed. And her laughter was as polished as she

was. "Oh, honey, the public is what will save you if you go to trial. They'll be the ones judging you. Now, I don't want to know if you did it or not."

"I didn't do it!"

"Honey, all my clients say that." Olivia gave her a little smile and then sighed. "But you actually didn't do it, did you?"

"No. I have no idea what happened. I was all alone when I went into the water." Darcy found herself blurting out her story and even the impeccable Olivia Townsend had to hide a laugh when Darcy mentioned throwing up on Wade Faulkner.

"I asked him to get me a lawyer," Darcy said as she finished up. "Did he hire you?"

"Yes and no. His cousin is my firm's biggest client. When Ryker Faulkner calls in the middle of the night, you pick up."

"How am I going to pay for you?" Darcy bit her lip. "I'm sorry, that makes you sound like a prostitute."

Olivia laughed fully. "I like you, Darcy. Don't you worry about payment, Mr. Faulkner is taking care of it."

"But he's just working for the Coast Guard. He can't afford you either."

"The other Mr. Faulkner."

"But he doesn't even know me."

Olivia shook her head. "Don't look a gift horse in the mouth. Now, from what you've told me, they won't find anything on your boat. You should be out of here by tomorrow evening. I'll try to keep you in this room as opposed to a jail cell."

❧

DARCY HAD BEEN SERVED BREAKFAST. The sounds of the police station came to life as the night turned to day. Finally, there was a knock and the door opened. Detective Chambers strode in and set a bag on the table. He knocked on the two-way glass and turned back to them. "You are now being recorded, and I will be reading you your rights for the record."

Darcy looked to Olivia whose face had turned to steel. She didn't look like someone who had sat in that room with her for ten or twelve hours. Her entire person was a display of silent confidence, and it soothed Darcy as the detective took a seat.

"Is this your knife?"

"My client will make a statement and then we are leaving unless you plan on charging her," Olivia said for her.

Detective Chambers leaned back in his chair and Olivia looked to Darcy who recounted the events of last night. When she finished, the detective leaned forward. "I need to know if this is your knife."

Darcy looked at it, but it was hard to tell. Diving knives all looked the same. "Is that the one I gave to Wade?"

"Don't say another word." Olivia cut in. "Detective Chambers, we can dance around this all afternoon. Lay your cards on the table, and we will try to help the best we can."

Detective Chambers's eyebrows rose over his honey-colored eyes. "That's a first. Are you ill, Olivia?"

"It's a one-time offer that's on the table for ten seconds." Olivia sat back and crossed her legs. She looked serene while Darcy's heart pounded.

"Fine. This was found on your boat. Can you take a look at it?"

Darcy leaned forward. "Can I pick it up?"

"Yes."

Darcy picked up the clear evidence bag and immediately saw the blood on the tip. She wanted to hurl it as far away as she could, but this was important. She turned it onto its hilt and looked at the bottom. Darcy then let out a sigh as her body relaxed even though she was still shaking with nerves. "No, it's not mine."

"How do you know?" the detective asked, leaning forward to take the knife back from her.

"Because I mark all my knives with my initials. It's hard to see because of the black handle, but I cut them in. Most diving knives look exactly alike, so I make sure mine are marked."

"Why bother doing that?" the detective asked.

"Sometimes I hire help or I take people diving for extra cash. I don't want our equipment getting mixed up. Take a look at all my knives. My initials are on everything I have. Oxygen tanks, knives, flippers, masks . . . everything."

Chambers turned to the mirror and gave a nod. Someone was going to check.

"My client has been truthful. Now it's your turn," Olivia demanded. "Where was this knife found?"

There was a knock on the door and a second later a young detective hurried in and whispered in Chambers's ear before leaving again.

"It appears you are correct, Ms. Delmar. You do mark everything. We found DD on the bottom of every knife out there, including the one you turned over to the Coast Guard. Every knife except this one, and this is the one used to murder Leon Snife. It was found in your bench storage hidden in a flipper."

"That's . . ." Darcy began, but Olivia put her hand on Darcy's arm, and Darcy immediately closed her mouth.

"I think we can both agree my client wouldn't leave

something like that out in the open where it could be found. It's clear to me it was planted and someone is trying to frame my client."

"Mr. Faulkner and the rest of the responders all stated that the boat was locked down tight when they got there. Mr. Faulkner pulled your client from the water after searching the boat and finding it locked. Ms. Delmar, was that bench seat locked?"

Darcy shook her head. "No, I never lock it. I have flippers and some quick access stuff in there. A couple masks, some emergency oxygen, nothing worth much money. I keep it open in case I need to reach it quickly."

"Who would want both you and Mr. Snife out of the picture?"

Darcy almost passed out from conflicting emotions. Relief set in as it sounded as if the detective believed her, but then fear hit. Did someone want her out of the picture also?

"I don't know. W-well," Darcy stuttered as her mind went in different directions. "I mean, I don't know anyone who wants *me* dead."

"But someone wanted Leon dead?" the detective asked as Olivia put her hand on Darcy's arm, quieting her.

"I need a moment with my client," Olivia stated before leaning in close and whispering to Darcy. "Do you have any actual knowledge on this?"

Darcy nodded and Olivia sat back. "My client will help you, but we require a little help in return."

"What kind of help?" the detective asked as he let out a sigh and Darcy felt pretty sure Olivia was about to get her way.

"Why don't you bring the district attorney in here so we don't have to waste any time?" Olivia said with a smooth grin that was anything but kind. It was more like a cat that'd just eaten a mouse.

Darcy expected to wait for the DA, but the door opened just seconds later and a man in an expensive suit with perfectly swept and cut brown hair walked in. "Olivia," he said, sounding none too pleased.

"Gerald, darling, how are you?" Olivia grinned in a way that made Darcy think that the mouse she'd just eaten was especially tasty.

Gerald shifted so slightly. Darcy would have missed it if she weren't examining the new person in the room. He looked to be in his late thirties, possibly his early forties. And while he was an attorney, he had the air of a politician. Must be the district attorney. Why was the actual DA here and not an assistant?

"I assume you've examined the evidence and know the case against my client is weak. And by now, as much as you are hoping for a splashy headline about already having the murderer in custody, you are realizing my client didn't kill Leon Snife. Am I correct?" Olivia asked with a little cock to her head.

Gerald's lips thinned a little, but he said nothing as Olivia continued.

"So, here's what we're going to do. My client is offering to help you by telling you everything she knows, and in return, you will grant her immunity for any harm done to Leon Snife as a guarantee you don't take what she gives you and try to use it against her."

Darcy's eyes went wide. They'd do that? She looked at Olivia, but Olivia kept her eyes locked on the DA's. The two were in a staring match for Darcy's life and as the silence wore on, Darcy was scared to even breathe.

5

WADE SAT PATIENTLY in the police station lobby. He'd been there since he'd given his official statement over twelve hours earlier. Wade was resting his eyes when someone sat down next to him. He opened his eyes and found his very elderly great-aunt and her husband sitting there. Marcy Faulkner Davies was well into her senior years, as was his Grandpa Scott, who was Marcy's brother, and his Great-Uncle Kevin.

Growing up, Wade and his brother, Trent, and all the Faulkner cousins had been told by their Great-Grandma Faulkner that her only daughter, Marcy, had abandoned the family. They had been led to believe that Marcy didn't care about them and cut herself off from the family. It wasn't until Wade's cousin Gavin had a friend who needed help that they learned a different story. Gavin had sucked it up and gone to a conference in Charleston to find their cousin Layne Davies after his friend, Walker Greene, had been shot. Layne was an expert in physical therapy for gunshot wounds and had agreed to help Walker. While Gavin was asking for help, they learned Great-Grandma wasn't so great. She was mad that Marcy chose to stay in their hometown of Keeneston, Kentucky, to marry the love of her life instead of moving to South Carolina to help babysit Wade's parents as babies—parents who had moved with his aunts and uncles to Florida upon retiring and whom they hadn't seen much since.

Great-Aunt Marcy had tried to keep in touch, but his great-grandmother had told everyone she'd left them. There was no reason for it except for spite. But once Layne and Gavin got talking, they discovered the truth, and soon the estranged sides of the families were eager to meet. And meet they did. When Gavin's love, Ellery, needed help, their Keeneston cousins were there in a heartbeat. And since the reconnection, Wade and the rest of the Faulkner cousins couldn't imagine life without their Keeneston Davies cousins.

"Aunt Marcy, Uncle Jake, what are you two doing here?" Wade asked, smelling apples and cinnamon wafting up from the small basket at Marcy's feet. Her old, wrinkled hand came out and squeezed his.

"We heard your lady friend is in trouble. I thought I could help," she said in her sweet old voice as she patted his hand. "Have you heard anything yet?"

"Not yet. She has the lawyer Ryker hired with her, though, so that's good. And she's not my lady friend. I'm just helping her out. She's not from here and doesn't have anyone to turn to," Wade said, resting his large hand over hers.

"Son, you don't sit in a police station all night and day for just some lady," Uncle Jake said with a shake of his head.

"Well, let me see what I can find out," Marcy said, standing up slowly. She gripped her cane in one hand and the basket in the other.

"They're not going to tell you anything, Aunt Marcy," Wade said sadly, but Marcy ignored him and headed to the information desk.

"Watch and learn, son," Jake said, sitting back and watching his wife. Wade watched the transformation from guard to blushing young man in awe. The officer on duty picked up the phone and a minute later was talking to Marcy as she pulled the towel from the freshly baked apple pie and handed it over to him. Five minutes later and another officer was hurrying around the desk to escort Marcy back to her chair as half the officers from behind the information desk called out their thanks to her.

"What just happened?" Wade asked Jake as Marcy drew closer on the arm a young strong officer.

"Apple pie is an amazing thing," Jake said with a grin as his wife was seated once again.

"We'll let you know as soon as she's released, Mrs. Davies. And thanks again," the officer said before turning and hurrying back to his desk.

Marcy turned a sly grin to Wade. "Apple pie works wonders bribing nurses and police officers, dear. I left the recipe with your cousin Tinsley. We can stay another hour but then we have to head to the airport to catch our flight home."

"So, what did the apple pie learn?" Wade asked with a chuckle.

"That the murder weapon was found in the only unlocked part of the boat. There are no fingerprints on it and it's the only knife that didn't have your lady friend's initials on it. There's no evidence other than the knife being found on the boat, linking your lady friend to the murder. However," Marcy said, leaning toward him and lowering her voice, "the DA is in there now and apparently he and your girlfriend's attorney had a thing a couple years ago."

"She's not my girlfriend," Wade defended.

"Son, I thought we'd already established she's *something*, otherwise we wouldn't be here bribing the police," Jake said as he stared him down. Well, okay, so maybe Wade felt *something* for Darcy.

"Anyway," Marcy continued, "the DA and Miss Olivia, your not-your-girlfriend's attorney, were dating until they went up against each other in court and Miss Olivia whopped him good. He couldn't handle that and broke it off with her. Now he does everything he can to beat her."

Wade's stomach fell. "So Darcy is going to get railroaded because of his ego?"

Marcy shook her head. "He does what he can, but Miss Olivia beats him every time. The word is she has him by the biscuits on this case and is pushing for full immunity in return for your Darcy's help with the case."

"Why would she need immunity?" Wade asked as he processed what Marcy was telling him.

"She doesn't," Marcy whispered. "Jimmy, that sweet young man who walked me back here, was telling me Olivia's doing it just as a big slap in the face to her ex and because she doesn't trust him with anything learned from Darcy's story. But Jimmy and the rest of the guys think your Darcy will be out within the hour. Now, until she's released, why don't you tell me a little about your cousin Ridge? Does he have a girlfriend?"

"Here we go again," Jake muttered as he leaned his head back and closed his eyes.

"Don't mind him. So, about Ridge . . ."

DARCY SIGNED her name to the document that guaranteed her immunity, and Olivia barely restrained her gloating as Gerald leaned against the far wall. "So, who wanted Leon dead?" Gerald asked as soon as the document was signed.

"Everyone," Darcy answered after Olivia gave her the go-ahead. "No one liked him. He gave dirt a bad name."

"That doesn't answer the question," Gerald began, but Darcy was feeling empowered now that she couldn't be arrested for his murder.

"And if you wouldn't interrupt me, I would tell you more," Darcy snapped. She was exhausted and scared. She'd either yell or cry soon if this didn't end. Neither would be good, and she wanted to be out of here before she snapped. Next to her, Olivia smiled and gave her a wink.

"There are tons of amateurs around. They come and go, so unless they're serious hobbyists I don't know them. I can write a list of the ones I know. Now, as for professionals, Jules Discoveries is here. I don't know if Jules himself is here, but I saw one of his boats earlier. Jules Discoveries is a huge, corporate-financed operation owned by a Frenchman named Jules Chasseur who claims he's a descendant of Jacques Cartier, the famous French explorer. However, no one believes him or cares, for that matter, but he uses it to get corporate sponsorships for exploration. And I ran into Hugo Lopez, the owner of Tesoro, Inc., at the marina two days ago."

"And they both want Leon dead?" Gerald asked as the detective took notes.

"Yes. But as I told you, those are just the two I know to be in town. Both of whom I have heard threaten Leon's life before. Hugo actually had him by the neck threatening him two months ago in Key West. Then Jules wanted to cut off his head," Darcy told them with a roll of her eyes. "As I said, he's very into French history."

"Why did they want to kill Leon?" the detective asked before Gerald could.

"Because Leon steals. He's a thief who slinks behind while we do all the research and work. Even if you claim the discovery with a marker, he swoops in and either steals the artifacts from under the water or suddenly your marker disappears and Leon is there with a television crew, pretending to be discovering it for the first time. He sells items on the black market or auctions them from countries that don't care about the treasure's origin *or* the country's laws where the treasure was found. He'll steal it from the bottom of the ocean and hightail it to a country that will sell it even if a government has a claim on it. He's done that to me, Jules, Hugo, and to Cash Olweck."

"Who's Cash Olweck?" Gerald asked, no longer sounding annoyed with her.

"He owns CMO Expedition."

"The treasure hunters with the television show?" Detective Chambers asked as he looked up from his notes.

Darcy nodded. "Yes, but I haven't seen him in Charleston. However, with news of Leon's death, everyone will show up. Treasure hunters may be rivals, but we're a tight group."

"Why does he have a motive to kill Leon?" Gerald asked, taking a seat next to Detective Chambers.

"Rumor has it Leon planted fake treasure where Cash was looking. Replicas. Good ones, and not many, but enough for Cash to get excited about the find. All the promos for the show were about how excited Cash was to find these artifacts, which he believed were indicators of an even bigger treasure from an ancient shipwreck nearby.

Cash was embarrassed on television when the archaeologist onboard revealed them to be fake."

Gerald's eyebrows rose, but then his eyes narrowed. "Where do you fit into this?"

Darcy felt a shiver run through her. "I don't know. That's what I don't get. I haven't made enemies. I'm kind of a loner. I'll join some hunters at a bar every couple of months, but I don't hang out with them and I don't get involved in their drama. I honestly have no idea why I was framed."

"What were you looking for, Ms. Delmar?" Detective Chambers asked as all eyes turned to her, including Olivia's.

"I don't want to say. It's something I've been working on since I was sixteen. I can't have a record of it until I know if it's real or not." Darcy turned to Olivia. "I don't have to tell them, do I?"

"No, you don't. But, Darcy, did it ever occur to you that someone knows what you're after and is willing to kill for it?" Olivia asked as Gerald and Detective Chambers nodded in agreement.

Darcy shook her head. "But no one knows what I'm working on. At least, I don't think they do."

"If your hunt is the motive for the murder, we need to know what it is," Gerald said, leaning toward her. "Now."

"I can't. I have to make the claim first or whoever this person is could steal it out from under me like Leon did."

Olivia put her hand on Darcy's. "I'm worried for your safety. How much time do you need to make your claim?"

Darcy leaned over to Olivia who got the hint and leaned in to listen. "I need to dive again, then I can know for sure and make my claim as soon as the courts open tomorrow," Darcy whispered, now even antsier to get out of the police station than she was before. "But that's only finding the first part of the treasure. I can't risk telling them anything about the second part until I find it."

Olivia leaned back and turned to the men. "Okay. Give my client until the close of business Monday to file her claim. As soon as she has filed said claim, she'll share all she knows about what she's found and why she was diving last night. Deal?"

"Deal," Gerald said. "But we want to be notified as soon as you find it. Call from the boat, and we'll put an officer on it until your claim is approved. Then you tell us what you found and why someone would kill for it. And, I don't want any statements saying you've been cleared. I know that might hurt your reputation short-term, but it will help solve the case if the killer thinks we're looking elsewhere. Can we agree to that?"

"How about a 'no comment' if asked?" Olivia countered, and Gerald agreed.

"Can I go now?" Darcy asked. She needed to get into the water soon.

Gerald nodded and Olivia instantly stood and brushed the wrinkles from her suit. "It's been a real pleasure, gentlemen." With a grumble, Chambers and Gerald Hemmings left the room. "Brush your hair, put on some lip gloss, and try to look happy. We have no idea if there's media out there or not."

Darcy hurriedly did as Olivia ordered and soon Olivia was leading her from the interrogation room and out to the lobby. "Miss Townsend!"

"Yes?"

"There's someone in the lobby waiting for your client."

"Thank you—"

"Jimmy, ma'am," the officer said as he blushed slightly.

"Thank you, Jimmy. That's very kind of you to let us know."

Darcy was in awe. Olivia had grown men shaking and young ones blushing. She didn't know how she'd thank Wade and his cousin. If she found what she was hoping to find, she'd give them something from it. It was the only thing she had to offer them.

"Too bad he's not waiting for me," Darcy heard Olivia say. Darcy looked around Olivia and saw Wade stand up along with an elderly couple sitting next to him.

"That's the Coast Guard man who helped me. Wade Faulkner. What is he doing here?"

"Are you complaining? Because if you are, I'll gladly do this pro bono if I get him in return."

Darcy couldn't tell if Olivia was joking or not, but it didn't sit well. "No," she said more sharply than she intended.

Olivia gave a little laugh but didn't seem offended. "I don't blame you. Call me before you call Chambers after finding your treasure. I'll help you get the claim filed. I must admit you have me very curious. Good luck, Darcy."

"Are you Miss Townsend?" the sweet-looking old lady asked.

"Yes, can I help you?"

"I'm this young man's great-aunt and I wanted to give you this for helping his lady friend here."

The woman reached into her basket and pulled out a pie —apple from the smell of it. Olivia took the pie graciously, took a deep sniff before she turned to Darcy. "Free legal services for life?"

This time Darcy laughed as Olivia sauntered out of the police station and right into a group of local reporters.

"And you must be Darcy. I've heard so much about you.

I'm Marcy Davies and this is my husband, Jake Davies. You must be famished. I made this little basket for you and Wade. He's been here all night and day, you know," Mrs. Davies said as she handed the basket to Wade. "Why don't you two go out back? Jake will get a car and meet you."

"You don't mind, Uncle Jake?" Wade asked.

"Of course not. It's not the first time we've hidden a relative from the press, or helped out a relative when someone was trying to kill them for that matter. It's good to feel useful again," Jake said with a shrug as he took off to hail a cab.

"Thank you so much, Mrs. Davies. I am starving," Darcy said, not knowing what to think about being Wade's "lady friend." Although, it did make her stomach flutter knowing he'd been sitting here all night waiting for her. And she was pretty sure those flutters were not hunger pains.

Wade bent down and kissed his great-aunt. "Thank you. I love you."

"I love you too," Mrs. Davies said, patting his cheek with her hand. "You be sure to let me know when to come back."

"I'm sure we'll be doing something for Christmas," Wade said as he placed his hand on the small of Darcy's back. She tried not to lean against him, but he had that warm strength in his touch that drew her to him.

"Not for Christmas, dear. For the wedding. Now you two go find your little treasure. We'll be pulling for you. And if you need a break, you're both welcome in Keeneston."

Wade said goodbye, and as they walked to the back, Darcy didn't dare ask about the wedding Mrs. Davies had mentioned.

6

WADE DIDN'T KNOW how to fill the silence after his aunt all but declared he and Darcy would be married. A little early, considering just twelve hours earlier Wade had thought she was a murder suspect. Marriage wasn't on his mind after seeing Darcy dressed and feeling her body under his hand. Something else entirely different was.

"Are you okay? Did they give you immunity?" Wade asked as they walked down a flight of stairs leading to the basement exit.

"How did you know that?" Darcy asked, shocked.

"You haven't had my great-aunt's apple pie yet. Apparently, she can get more information with it than the CIA."

Darcy laughed, and Wade had never heard a better sound. He gulped then as he thought his aunt might be on the right track. Or was he just interested because he desired the love his cousin Gavin had found?

"Yes, they gave me immunity. I can't tell anyone I'm cleared of the charges, though. They're hoping to draw out the real murderer by making him or her think I'm the main suspect. They did promise to help me after an arrest is made. And speaking of help, thank you and your cousin for the attorney. Olivia is . . . well, there are really no words. The best I can come up with is a pit bull in a designer skirt."

"You're welcome. I will also thank Ryker for his help. Although, I think I might have to buy him a new boat. I'm to blame for his boat having death cooties."

Darcy laughed again and Wade opened the door for her. Uncle Jake was riding in the back of the cab as it came around the side of the police station. Wade led Darcy out of the doorway, and they stepped outside into the hot sun. The cab pulled to a stop and Uncle Jake got out with a smile. "Here you go, son. Good luck to you two. Let us know if we can help. And a fall wedding would be beautiful. It would give us guests a little break from this heat." With a little whistle, Uncle Jake slowly headed up the alley to the front parking lot, leaving Wade once again speechless. Was this what his cousins in Kentucky were complaining about? They said the town was a little overly involved in their relationships.

"Oh no," Darcy said, drawing his attention away from his embarrassment.

"What is it?" Wade asked as he opened the back door for her.

"I don't have anywhere to go. The police have my boat. I live on it. My equipment is there. How am I going to—?" Darcy snapped her mouth shut and slid into the backseat.

Wade hurried around to the other side and got in. "How are you going to do what?"

"Nothing," Darcy said as she chewed on her bottom lip.

"I have a boat at the marina you can stay on," Wade offered, hoping she'd trust him enough to tell him what was going on.

"You do?" Darcy asked as her face lit up.

"Yes. I'll take you there now and text my cousin Harper for some clothes. You're about her size." Wade gave the taxi driver the address for the nearby marina and then turned back to see that Darcy was nibbling on her lip again.

"I don't want her to drive down here for that," Darcy said, looking a little nervous.

"I thought we could take the boat up to Shadows Landing. I have my own slip there that you can stay at. I know the sheriff so there shouldn't be any police hassles. If the people who did kill Leon are around, then they won't be looking for you there. Plus, my car is there."

Wade watched as Darcy processed it all and then nodded slowly. They drove the rest of the way in silence. There was clearly something on her mind. Every now and then, she'd turn from the window to look over at him and then would make a little noise as if having an internal debate before turning away and looking out the window again. He just wished she would tell him what was on her mind.

How could she take the leap and trust a man who thought she could be a murderer just a couple hours ago? Darcy sighed as she looked back out the window. Food, money, clothes, her livelihood, and the treasure . . . everything was flying through her mind at super speed as she tried to figure out her next move. No, that wasn't true. She knew what her next move needed to be. She needed to dive down and find her clue, hide it, and then make the claim on the rowboat.

But she couldn't tell Wade that. He was a straight arrow. He wouldn't put up with what amounted to stealing from the state of South Carolina. Her fingers were crossed for luck that the clue would indicate the main treasure was outside of the state's waterways. Anything found inside the state's territory was just a mess. The state would want it. She would want it. In the end, she might get a finder's fee or some split, but no real say in what happens to the discovery. However, if it were outside the state's territory, that was another matter. A matter that the courts would decide, and she would have a better chance of retaining total control over the treasure.

Darcy brought herself back to the present as the taxi came to a stop at a small marina near the Coast Guard station. She went to grab her purse to pay but then realized she literally had nothing.

"Here you go," Wade said, handing the driver some cash before getting out. Left with no other option, Darcy followed.

Wade pressed a code into a gate, and they began to walk down the floating dock. "I'm the third on the left," Wade said as her eyes began to count. There it was. It wasn't as nice or as fast as the boat he'd borrowed from his cousin, but it was nicer than her thirty-year-old boat that was now in police custody.

"I discovered sometimes it's easier to boat into work than drive. And if I'm on call, I can just stay on the boat near the base," Wade explained as he stepped on board and held out his hand for her to take.

Darcy placed her hand in his, and he instantly curled his fingers around her hand. She easily climbed on, but then Wade took a moment to let go and when he did, she felt the loss of his hand. "This is a great boat," she said instead of reaching for his hand again like she wanted to.

"Thanks. I got it last year. Let me get you a spare key," he said, using his key to unlock the cabin door. His boat, unlike hers, had a flying bridge above the cabin where she would operate the boat. Her cabin was cramped and completely underwater. But Wade's boat would have some windows in his.

She looked around while Wade went inside the cabin. She took in the engine and the locked storage bench. Maybe the key would open the bench and she could *borrow* some scuba gear. Then later that night, she could slip away and find what she'd spent years and years searching for.

"Here you go. There's some food in the cabinets and some beer and water in the fridge. There's scuba and snorkeling gear in there," Wade said as he pointed right to the bench she'd been looking at. Did he know? Wade motioned for her to get the ropes and she did while he climbed up the ladder to the bridge. He started the boat as she got everything ready to go.

When he pulled away from his slip, Darcy took a deep breath and made her way up the ladder to join him. She expected him to ask about her dive, but he didn't. Instead, he was quiet as they got farther away from the marina and he navigated his way through the harbor.

"Do you know the history of Shadows Landing?" Wade asked finally.

"Not too much. I just know there were some pirates there," Darcy said, relaxing. She loved talking about history and found the history of small towns just as fascinating, if not more so, than the history of large cities.

"It was a small farming community until pirates discovered the benefits of hiding there. The river is deep enough that during high tide you can sail a ship loaded down with stolen goods to our town. There's a little jag that looks too narrow for a ship but is, in fact, the perfect size to hide one. And, it just so happens to be inaccessible during low tide. The authorities would sail on by and never know pirates were anchored there."

"Which pirates?" Darcy asked, getting into the story.

"The usual suspects. In fact, Skeeter, the local ghost tour operator, says Anne Bonny has spoken to him and an old pirate named Eddie lives in his house with him."

Darcy grinned. Everyone had a ghost in South Carolina. Savannah was just as bad. With a roll of her eyes, she laughed. "And let me guess, Blackbeard, too."

"We know it for a fact. They built the church and Reverend Winston has the signed decree from the founding pirates. Blackbeard, Black Law, all of them."

Darcy's heart stopped. "Black Law?"

"Yeah. He was a regular in Shadows Landing. The bar that my cousin runs is said to have been his home at one time."

"Can I see it?" Darcy asked as she practically jumped up to push the boat to full throttle.

"Of course. She's the one I thought you could borrow some clothes from. So, you're a Black Law fan?"

"I wouldn't say *fan*. I studied him in history. His boat sank somewhere around here, didn't it?"

"Yes. Skeeter knows more about it, though. He has a story about the night it sank."

"We have to find him!" Darcy gripped Wade's arm quickly and rather hard from the surprised reaction she got from Wade.

7

WADE LOOKED at her then and she knew she'd gotten too excited and blown any attempt to appear nonchalant at the mention of Black Law.

She slowly let go of his arm. She could see the wheels turning in his head before he gave her a half smile. "Why don't you just tell me what's going on, and I'll help you?"

Darcy knew she was biting her lip, and she let go so she wouldn't draw blood. Could she trust him? "Even if it might fall into the gray area of the law?"

"Are you going to kill someone?"

"No!" Darcy said, shocked that he'd even ask.

"Hurt someone?"

"No!" Darcy said, even more insulted this time.

"Then I'll help you, but you're going to have to take a leap of faith and tell me what's going on."

Wade sounded so patient and understanding that it made Darcy feel bad for not telling him sooner. She took a deep breath and gave in. She was tired of doing this alone. "When I was a little girl, a boat was found off Key West. It was filled with Portuguese treasure. I knew instantly I wanted to do this. I wanted to find a piece of history and bring it back from the depths of the ocean."

Darcy took another breath and then let out a long exhale. "I began researching lost ships, and after a year I found one that spoke to me. We were on vacation on Isle of Palms right outside of Charleston, and it was as if I lived every second of the tale. It was from an ancient book that had been put online as part of a library program. The book was from 1724 and told the story of locals affected by pirates. I read a story of a young man by the name of Timothy Longworth. He'd been out fishing when Black Law captured him and his two friends. The story went on to say that the boy somehow escaped in a rowboat with his friends and they were almost home when Black Law caught up with them and killed them."

Wade nodded. He didn't seem surprised to hear this tale.

"Have you heard this story?" Darcy asked.

"Not about the boy. But I know at some point in time Black Law came to Shadows Landing upset about a sunken ship. Like I said, Skeeter knows the story."

"He does? *This* story?" Darcy asked, excited once again. "This is *that* story. While two of the boys were killed and never found, a third made it to shore only to die shortly after. Black Law disappeared after the rowboat the boys were in went down. There were witnesses who saw it and who tried to chase Black Law, but he just disappeared."

"Let me guess. He disappeared somewhere near Shadows Landing," Wade stated.

"That's my guess. The important part of the story was that he had no ship."

WADE WAS quiet as Darcy held her breath. He could see her

willing him to connect the dots, but he'd already had. A local boy had sunk a pirate's ship and tried to escape home. "But why are you looking in the river for the boy instead of the ocean for the ship?"

"Black Law also had a place he sometimes stayed at in Florida. Over the years, I have traveled there and found reports of him saying his ship was lost at sea because of a boy. But the sea is too big. I have to find the boy to see if there's a clue to the whereabouts of the ship he sank. Was it a regular rowboat? Was it a small sailboat? All that information will help me determine how far he could have traveled and give me a starting point to search."

"Why do you think there was treasure on the ship that sunk?" Wade asked.

"Because I was doing research in this small town in Mexico when I found what I was looking for. It was a letter to this woman's sister in the neighboring village. It was from a maid at the large plantation that ran the area. The owner was an incredibly wealthy landowner. It stated that there had been quite the ruckus at the house when a new *condesa*, or countess, who was supposed to arrive to marry the master didn't show up. Instead of a bride with a large dowry arriving, a donkey was found roaming around the docks wearing a pearl necklace. Attached was a letter from Black Law, apologizing for the fact that the master will need to find a new bride. It was also said Black Law left some gold coins, but those never made it to the master."

Wade listened to the story and it made sense. "You think the ship was laden with a rich dowry and sunk on its way . . . to where?"

Darcy was practically bouncing around. "Boston."

"Why Boston?" Wade asked as he listened closely to her story.

"I went to Boston and researched. Massachusetts has been remarkable about preserving history. I found a court order sentencing a man to hard labor for, in today's language, laundering pirated goods. For a year, I studied everything I could about this man and discovered he was basically a fence for expensive fabrics for wealthy Bostonians all the way down to supplying food for the poor. All supplied by pirates, including . . ."

Darcy turned her palms up as she fluttered her hands with excitement. "Black Law," Wade said, filling in the gap.

"Exactly."

"So you think Black Law was on his way to Boston to launder the dowry of some countess when he pressed Timothy Longworth into service. Timothy escaped when the ship sank but he had enough knowledge about the pirate that Black Law hunted him down. Is that right?" Wade asked as he tried to envision the river he was cruising up as if it were 1719. They were approaching the location of the murder and he saw when Darcy realized it. Her whole body went tense even though all the boats were now gone.

"Yes, but there's more. I visited the boys' small town, too. It's just right up here. I found reports that William, Timothy's cousin, had made it to shore before he died from a bullet wound. He told his aunt and uncle, Timothy's parents, that Timothy had a note for them in his pocket that was important, but he couldn't get it when he was escaping."

"What was the note?" Wade asked as he got into the story.

"I don't know. No one does. It was just a small aside I read about and as far as I know, nothing happened after that."

"What about when they found his body?"

"His body was never found. When I was diving last

night, I was looking for that note," Darcy said, lowering her voice even though no one was around.

Wade had to admire her tenacity. She wasn't one to give up. "Did you find it?"

Darcy shook her head. "But I found something."

Wade turned slowly so he could look at her. "Really? What did you find?"

"A very old rowboat. I tagged it with my GPS marker, but I can't yet verify its provenance. If it's as old as I think it is, then I might have found Timothy Longworth."

Wade knew he was staring. He couldn't believe it. Shadows Landing was full of tales of sunken treasure, buried treasure, or pirate ghosts. He'd never believed them before. But now . . . they needed to see if what Darcy had found was a centuries-old rowboat or something more modern.

"Who else knew you were looking for Black Law's treasure?" Wade asked as suddenly last night was beginning to make sense.

"No one. At least not that I knew of. But I've had a feeling I was being followed. That's why I thought you were Leon when I saw you underwater. I thought he'd somehow figured out I was onto something big."

Wade thought for a moment, but he already knew the answer. "Someone else knows what you're looking for, and they're willing to kill for it."

DARCY SWALLOWED HARD. She'd come to that realization as well. It was another reason she wanted Wade to know the truth. "I think so, too. I wanted you to know in case something happens to me."

"Nothing will happen to you because I'm not leaving

your side until we find out who is behind this. I'm calling in some vacation time."

"Vacation time?" Darcy asked as her heart sped up. He wanted to protect her.

"There are only two ways to end this threat against you," Wade said as he sped the boat up and veered sharply around a corner. "One, we find the person responsible for killing Leon. However, there isn't nearly enough evidence to provide a lead right now."

"What's the second option?" Darcy asked.

"We find the treasure."

8

WADE COULDN'T BELIEVE he'd said that. *Find the treasure*. As if there was really sunken treasure people were being murdered for. But there was a part of him that believed it could actually be true.

"Really?" Darcy asked stunned.

He'd said it mainly so he could spend time with her and make sure she was safe. They'd dive a couple of times together. See there was nothing at the bottom of the river and he would keep her safe.

"Sure. So, what do you want to do first?" Wade asked as he approached Shadows Landing. The look of pure happiness on Darcy's face meant going along with this wild goose chase was worth it.

"Can you introduce me to Skeeter? I've learned there's a grain of truth in all of the old ghost stories. Tonight I'd like to go back to the dive and see what I can find. I told Olivia and Detective Chambers I would let them know the second I find something."

The way Darcy snapped her mouth shut made him realize there was more to this story. Even though she'd told him all she'd done and all of her theories, there was something she was holding back.

"Sure. At this time of day, Skeeter will be at the bar I was telling you about."

"The bar that is rumored to have belonged to Black Law."

"Oh, it's more than just a rumor. Harper will show you."

DARCY LOOKED AROUND in awe as they walked out of the Shadows Landing Marina, cut through a park, and popped out on Main Street. The town was small. No more than a couple of city blocks. But it was cute and old. The old buildings are what gave the town a feel that it was stuck between the past and the present.

Darcy looked to her right and saw Gil's Grub and Gas. She looked to the left and her stomach rumbled at the smell coming from the Pink Pig BBQ. But it was what was next to the two buildings that caught her attention.

"Next to the Pink Pig is the historical society. The guy who runs it, *Dr.* Stephen Adkins, is a stuck-up prick, but he knows his history. It would be a good place to do some research. As well as across the street at the Daughters of Shadows Landing. Some of the members there claim the heritage of a pirate or two," Wade told her as if he could see her already veering toward the old buildings.

"My cousin's bar is there," he said, pointing to an old brick building painted a dark gray. "And my other cousin, Tinsley, has an art studio directly across the street and next to the historical society."

That was great and all, but the chance to explore Black Law's actual house was too much of a pull. Darcy practically bounded to the door as Wade hurried to catch up. Darcy opened the thick wooden door and stepped into the dim interior. She had to admit it was a disappointment. It wasn't as if she expected Black Law to step from the shadows, but it was a little of a shock when a big man, well over six feet wearing nothing but overalls and a hat that said *COCKS* on it, stumbled out of the shadows instead. Apparently, he was a fan of the University of South Carolina football team.

"Ahoy there!" he bellowed as he waved a hand with a missing finger as an impressive beard shook with his call.

Darcy stood with her mouth open as he stumbled forward.

"Ahoy, Gator," Wade called out in greeting from behind Darcy. "Have a good catch today?"

"You betcha. Ol' Bubba is feeling real feisty. He got into Miss Ruby's kitchen somehow. She came home from church and found him eating her freshly made red velvet cake. She thought he'd eaten a dog or something with all the red, but luckily we figured out it was the cake," the man who apparently went by the name Gator told Wade.

"Who's Bubba?" Darcy asked.

"A big ol' gator. Don't worry. He's only mean if he's in a mood. But he was sweet as a kitten after having Miss Ruby's cake. And Miss Ruby paid me well and even gave me one of her apple pies. I'd do anything for a slice of that pie."

"What is it with apple pie?" Darcy whispered as she shook her head in confusion.

"It's darn near transcendent, and I don't mean in Immanuel Kant's way, but more along the lines of Plato's ideas on divine objects that transcend this world," Gator said as he hooked his thumbs under the straps of his overalls.

"Where the hell did that come from?" a woman from

behind the bar asked as she threw a wet rag at Gator that hit him on the side of his face.

Gator shrugged. "I spend a lot of time waitin' on gators to show themselves so I went to the library and Miss Allison recommended this book on philosophy. It's really got me thinking"—he scratched his head—"though it's not nearly as entertaining as the latest graphic novel. But it got me thinking, all philosophical like, about my legacy. I think I should write a graphic novel about a new kind of hero— Gatorman. He rescues damsels in distress and towns held hostage by mutant alligators from the murky water's deepest depths."

"Go for it," Wade said with a grin as he placed his hand on the small of Darcy's back. She unconsciously leaned back into his hand as the bartender's eyes grew wide.

"Wade," the woman behind the bar said slowly. "Who's the girl you have your hand on?"

Uh-oh. Darcy never thought to ask if Wade had a girlfriend, but why would she? It wasn't as if they were together, even if she wished they were.

"Darcy Delmar, meet my cousin Harper Faulkner. Owner of the bar and Black Law's former house."

"Dammit, Wade. Did you bring me another ghost freak? Skeeter's bad enough." Harper snapped her head in the direction of a man in worn-out khakis with an *I Believe in Ghosts* T-shirt. Harper's brown hair had some blonde highlights in it that stood out under the bar lights along with her don't-mess-with-me attitude. "The last one tried to get married to Black Law's ghost here."

"Married to a ghost? Are you serious?" Darcy blurted out.

Harper raised one eyebrow over her dark green eyes and

stared her down. "So, you don't believe you can have sex
with a ghost or get married to one?"

"No," Darcy said instantly. "Is that a thing?"

"Oh, it's a thing. But most ghosts wait for the ghosts of
their loved ones and don't bother mortals. They believe
themselves superior to us mere mortals," the man she
guessed to be Skeeter said as he came to the bar to join them.

"If you're not a ghostie, then what's going on?" Harper
asked, never once saying it was nice to meet her.

"Didn't Ryker, Great-Aunt Marcy, or Uncle Jake tell you
what's going on?" Wade asked, pulling out a wooden bar
stool for Darcy.

"Just that you had a Coast Guard emergency and you
saved a woman . . . *oh*."

"Hi. I'm the woman," Darcy said, holding out her hand
to shake Harper's. "He tried to save someone else, but he's
dead. Luckily they let me out of jail." Darcy dropped her
hand when Harper just stared at her.

Gator took a giant step backward and Skeeter scooted to
a barstool a little farther away.

"I didn't kill him. That's why they released me. I mean, I
could have killed the thieving jerk, but I didn't. I'm actually
quite nice. I don't like killing things." Darcy snapped her
mouth shut. She was blowing it.

"So, you kill things but don't like it?" Harper asked
slowly as her hand slowly grabbed an ice pick.

"I mean like spiders! I've never killed an actual person.
That was my dad. He's the only one who killed people."
Darcy shook her head. "In the military. Only bad guys."

Suddenly Harper broke out in a loud laugh. She
dropped the ice pick and poured a shot of tequila. "Here,
you need this."

Darcy took the shot and tossed it back. It burned, and she sputtered, but it brought her back from the hole she'd dug herself. "I'm sorry. Let me start over. My name is Darcy Delmar. I am searching for a treasure that once belonged to Black Law. I don't want to have sex with him. I'd rather have sex with Wade—" Darcy's mouth slammed shut again, and Harper poured her another shot. Darcy grabbed it and tossed it back. It didn't even burn this time.

WADE WAS HOLDING BACK LAUGHTER. He felt bad about it, but he'd never seen anyone stumble through a simple introduction so badly before. He found it adorable. And he was also incredibly turned on. Darcy wanted to have sex with him, and the feeling was mutual. Very mutual.

He also saw the way Darcy plopped onto the stool, took the bottle from Harper and poured another shot. "Okay there," Wade said, taking the shot from her and tossing it back himself. "Darcy, no one will be stealing the treasure here, right guys?"

"Are you sure she ain't no murderer?" Gator asked as he eyed her suspiciously.

"Fairly sure," Wade said and then grinned when Darcy skewered him with a look. "You can't be mad at me. You want me too badly," Wade whispered for her ears only. Her face flushed bright red.

"I know all about Black Law," Skeeter said, moving closer.

"What about the night his boat sank, and he killed the boy Timothy Longworth?" Darcy asked, clearly forgetting her embarrassment.

"Ah, I know the story well," Skeeter said.

"Well, come on then, Skeeter," Harper said with a roll of her eyes at Skeeter's dramatic pause.

"A beer would go a long way in helping me remember." He grinned. Harper rolled her eyes and filled up a mug. "Ah, the memory is clear now. The story goes that one night, almost as dawn broke, Black Law and about ten of his men arrived in Shadows Landing in a rowboat. Black Law stormed through town waking people with his ranting. He claimed a boy had sunk his ship."

"Timothy Longworth," Darcy whispered. Wade saw her move to the edge of her stool in anticipation. "What was on the ship?" Darcy eagerly asked.

"Black Law claimed it was filled with the finest dowry ever seen for the countess of something or another. Said she was the plainest woman ever seen so the dowry was supposed to make up for it," Skeeter snickered. "Then Black Law proceeded to get drunk, and as people began to question him, he pulled out a wooden box and opened it, revealing the largest emerald anyone had ever seen."

That's right. Wade couldn't remember all of the story, but now it was coming back to him. "Isn't there some legend about that emerald?"

"Yes. They say Black Law hid it in his house. No one has ever been able to find it," Skeeter answered.

"But what about his ship? Where did it go down?" Darcy asked, ignoring the fact there could be a massive emerald right here in this bar.

"The story goes Black Law bemoaned the loss, as it was only two leagues from here off what is now the Isle of Palms."

Darcy silently reached for Wade's arm and squeezed it hard. Skeeter's story must have meant something to her, and he was excited for her. He could see she was at the edge of her seat, energy humming through her body.

"Where did you learn this?" Darcy asked Skeeter.

"It's all in the historical society. You just have to know where to look in the archives," Skeeter told her.

"Can you show me?"

"Can you get me another beer?"

Darcy whipped around to look at Wade. "Can I borrow five dollars? I'll pay you back when my purse gets released from the evidence lock-up."

Wade didn't care about the five dollars. Suddenly her fantasy tale of pirates and treasure was starting to sound a little more real. He pushed five dollars over to Harper who poured two more beers for Skeeter.

Skeeter toasted Darcy and Wade and then said, "I'll meet you there tomorrow at ten in the morning."

"Do you really think there's a missing emerald here?" Harper asked after Skeeter and Gator went to play darts.

"Could be. I've found plenty of articles and diary entries supporting the fact that Black Law did steal a massive dowry," Darcy told Wade's cousin.

"We might have to look for it," Harper said, surprising Wade. Harper had always been a cynic. He was surprised she wasn't calling the whole thing a stupid story.

"So," Wade began as Harper placed her elbows on the bar top, "I have a favor."

"Does this have to do with Darcy's things being in police impound?"

"Yes. Can she borrow some clothes?"

Harper shook her head. "Home for homeless girlfriends. I swear. Between you and Gavin, can't someone bring home a girl that has her own things?"

He saw Darcy fold under the scrutiny. "Harper," he said, his voice heavy with warning.

"Did she murder someone, too?" Darcy asked, referring to Gavin's new wife, Ellery.

"She was cleared of it," Harper said as she laughed. "So, what are you doing in Shadows Landing?" she asked as she held Darcy's eye. Wade wanted to come to her defense, but Darcy squeezed his arm, letting him know she would handle his cousin.

"It's a long story," Darcy told her.

"And I want to hear it."

9

DARCY LEANED BACK from the bar after telling Harper about the previous night. Harper hadn't interrupted. She hadn't asked questions. Instead, she was quiet until a brilliant smile broke out over her face. "Any woman who goes after my cousin with a knife is a friend of mine. He used to pull my pigtails when I was young."

"You'll help?" Darcy asked way more hopefully than she wanted to admit. It felt good to be believed.

"Sure thing. Provided you help me look for that emerald."

"I'd love to," Darcy said, meaning it.

"I'll grab some things for you and be right back."

Darcy turned to Wade and smiled. "She believed me."

"Everyone will believe you. There's no story too crazy not to be believed in Shadows Landing."

Darcy took a deep breath. She was energized and ready to go. She was with people who believed her and weren't trying to steal the treasure out from under her . . . as far as she could tell. But she was still anxious. She needed to do something and fast. If Black Law's life in Shadows Landing was common knowledge, whoever did kill Leon would know about the treasure, and it would only be a matter of time before they showed up.

"Hey, Skeeter," Darcy called out as Skeeter and Gator both turned around. "What would it cost me for you to not repeat Black Law's story to anyone for the next month?"

"How about if you find the treasure, you give a shout-out to me and my ghost tours for helping with your research," Skeeter suggested.

"That's it?" Darcy asked, surprised. She thought he'd want money. All the investors and hangers-on around treasure hunting always wanted a piece of the pie.

"No."

Ah, well, here's the money angle. "What else?" Darcy asked.

"A case of beer would be nice."

Wade chuckled next to her as Darcy hurriedly agreed. "I can't believe that's all he asked for."

"No one in Shadows Landing is after your discovery. We'll help in any way. Speaking of help. I've noticed your leg hasn't stopped bouncing. Are you wanting to dive soon?"

"Would you mind if we go now? I'm not hungry or tired anymore. I don't think I'll be able to rest until I find what I am looking for and have a court order in hand." Darcy looked at the clock. It was after six in the evening already. Just over fourteen hours and the courthouse would be open.

"No problem. I have energy bars on the boat that we can eat before we dive."

"You don't have to dive," Darcy insisted.

"I'm not letting you go down there alone. End of discussion."

"You can't end a discussion you don't have a right to be in," Darcy said as Harper set a duffle bag on the bar top.

"Don't waste your breath. My brother and cousins never listen when we girls tell them to butt out. Just ignore them and do your thing. Do you need any help? I close up early on Sundays."

"Wouldn't hurt to have a lookout," Wade suggested, but Harper was looking to Darcy for an answer and Darcy really appreciated that.

"Wade is right," she said with a roll of her eyes. "A lookout would be good, but I don't want to wait. I can give you the coordinates, and you can meet us after you've closed."

"Sounds good. I'll see you around ten. Will you still be out there by then?"

"Yes. It'll take a little while for me to get everything together. You don't happen to have a wetsuit in there, do you?" Darcy asked. The need to get underwater was almost overwhelming.

"Wade, watch the bar for a second, and I'll take Darcy to my house and grab more things. I only stay upstairs if it's been a super late night, so the clothing selection I have to offer you is pretty sparse."

"Great, thanks," Darcy said, giving Wade a smile as she moved to leave. She figured if they hurried out, he'd be stuck watching the bar.

Harper was already around the bar and leading Darcy out the back door before Wade could protest too loudly. "Now that we're alone, you can tell me what's really going on with my cousin."

"What? Nothing." Darcy's voice cracked and she was suddenly interested in the sandy grass under her feet as they moved through a gate in the back fence.

"Right. He's only taking a leave from work to help you out and *nothing* is going on," Harper said sarcastically.

"It's just that I have a lot on my mind right now, and no matter how attractive he is . . . who's that?" Darcy asked quietly as they approached a house.

"My other cousin, Ridge. He's a builder and is building a new front porch for me. He's single, too." Harper winked at her.

"No thanks. Wade is—" Darcy cut off what she was going to say and Harper just laughed.

"Ridge, meet Wade's girl, Darcy."

"Wade has a girl? When did that happen?" Ridge was the same height as Wade, only he had slightly lighter green eyes. His brown hair was short, and he wore jeans and a tight white T-shirt that was covered in wood shavings.

"Darcy Delmar, this is Ridge Faulkner," Harper said, introducing them. "And it happened last night when he thought she murdered someone. Don't worry, she didn't do it."

Darcy didn't know whether to love or hate Harper as Ridge just looked at her and then shrugged. "Nice to meet you. After hearing Wade talk last night, I was afraid he'd bring home some boring girl to settle down with. Good thing I was wrong."

"What does that mean?" Darcy asked Harper as they made their way to her bedroom.

"Oh, nothing. The guys were teasing Wade because he said he was ready for something serious. Wade is a really easy-going fun guy so they didn't believe him. Tinsley and I did, though. Wade may be the fun one, but underneath it, he's always the one who wanted a deeper connection with people. Underneath that party-guy attitude is someone who would rather be one-on-one and share things. His past girlfriends never shut up about how great he was." Harper rolled her eyes and pulled out a wetsuit, a swimsuit, and a few basics before tossing them to her. "Are these okay?"

"Perfect," Darcy said as she put them in the duffle bag. And maybe Wade was too, but right now she couldn't find out. Not when everything she'd been working on her whole life was within her grasp.

IT WAS STILL SLIGHTLY light out when they dropped anchor near the location of the GPS beacon. Wade and Darcy looked around as if they thought someone was following them. "Do you think it's safe to dive?" Darcy asked him.

"We can wait until later if you'd like," Wade suggested but felt better going down while they still had the setting sunlight to make it easier to see underwater. Not that it would help much in the murky water.

"No, I want my claim. We'll call Olivia and the detective as soon as I determine that this is it."

"Then let's change. I'll stay out here and keep watch," Wade suggested as they climbed down from the bridge. Darcy went into the cabin, and Wade pulled off his T-shirt and stepped into his wetsuit. He left it hanging at the waist as he checked his scuba gear. He'd need to get more oxygen if they were to dive again the next day. Luckily, he had enough for the night.

"I'm . . ." Darcy paused, and he saw her eyes linger on his bare chest, "ready."

If he didn't get it together, he'd be *ready* too. He had to turn his eyes from her curves as he put his arms into the wetsuit and reached behind to zip it up.

"Do you need help with your gear?" Wade asked as he equally hoped she'd say *yes* so he could touch her again and *no* because it might prove embarrassing if she looked any farther down than his chest.

"I've got it." Darcy paused. "Do you think we should arm ourselves in case they come back?"

"Already got it covered," Wade said as he strapped a knife to his forearm and another to his thigh. He finally turned around and saw that Darcy looked relieved that he was armed. "I've got your back. You do what you need to do."

"Okay then," she said, grabbing an underwater bag they'd filled with tools, including a small hand-held metal detector they'd borrowed from Gator. "I'm ready."

Wade waited for Darcy to enter the water before locking his boat up tight and jumping in. He gave her a nod and she went under.

DARCY KEPT the flashlight on even though for the first little bit of the dive she didn't need it. Wade swam close behind her and off to her side. She felt much safer with him diving with her. At the same time, it was hard for her to trust a stranger, and today she'd trusted many. Knowing exactly where the beacon was, Darcy swam straight to it. In the light of her flashlight, she saw her flag and relaxed a little. It was still there. She slowed next to the boat that was sticking butt up from the river floor. She reached into her bag for her equipment as Wade swam around the boat, checking it out.

She flashed her light at him, and he came over to her. She handed him a paintbrush she'd borrowed from Ridge and showed him what she wanted him to do. Soon Wade was gently brushing silt, sand, and mud from the end and underside of the rowboat. As he worked, her heart raced as large splintering holes were finally able to be seen. This *had* to be it.

Darcy took out the metal detector and turned it on. While the boat was interesting, it wasn't what she was after. She was after Timothy Longworth and that note he was supposed to have left for his parents. Hopefully, Timothy would still have a gun or knife or some kind of metal on him. Otherwise, she'd never find his final resting place.

Timothy had probably been thrown from the boat. He could be anywhere. And just like that, Darcy's hope faded. Still, she had to try. She turned it on and worked behind Wade. Then she worked off the right side of the rowboat. Nothing. The waters had grown darker and Wade was still working on brushing the silt from the bottom of the boat.

Hope faded as time went by, yet Darcy refused to give in. They still had diving time left, and she was going to use every minute of it. Darcy swam toward the boat. The inside was filled with so much silt she couldn't see the benches. She held the metal detector at the top, which was really the back end of the rowboat, and began a slow, methodical sweep. She knew there were metal rings and metal strips holding the boat together and wasn't surprised when the detector went off over the areas she knew metal to be. As she worked her way down slowly, hope faded once again.

The loud beeping sound suddenly surprised her as the light flashed on the metal detector. She was a couple feet away from the boat down in the riverbed. The location didn't make sense for it to be part of the boat.

Darcy dropped the metal detector and dove down. With the flashlight in one hand, she used her other to dig. At some point, Wade joined her and tapped her. Darcy almost jumped out of her skin. Her heart was pounding, and all she could hear was her pulse. She pointed down at where she was digging, and Wade held her flashlight. With Wade holding both of the lights, she could use two hands to dig. A piece of fabric was the first thing that finally broke through the thick riverbed.

Darcy shot a look to Wade, who was focused on the fabric with wide eyes. Using her hands, she continued to dig before she was suddenly slammed into the rowboat. Water rushed by her. Sand and silt covered her mask as Wade frantically grasped for her. What the hell had just happened?

Wade turned off the flashlights and in the distance, she could see a spark sinking in the water. Wade grabbed her and hauled her behind the boat a second before the underwater explosive went off. Wade tried to grab her, but she fought him off. She had to get to Timothy before the explosions destroyed the boat.

Darcy swam and saw the fabric was exposed. Instead of being hidden by mud, the explosives had uncovered what she was looking for. A tattered jacket and some boots were now visible. It appeared Timothy's foot had been caught inside the rowboat when it had sunk. She grabbed the coat and felt the weight of something that wasn't just fabric. Another spark, this time closer, was sinking toward them. Wade grabbed her and she let him. She had what she needed. Only this time there was a second spark and then a third. Frantically she and Wade looked around. There were explosives sinking all around them.

10

WADE STOPPED SWIMMING as the explosives dropped. Their pattern indicated the person didn't know exactly where he and Darcy were, but they knew they were getting close. His eyes went back to the rowboat. He'd gotten a lot of it unearthed, and that might protect them. He pulled Darcy toward the rowboat. She was shoving an old coat into her bag and tying it tightly around her front as if she were carrying a newborn.

Wade dropped her hand and grabbed the top of the boat sticking out of the riverbed. He pulled with all his strength as the first charge went off. The powerful rush of water shoved them both forward and into the boat, which rocked backward, loosening the stuck end. The blast shook his body and rattled his teeth, but it had helped his efforts. The old rowboat was now much easier to move, and he pulled on it for cover. Darcy had picked up on what he was doing and turned to help. Together, they pushed and pulled as the boat slowly freed itself from the riverbed.

Wade looked up in time to see the spark fading into the explosive. He shoved Darcy under the boat a second before the explosive went off. Wade didn't make it under the cover of the boat. As the water rushed past him, he held tightly onto the metal outrigger that the oar had sat in. The metal ripped into his skin as the explosive's energy tried to tear him away. Air was pushed from his lungs as Wade gritted his teeth in pain. He dove under the boat as soon as the explosive pulse had passed. Darcy was frantically grabbing him and pulling him under as another charge went off.

The water raced under the boat as Darcy and he held onto the wooden seat to keep the boat over them as a turtle hides in its shell. Time and time again the charges went off. But then they seemed a little farther away and finally, they were gone. Their flashlights were gone and they were in complete darkness as they waited for another charge. None came.

Wade reached out for Darcy. He felt her back and then her arm. She turned so she was facing him, and he laced his fingers with hers. It was time to get out of there. They couldn't simply surface in case the person who tried to blow them up was waiting for them.

Darcy began to swim upward, but Wade pulled her back to his side. He kept to the riverbed and began swimming toward the shore. Slowly, the riverbed began to slant upward as the water grew shallower. He paused before they broke the surface and turned Darcy toward him. He could see her now, and he held up his hands to indicate that she should stay put.

Wade slowly rose from the water. He only risked poking his head above the waterline enough to look around the water's surface. He saw a new boat, but it was one he recognized. Harper was there, and she wasn't alone. Harper and Wade's brother, Trent, were yelling his name.

He tapped Darcy on the head and she broke the surface.

The light was almost gone, but he could see the fear in her eyes as he spit out his regulator and pulled off his mask. "It's safe. That's Harper and my brother, Trent."

Wade pursed his lips together and let out a loud whistle. Trent and Harper immediately stopped yelling and began looking around as Darcy took off her mask, too. "What the hell was that?" she asked, her voice frantic with fear.

"Explosives. Someone was waiting for you to show again and finish you off. My guess is they have a camera nearby or they were staked out," Wade said as they began to swim toward Harper's speedboat.

"Are you okay?" Trent yelled out.

"We're a little shaken up, but not injured. Unless you are?" Wade asked Darcy, realizing he'd been so concerned with the attacker he didn't know if she was injured.

"I'm okay," she said, but she was breathing hard and shaking.

"We're okay now. We're safe."

"Wade, I think I found it," Darcy whispered.

"Found what? We already found the rowboat."

"No, what I was really looking for. I think I found Timothy's jacket, and if it's true he left a message for his parents, that message might have a clue as to the whereabouts of Black Law's ship."

"Then we can't open it here. If they have a video feed on the area, we need to get the police here and get somewhere safe before you even mention it again." Wade's heart pounded. They weren't out of danger. They were even deeper in the mystery and danger now.

"Please," Darcy begged as they drew near the boat. "You can't tell anyone I found it. By law, I have to turn everything over to the state."

Wade paused in his swimming. He knew the salvage law,

and he couldn't ignore it. "Will you turn it over after you've examined it?"

Darcy bit her lip and didn't look at him. "After a couple days," Wade offered, feeling horrible about not strictly following the law.

"I'll turn it over immediately if it has no value to the hunt. If it does, we'll re-evaluate. But I promise I will turn it over as soon as possible," Darcy said, practically begging.

"Let's see what it is, and then we'll decide. And we will tell the police we have it. Just not the Charleston police."

"What? We can't. They'll take it," Darcy cried as Wade held up a hand to calm her.

"Sheriff Granger Fox of Shadows Landing is a very good friend. We'll technically turn it over to him, and I bet he'll be nice enough to hold on to it for us. Then we won't get in trouble legally. Deal?"

Darcy was quiet as Trent and Harper were telling them to hurry up. "And you trust him?"

"With my life."

"How about with my life?"

"No question."

Darcy took a breath. "Okay. I'm trusting you, Wade. Please."

She didn't have to finish. She was begging him to not break that trust and hurt her career and her life.

DARCY'S HEART was in her stomach. Someone was trying to kill her. She might have what she'd been working for in her bag, and now she was going to trust someone she'd met not even twenty-four hours before. Plus she was going to hand it over to someone she'd never met.

"Are you two okay? I had this feeling I needed to come

out here, and so I handed the bar over to Tinsley and was heading to my boat when I saw Trent and waved him down," Harper rambled as Trent reached down to pull Darcy up and into the boat.

"Then we heard these explosions," Harper continued, "and we were so scared something happened to you two."

"Did you see who did it?" Wade asked as he climbed into the small speedboat.

"Two people in hoods," Trent said. "Harper tried to get a picture of the boat, but it's not clear. What is going on?"

Harper looked guiltily at them. "I didn't tell him since you told me not to tell anyone."

Darcy reached out for Harper. "Thank you." She turned to Wade and saw the blood dripping from his hand. "You're hurt!"

"It's nothing," Wade said, trying to act as if he weren't standing there bleeding.

"I'll fill your brother in while you get that bandaged up and call your friend. Then I'll make my phone calls," Darcy said, sounding resigned. She didn't want to do any of this. She wanted to hurry inside the cabin of Wade's boat and search the jacket she had taken.

"Fill me in on what?" Trent asked as he pushed his hair back from his face. He was looking between them as Wade instructed Harper to tie up to his boat.

"It started twelve years ago," Darcy began as Wade and Harper climbed onto Wade's boat. Darcy clung to the underwater bag as she filled Trent in on everything that had happened. She felt both relieved and petrified every time she told someone else the story. What if they went after her treasure? But at the same time, there was great relief in having others to talk to about her search.

"Granger and Kord are on their way," Wade said, coming

out of the cabin with Harper and a fresh bandage on his hand.

"I'll call Olivia to give her a chance to arrive before I call the detective," Darcy said as she stood up from the bench on the speedboat. Trent stood with her and held out his hand to help her onto Wade's boat.

"I think you're doing the right thing," Trent said for her ears only. "Wade is a good guy. He'll help you as much as you let him. And trust Granger. He'll go to bat for you."

Darcy didn't know why, but that was the reassurance she needed. She watched Wade put their gear up as she reached for a towel. He kept an eye on her, and she knew he would do everything he could to help her. She hadn't ever had that kind of support before. It was . . . freeing.

"So, let's see it," Wade said to her as they all gathered around.

"See what?" Darcy asked, lost in examining her surprisingly strong feelings for Wade.

"You. Take off your wetsuit to make sure you're not injured," Wade said with a grin that shot Darcy's thoughts right back to the warm fuzzies she got when she thought about him. But then he zipped down his wetsuit and let it hang from his waist again, and the warm fuzzies became incinerated fluff.

Trent looked at him and gave him the thumbs-up.

"Oh," Darcy said as she bit her lip. It felt intimate, even though she'd taken off wetsuits in front of hundreds of people before.

"Come on, Darcy. We'll go inside and get you changed and checked out," Harper said as she stepped into the cabin. Half of her wanted to scream, "Thank you!" The other half wanted to strip naked and leap into Wade's arms.

Instead of doing either, Darcy stepped into the cabin, and Harper started laughing. "You *so* like my cousin."

"What?" Darcy asked, completely caught red-faced.

"You were looking like you wanted to lick Wade dry." Well, crap, now Darcy couldn't get that image out of her head. She wouldn't need a towel to dry off. She was so hot at the thought of licking Wade's naked body that she was sure all the water had evaporated from her flushed skin.

"Tell me about the sheriff," Darcy said instead of answering as she changed.

"Granger is a great guy. He and Kord King run the department. You can trust them. And I don't see any serious injuries. You have a bruise here or there, but nothing serious," Harper said, before sitting down and waiting for Darcy to finish getting dressed.

"Even if I have something that I should technically hand over?"

"What did you steal? Is it wrong that makes me like you even more?" Harper asked, moving to sit at the edge of her seat.

Darcy laughed. She liked Harper. Tough on the outside, kind on the inside. "It's a jacket that has something heavy inside it. The reports I read from the lone survivor was that Timothy told them that he'd written a note for his parents, and it was very important they get it."

"What happened to the survivor?" Harper asked.

"Died very soon after being rescued."

"Now, this is really getting interesting. No way can you hand that over yet. Can't you just toss it back in the water after you have a chance to look it over and leave the state to find it?" Harper asked.

Now Darcy was sure she and Harper were going to be good friends because that was the exact plan Darcy had.

"That's what I want to do, but Wade said we should turn it over to this Granger guy so we are technically following the law."

Harper made a face, telling Darcy what she thought about that idea. "Wade would. For all his happy-go-lucky ways, he's actually a straight arrow. But, it's a good plan if you don't want to end up in jail. Granger and Kord will work with you. They'll listen. Speaking of them"—Harper pulled up a blind and saw the flashing blue lights of a police boat —"they're here."

"I'll make my calls then." Darcy picked up her phone and placed her call. "Olivia, it's Darcy. I found the rowboat and someone tried to kill me with underwater explosives."

11

Olivia promised to call the detective and would meet her on the water as soon as possible. When Darcy stepped out onto the deck, she was met with two new people. Both men were over six feet and physically fit. And both were wearing jeans and a brown polo shirt that had a gold badge embroidered on the chest with Shadows Landing stitched around it.

However, that's where the similarities stopped. One was in his thirties with tanned skin, a chiseled face, and wore a cowboy hat. The other was in his twenties, had smooth dark skin and black hair trimmed almost to his scalp with perfect trim lines, and sexy full lips.

"So, that's the deal," Wade was saying when Darcy walked out. Both men had looked at her the second she began to open the sliding door.

Wade reached out for her, and she slipped her hand into his. It felt natural. Safe. And when he used his thumb to gently rub the palm of her hand it made her feel very hot even as the night air had a cool breeze to it.

"This is Darcy Delmar," Wade said, smiling down to her. "These are my friends. Sheriff Granger Fox is in the hat."

Granger tipped his hat, "Ma'am."

"And the good-looking one is Kordell King, but everyone calls me Kord," Kord said with a wink as he reached for her hand. "And what can two humble servants of the law do for you?"

Darcy laughed. Humble and Kordell didn't go together, and for some reason that made her relax. "I'm guessing Wade told you what's going on?"

Kord's charming smile dropped as Granger gave a single nod. "What's this object you need to officially hand over and then we *misplace* for a couple of weeks?" Granger asked, cutting right to the chase.

"You'd do that?" Darcy asked with disbelief.

"We always like messing with the Charleston cops. It's fun to see them get their Kevlar in a bunch," Kord said, grinning once again.

Granger's lips twitched in what Darcy thought was agreement.

"Okay. I saved what I think to be Timothy Longworth's coat and it's heavier than it should be. Now, it could be nothing, but I am hoping it's holding a clue to Black Law's sunken boat in its pocket."

"What should we do with it?" Granger asked.

"Can you keep it someplace safe? Put it somewhere no one can find it until I have a chance to examine it?" Darcy asked hopefully.

Kord looked to Granger. "You thinking what I'm thinking?"

"The church," Granger agreed with a nod.

"The church! Why would you put it there? Isn't there an

evidence locker or something you can put it in?" Darcy asked.

"Pirates paid for the church and there're hidden places all over it. The Rev will know where to hide it," Kord said, sounding as if it were no big deal.

"Wait, I don't want anyone else to know about it."

"Ma'am, if I put that in evidence, everyone will know about it. My secretary, bless her heart, loves to talk," Granger said. "Plus, if anyone from Charleston PD comes to visit, they'll be nosy. It's best to keep it out of the station. You can trust Reverend Winston. Shoot, the man just led a group of senior women in a sword battle to help Harper's sister-in-law. Hiding something to do with a Shadows Landing pirate? That will be his honor."

Darcy looked at everyone and they were all nodding, including Harper. "I'd trust Rev more than Kord."

"But who do you call in the middle of the night when you hear something outside?" Kord smirked.

"One time! Geez, let it go." Harper rolled her eyes. "And let's not forget you screamed, and we had to call Gator to remove Bubba from my backyard."

Darcy laughed, especially after meeting Gator and hearing about Bubba. "Okay, fine. I guess this is six degrees of trust or something."

"Don't look now, but Charleston is on their way," Granger said with a sigh. "Kord, you stay here and liaise. Trent, can you and Harper take me back?"

"You bet," Trent said before helping Harper onto her boat.

Granger turned and faced Darcy, and she saw someone who was stubborn and luckily, it appeared that stubbornness was on her side tonight. "Get it for me. Hurry."

He said it completely calmly, but because Granger was so calm Darcy knew her time was about up. "Here," she said as she turned over her future to him. "Be very gentle with it."

"We'll meet you at the church tonight!" Harper called from the boat as Granger stepped on and shoved off from Wade's boat.

As soon as they were clear, Trent shot off. He was leaving no chance for the Charleston PD to talk to them.

"You expecting someone else?" Kord asked as he squinted. "I've never seen hair not move before on a boat going that fast. Nor a woman dressed quite like that to take a boat out."

"That must be Olivia Townsend. She's my lawyer."

Kord let out a whistle. "Is she single?"

"I don't know. I never asked." Kord had a way of making her forget what a tense situation she was really in and she appreciated that.

WADE AND KORD got to work securing the police boat and the expensive speedboat Olivia was driving.

"Ma'am, I am at your service to assist you in *any* way," Kord said, shooting a full dazzling smile to Olivia as he put his hands around her waist and easily lifted her up and over the water and onto Wade's boat.

Darcy stared in disbelief as her unflappable attorney blushed before brushing imaginary wrinkles from her tight pink pencil skirt. She was in full courtroom attire and Kord was right, her blonde updo didn't have a hair out of place.

"Thank you . . . deputy?"

"Deputy Kord King," Kord introduced himself.

"Olivia Townsend. Miss Delmar's attorney," she said

before her face transformed from kind to determined. "Detective. I see you brought company."

Darcy looked back to see Gerald Hemmings standing in his suit. Apparently, lawyers never took them off.

"Want me to throw him overboard?" Kord asked quietly. Darcy heard Wade snicker next to her, and Olivia tossed him a dazzling smile.

"What's he doing here?" Detective Chambers asked as he stumbled onto the boat.

WADE STEPPED IN, knowing this could be a delicate situation, and he wanted to make sure Shadows Landing stayed in this investigation.

"I called them when we were attacked. Shadows Landing is closer than Charleston and I was hoping Deputy King would spot someone trying to flee north while you covered the south," Wade explained. From the corner of his eye, he saw Olivia and Darcy with their heads together. He needed to give them time to discuss whatever they needed.

"Sir, this is Deputy Kordell King of the Shadows Landing sheriff's office," Wade introduced as Kord put on his best professional face.

"Detective Willie Chambers," the detective grudgingly introduced.

"Sir, it's a pleasure to be working with you," Kordell said in a humble tone Wade had never heard before. Kord was one of the nicest guys in the world, but modesty was not his usual approach.

"Kordell King . . ." the man in the suit muttered as he climbed aboard. "Didn't you play football?"

"Yes, sir," King said proudly.

"You were one hell of a player. I'm Gerald Hemmings. I'm the DA handling Miss Delmar's case."

Gerald shook hands with Kord and then turned to him. "Wade Faulkner, Coast Guard."

"That's right. I read your report. What are you doing here?" Gerald asked.

"I was wondering the same thing," the detective said, pulling out his notepad as a second police boat drew closer.

"I went diving with Miss Delmar. She was adamant that she had found something, and since I'm a master diver, I thought I would assist," Wade said easily. It was mostly the truth. He maybe wouldn't have assisted if he weren't so fascinated by Darcy and her love of this treasure. Her passion for the history of the boat was something he not only respected but found very sexy.

"And what did you find on your dive?" the detective asked as Darcy and Olivia joined him.

"I found a rowboat," Darcy said with a smile. "And it's quite old. My guess is from the early 1700s."

"Is this what you told us you were looking for?" the DA asked.

"Yes. It's a part of colonial history," Darcy answered with pride. "And I found it."

"Miss Townsend said something about explosives," the detective said, bringing the interview back around to the criminal aspect.

"Yes, sir," Wade answered before telling them what happened. As he reported the incident, he watched the Charleston police divers gear up. "You can pretty much tell where they were set off by the dead fish on the water, but would you like me to show your men where the rowboat is located?" Wade offered after finishing his report.

The detective looked up from his notes as if he didn't

realize others were around. "Yes, that would be good." The detective turned to Kord. "Did you see anyone?"

"No, sir. Did you?"

Detective Chambers looked a little surprised at being asked, but then shook his head. "Nothing suspicious. We have all the boats we passed on camera, so we'll look into them."

WADE PULLED up his wetsuit and borrowed some oxygen from the police divers. It took thirty minutes to show the divers the rowboat and also the area where the charges went off. Wade left the divers marking the river bottom with little flags as they took underwater photos of the destruction and the boat.

As they collected what evidence they could, Wade made his way back to the boat. When he climbed back up, he found Kord regaling Gerald with football stories while Olivia worked feverishly on a laptop.

"Are we all done here, detective?" Wade asked as he put the oxygen tank back on the police divers' boat before jumping in the water and swimming back to his own boat a couple yards away.

"I want to hear what the divers say first. Then you may go," the detective told him as Darcy climbed aboard. The detective suddenly turned to her. "Where are you staying?"

"Here," Darcy said as Olivia looked up.

"Why?" Olivia asked, although her tone indicated it wasn't a question the detective could ignore.

"Just in case we need to get in touch with her."

"You call me, and *I'll* get in touch with her. Understand?" She smiled sweetly when it was anything but.

The detective held up his hands. "We're on the same team."

"We'll see. First, you need to do your job and find out who is trying to kill my client. For her safety, her whereabouts or any contact information will not be put into any report. Solely my phone number."

Darcy stepped closer to Wade as the detective agreed. Wade would make sure she was safe. He wouldn't leave her side until whoever did this was caught.

"Detective!" A diver had surfaced and swam toward them. "We saw the boat. Looks old like you told us. We're about done here. Looks like dynamite was set off for sure. Not much is left. Found some bits and pieces, but I don't know how much we'll be able to give you."

"It only takes one piece of evidence," the detective tried to say with hope. He turned to them then with his lips thinned as if he were deep in thought. "You all can go now. I'll call if I need anything more. I take it you'll be making a claim tomorrow in court?"

"Yes, she will be. I have already emailed you a copy," Olivia said, shutting her laptop. "My client will be signing this as soon as she gets on dry land, and we will be at the courthouse the second the doors open to make the claim. Also, my client wants her diving equipment, including a professional metal detector, clothes, and purse, back."

"I'll meet you there in the morning. I can't get the clothes yet, but the metal detector and purse I can release. I want to keep an eye on who else is there when you make that claim," the detective told them as he made his way back to the police boat.

"You can make the claim, Miss Delmar, but you know the state will take it over, don't you?" Gerald asked before climbing on the police boat with Chambers.

"Yes, but I still get my name attached to the find and a small percentage of the find."

Gerald's forehead wrinkled in thought, but then he just nodded once and got on the boat. "An officer will be staying the night."

"I will be here for a little while myself," Kord called out and then winked at Olivia. "It's romantic in the moonlight, isn't it?"

"Yes, the floating dead fish really set the mood," Olivia said sweetly back as Kord lifted her again and easily set her down gently on her boat. He gave her another smile and laughed.

"You're good."

"So I've been told."

"Such a player," Olivia said as she started up her boat.

"And a good one!" Kord called out.

"Darcy, I'll meet you at my office at eight. Goodnight!" Olivia gave a wave and shot off.

Wade just shook his head at his friend. "Coming on strong, aren't you?"

"It was the skirt and the laptop. Beauty and brains, my weakness." Kord sighed, getting back onto the Shadows Landing police boat. "I'll stay here until Charleston has everything in order. Hopefully, I can catch up with you at the church."

Darcy waved to Kord before they both climbed to the bridge. Wade maneuvered the boat away from the divers and other boats before opening it up. It was time to see what stories the dead told.

12

DARCY DIDN'T TALK on the way back to Shadows Landing. Instead, she twisted her hands and bit her lip. "Your find is safe. I trust everyone in Shadows Landing. They won't turn on you. They'll help you. This town is a little pirate-crazy after all."

"What if it's nothing?" Darcy finally asked. Wade reached out a hand and took hers in it while he steered with the other.

"Then we'll look some more. You still have all of the Shadows Landing historical books to look through." Wade squeezed her hand before letting go and maneuvering into the marina.

"We?"

"Yeah, we. Now, are you ready to find out if you were right?" Wade asked as he shut off the motor.

"It sounds silly, but I'm kind of afraid to see. What if I'm wrong? What if this was all for nothing?"

Wade secured the boat and held out his hands for her. She took them and he helped her onto the dock but didn't let go. He wanted to make it all better for her. "It doesn't matter. If there's nothing there, then we look at the historical society tomorrow. If there is, but it just says *love you, mom*, then it's still a find, still personal, and the Shadows Landing historical society would love it."

Wade kept his fingers entwined with Darcy's as they walked into town. It was natural, and he had to admit he felt as if he walked taller with her by his side. As they turned onto Main Street, though, Wade stumbled to a stop.

"What is it?" Darcy asked.

"Well, you're definitely not alone anymore."

Darcy turned to where the street in front of the church was lined with cars. "What does this mean?"

"It means my cousin or my brother told all of the others."

"Others?"

Wade could feel Darcy begin to freak out. Her body shook slightly, and he felt like killing whoever it was that notified the rest of them. The Faulkners were a tight bunch.

"My family," Wade said through clenched teeth. He loved them, but right now he was furious.

DARCY TRIED to pull her hand from Wade's grasp, but he didn't let go. She looked up and saw that his jaw was tight and his eyes narrowed as he looked at the cars parked in front of the old church with even older stained glass windows.

"Come on," he said as he began to walk faster. He was angry for her. And she hated that. She hoped when they went inside there was nothing to be angry about. She had been shocked to find more people there, but she liked Harper, Trent, and Ridge. How many more could there be? Darcy kept her panic in line by telling herself they were going to help her, and they weren't there to steal what she'd been working on for over a decade.

The door opened and a man wearing a white robe, clearly the pastor, stood with a Bible in hand at the top of the stone steps. He looked to be in his forties with smooth umber skin. His hair had soft coils on the top and was shaved down the sides of his head. And he had a smile. A big one. A warm one. Darcy's fears began to fade.

"Welcome! So glad you could join us as we say a private family prayer for the newlyweds. You must be Darcy Delmar," he called out to them. "I'm Floyd Winston, the pastor for our town's beautiful church here. Come in and pray with us."

Darcy looked up the steps at him and smiled. For that moment, she really did feel as if they were going to pray together. But then she noticed the people walking the street. People she hadn't noticed before because she'd been so focused on the church doors and then Reverend Winston.

"I thought there already was a weddin'," an old man in a power scooter with a massive engine on it said as he pulled to a stop on the sidewalk.

"Good evening, Mr. Gann." Reverend Winston smiled down at the man who had to be in his eighties. "The wedding is done, but we are having a family group prayer tonight to wish blessings on the newlyweds before they leave for their honeymoon in the morning."

Mr. Gann harrumphed, and with the twist of the handle of his scooter, he shot off down the sidewalk with a rather loud rumbling coming from what looked to be a muffler. Wade grabbed Darcy and pulled her safely to the side. "He used to build cars for dirt racing. He's a little speed demon on his scooter. Always watch your toes," Wade told her as he held her close to him. Oh goodness. Her leg was between his. Her hips pressed against his with Wade's hand at the small of her back pressing her even closer. Her hands rested on his chest and under her right hand, she felt his heart beating.

Darcy stared at her hands on his chest, taking in the way they conformed to his muscles before looking up. Wade was looking at her, and his green eyes seemed darker and softer than they had a minute ago.

"Darcy." He said her name on a whispered breath, but it was enough to rock her whole body to the core.

"Yes?" she whispered back, too afraid to break the spell.

"Lord Jesus, pray for this new couple to find the strength to rein in their passions long enough to pray for their beloved family. In Jesus' name, amen."

Darcy jumped back and Wade let go of her except for quickly taking her hand in his once again. How had that happened? She'd been so lost in Wade she'd forgotten, for just a second, her life's work.

"Sorry," she muttered as they began to hurry up the steps.

"I'm not," she heard Wade say and felt her heart speed up once again, and this time she knew it wasn't just because of the possible clue for the treasure.

"So nice to see you. Come right this way for our prayer," Reverend Winston said loudly before closing the thick wooden doors that Darcy thought looked as if they were riddled with bullet holes.

The door closed with a soft *thud* and then the pastor picked up a freestanding wrought iron candleholder. He blew out the candle, took it off the top of the four-foot tall candleholder, and shoved the holder through the twisted iron door handles.

"There. No one should bother us now." He grinned at

them both and stepped over to Darcy. "I can't wait to see what you found. My many times great-grandfather was a pirate who resided here. He wasn't a big name like Black Law, but they all knew each other. When Granger told me about what you found, I just have to say I couldn't wait to be a part of it."

"Really?" Darcy asked, amazed a pastor would want to hide something for her. Something that as of tomorrow should be turned over to the state.

"Oh yes. I just love history and puzzles. Right this way."

Darcy stopped as he led them to the stone wall behind the altar. Above it was a beautiful stained glass window that had to be at least six feet tall and three feet wide. Reverend Winston pulled aside a wall hanging and pushed on a stone. Suddenly the door swung inward. There were honest-to-God torches on the wall lighting up the narrow hallway with a soft glow that still left plenty of shadows.

"What is this?" Darcy asked as she looked all around the path that seemed to slope downward rather quickly.

"It's one of the many hidden passages in the church. The locations of all of them are passed onto each new pastor when the elder retires. This particular one was used to roll barrels from the river. Behind the church is a cemetery and then the small offshoot of Shadows River where the pirates would hide their ships since it was inaccessible during low tide."

"And this is where you've hidden my artifact?" Darcy asked as they continued to walk down the corridor, and from what she could tell, away from the church. The stones on the floor were worn and two iron rails, almost like train tracks that ran down the middle of the path, were similarly rounded down with time and use.

"Yes, there is a large storage room under the garden of

the church before it narrows and runs to the river. I had the artifact in a smaller hidey-hole but when more and more Faulkners began to show up, I thought it best to meet down here."

"This is amazing," Darcy whispered more to herself than anyone else as she ran her fingers over the rough stone walls lit with a torch every ten feet or so.

Wade walked directly behind her, and she felt him near her the entire walk down to the room. Before they made it to the room, she saw the light coming from under a door. Reverend Winston pulled out an old ring of large iron keys and placed one in the old lock. As the keys jingled, Darcy wondered what else they unlocked.

Then she heard the voices. Men and woman laughing, talking, and then silent in anticipation as the door opened. Reverend Winston opened the thick door and Darcy saw people around an old wooden table. It looked like it used to belong in an old farmhouse and could seat twenty. It was as battered and dented as the two long benches sitting on either side of it. But right in the middle sat the bag that contained Timothy's jacket.

"Oh my gosh! Isn't this exciting? I have painting ideas just flowing out of me." A cute woman who stood a couple inches shorter than Darcy's five feet five inches came bounding over to them. Her long, wavy brown hair had something white in it, and upon closer look, her clothes had lots of colors splattered on them. She must be a painter. Either way, she was adorable, and her big bright green eyes radiated kindness. "You must be Darcy. I'm Tinsley, Wade's cousin."

The woman practically threw herself into Darcy's arms as she hugged her briefly before pulling back. "And this is my brother, Ridge," she said as she waved over the man in jeans, work boots, and a heather gray T-shirt.

"We met earlier."

Tinsley turned and smacked her brother. "You didn't tell me!"

Even though the meeting room smelled of earth, Darcy caught a whiff of fresh-cut wood and leaned forward to smell it more. Ridge had the same brown hair as Tinsley, but his hair was shorter. It wasn't buzzed like Wade's. Instead, it was long enough to be pushed behind the ears.

"When Harper told us Wade had a friend needing help, and it was the nice girl I met earlier, I had to admit I was curious. Granger didn't want to let us join, but . . ." Ridge shrugged his wide shoulders and grinned.

"I tried to keep it quiet," Granger said apologetically. "But someone sent a text to the whole family." He shot a pointed look at Harper.

Harper didn't seem embarrassed at all. Instead, she smiled. "You said it could be a clue. The more the better, right? My brother, Gavin," she said, looking over at the man with his arm around a pretty blonde woman, "loves puzzles."

"Hi." He smiled as he held out his hand. "I'm Gavin and this is Ellery, my bride." Darcy shook hands with both as she smiled. How could she not? They were adorable together.

Darcy looked around and realized she had met everyone in the room except for the tall brooding man in the farthest chair. Wade saw her looking and introduced her. "And this is my cousin, Ryker."

Why did that name sound familiar? "Ryker! You got me Olivia." Darcy stepped from Wade's arm and rushed toward the man with ice-green eyes and dark hair. His dark suit made it so he seemed to blend into the shadows. The man's eyes went wide with surprise, but Darcy wrapped her arms around him anyway. He was so tall that even sitting she didn't need to bend over much. "Olivia is amazing, and there's no way I could ever afford her. You are so nice."

"Nice?" Harper snorted. "Ryker?"

"He's incredibly nice and caring. He's paying for my attorney, and he doesn't even know me," Darcy said, quickly coming to his defense.

"I was intrigued," Ryker grumbled. "Now, let's see what almost got you killed."

Darcy took a deep breath as she turned toward the table now silently lined by Faulkners, Sheriff Fox, and Reverend Winston.

13

DARCY FELT Wade come to stand next to her as everyone quietly eyed the bag. Her heart was pounding, and her hand shook slightly as she reached for the bag that was still damp from the river water. Inside was something three hundred years old. She shook her head slightly as she thought to herself. There was no way there would be anything inside. She was crazy for thinking so.

"Do you want me to do it?" Wade asked quietly, and Darcy realized she was standing there with her hand hovering over the bag.

"I got it. It's probably nothing."

Darcy took a breath and let it out. It seemed to echo around the room as she carefully opened the bag and pulled out the wet wool jacket. The weight was still there as she set the jacket, its round metal buttons now covered in algae, on the desk.

"Wow, that's really old. It looks like it's from colonial times," Tinsley whispered. Because everyone else was so quiet, her words filled the room.

"That's because it is. If I'm correct, this coat belonged to

Timothy Longworth and has been on the river bottom since 1719," Darcy said, hearing the trembling in her voice.

She moved the jacket so it was lying flat and she stared at the obvious lump in the right pocket. Darcy moved her hand slowly to pull back the pocket flap. It was a tight fit, but her fingers came across something hard and slimy. It wasn't very large and she was able to put her fingers around it. It took work to wiggle it free from the tight pocket. As soon as it was free everyone breathed in and leaned closer.

In Darcy's hand was a small metal box. It was probably five inches by three inches and had a small padlock hanging from it. Darcy set it down as if it might break at the slightest touch as she reached into the small bag she was carrying and pulled out a piece of soft cloth.

"What is it?" Harper asked.

"Looks like a jewelry box," Tinsley answered as everyone leaned even closer. Even Ryker stood to get a better look as Darcy wiped the sludge, algae, and slime from it.

"Silver," Ryker's deep voice said. "Do you want me to unlock it?"

"You can do that?" Darcy asked.

"I can try. I used to be pretty good at it."

"If he can't, I can give it a try. I'm not too bad myself, but as I remember, Ryker was the best at it," Granger told her before turning to Reverend Winston. "Can you go see if Kord is here and ask him to bring in the lock-picking set? If he's not here, it's in the glove box of my cruiser."

"Don't open it without me," the reverend called out as he hurried from the room.

Time seemed to slow. She was so close to finding out if her research and her hunch were right. Everyone seemed to pick up on her nervousness as Ridge tried to talk to her about building practices of the 1700s and how these tunnels could have been made. He talked and talked and his slow southern accent relaxed her as Wade gently rubbed his hand up and down her back in a silent show of support. Finally, an out-of-breath Reverend Winston and Kord, who wasn't out of breath, came into the room.

"Is that it?" Kord asked. "I kinda expected a big treasure chest."

"Give the picks to Ryker. You saw the bag. There wasn't any room for something large," Granger said with a shake of his head.

"I got carried away thinking about treasure," Kord said with a shrug. "I wonder what's inside."

Everyone got quiet again as soon as Ryker slipped the small pick into the lock. Darcy was pretty sure her heart stopped beating as he moved the pick around the lock. The *click* sounded as loud as an explosion, and Ryker froze for just a second before sitting back. "There you go."

Darcy swallowed hard and reached forward. By now she almost bumped her head with the rest of the table as everyone was so close. Darcy used her fingernail to pry the clasp loose from the box and lift it up and over the lock. She tried to pull the box top open, but nothing.

"It could be sealed tight," Wade said quietly. "Do you want me to try to pry it open?"

Darcy gave it another try, but it wouldn't budge. "Yes, but be careful."

"Can I have the flat pick?" Ryker handed it over to Wade, and Darcy felt herself shaking with anticipation as Wade cleaned out slime and sludge from around the top of the small box. Then he worked slowly around the top, slipping it in and wiggling it until finally the corner gave way. Everyone gasped as each inch was freed and finally Wade was able to pull the top open.

Darcy felt the world shift as she looked down at it. The first thing that she noticed was that it was dry. The second was the gold coin blinking up at them.

"That looks like a gold doubloon," Trent said as everyone nodded.

"Go on," Wade said softly. "Open it."

Darcy wanted to, but she was scared. *Please let there be more.* Darcy reached into her bag and pulled out a pair of soft gloves. They were Harper's for church, but she'd let her borrow them. Darcy didn't want any oil to touch any of the treasure. Carefully she lifted the gold coin. "Wade, there's another strip of cloth in my bag. Can you get it and place it on the table?" As Wade did what she asked, she looked closely at the coin. "The cross on one side and the L and 8 on the other side tell me it's Spanish."

"Is that good?" Ridge asked.

"Yes," Darcy said as she gently set it down on the fabric Wade had spread out. "Reports from the story say Black Law took a ship filled with Spanish gold and treasure from a rich count who was delivering his daughter to an even richer man in Mexico." Darcy knew her breathing was shallow as she was trying to explain while remaining calm. "Black Law killed the family and took the dowry."

"What's that inside?" Kord asked as everyone shifted attention back to the box.

"Oilcloth," Darcy told them as she felt the cloth used to keep things waterproof back then. Carefully she tilted the box over the table and gently pulled one corner of the oilcloth until it came out of the silver box.

"Did you hear that?" Reverend Winston said quietly as he raised his hands to Jesus. "Dear Lord, please let that paper sound be the item Miss Delmar is looking for."

"Amen," everyone said together, and Darcy carefully

unfolded the oilcloth. Her heart was beating so loudly she was sure everyone could hear it. It seemed as though time slowed, and no one breathed as she unfolded the final flap to see the paper inside.

"Thank you, Jesus," Darcy said with a whoosh of air as she looked down at a hastily scribbled note.

"What does it say?" Wade asked next to her.

Darcy didn't want to touch it so she leaned toward the table and read the flowing letters that made up the note aloud.

"*If I shall perish, it was Black Law who captured Samuel, William, and me. His ship rides low and lower shall it ride. No amount of gold, silver, or gems will save me. To my family, I shall miss thee, but I leave one last gift. As the snake's tail sounds, you spin me like a dancing master. He Loves Me So. As I love you. Goodbye and Godspeed. Timothy Longworth.*"

"Darcy, you did it!" Wade said, grabbing her hand as she stood staring at the note in shock.

"It's a clue," Darcy muttered as she stood up and looked around at all the happy faces.

"You were right. He left a secret message for his parents. You did it." Wade grabbed her up and twirled her around as he laughed. Darcy hadn't even breathed yet. Her mind couldn't process it. After all these years and all of the research, she had been right.

"What does it mean?" Tinsley asked as Wade set her down.

"I don't know," Darcy said as she looked back down at the note. She pulled out her phone and captured at least twenty photos before standing back up. "But I will."

WADE RESTED his hand on her hip as they read the note

again. "When a ship rides low it means it has cargo on it," he told them.

Darcy nodded next to him. "And lower shall it ride . . . I bet that means it's going to be sunk."

"The gold, silver, or gems line probably is telling his parents what is on the ship," Ellery said.

"And one last gift is the location of the ship," Gavin added.

"So, the rest of the message is how to find the ship," Ridge said as he pinched his lips in thought.

They all leaned forward again. "As the snake's tail sounds," Darcy read aloud. "Does that mean anything to you?"

Wade grinned as he pulled out his phone. He didn't have cell service, but what he was looking for was a picture he'd taken a year ago. "I think I have it," he said as he scrolled through the photos until he found what he was looking for. It was simply a picture of the ocean depths off the coast of South Carolina.

"What is it?" Ridge asked him.

"It's the name of a particular shallow off the Isle of Palms," he said, shooting a grin to Darcy. She had mentioned the Isle of Palms before. It was a small island across from Charleston. "Here it is."

Wade zoomed in and showed the picture to Darcy. He heard her suck in a breath as she saw what he was pointing to—Rattlesnake Shoal.

"What? What's that?" Harper asked.

"It's a shallow area about three miles from shore. Depths range from eleven to sixteen feet and it's called Rattlesnake Shoal. There's a long history of ships running aground there. But it's a well-known place. I don't think a ship could be sunk there and us not know about it," Wade explained.

He knew it well. He'd had to rescue people there before and it would be darn hard to not see a large boat sunk there. People would hit it all the time.

"So, the rest of the letter must be where to go after the shoal," Ryker said from where he had taken his seat again.

"*As the snake's tail sounds, you spin me like a dancing master. He Loves Me So. As I love you. Goodbye and Godspeed*," Darcy repeated. "Godspeed is something said to someone to wish them success."

"To find the ship," Wade said out loud as he thought about the phrase. "But I can't figure out the rest."

"I have to get to Charleston. Tomorrow morning I'm buying a new boat since someone put a dead body in mine," Ryker grumbled as he stood up. "I'll think about it and see what I can come up with."

"We'll text you from our honeymoon if we think of anything, too," Gavin said as Ellery gave Darcy a hug goodbye.

"I'll slip the jacket back into the water as well," Kord told them. "Unless you need it?"

"No, I don't. Thank you."

"No problem. I want to see that attorney again, so I'll pop down in the morning as an interested citizen."

"Thank you," Darcy said to him as she gave him a smile.

Soon everyone was heading out of the tunnel. Wade had a hand on Darcy's elbow as she held onto the box with both hands. Darcy hung back so Wade let his family leave first before asking her why she didn't want to leave.

"Reverend, can you place this in the hidey-hole you were talking about so only the three of us know where it is and how to get to it?"

"Sure thing. Right this way."

"Don't trust my family?" Wade asked, slightly hurt. He had thought they had gotten along great. In fact, she seemed as if she were already part of them.

"No, it's not that. It's just that I want to get to it easily, and I don't want to have to light all those torches every time I want to see it."

"Understandable. It is a hike to get there." Wade relaxed a little, knowing it wasn't personal as Reverend Winston showed them a stone in the wall that was hollow. Darcy slipped the box inside and pushed it back into the wall. "Amazing. You can't tell at all."

Darcy looked relieved and that's all that mattered to him. "Come on, let's go home," Wade said, taking her hand in his as they left the church.

14

"MY HOUSE IS JUST OVER THERE," Wade said, pointing in the direction of his small cottage-style house a couple blocks away. "I have a spare room if you feel like sleeping on land tonight."

Wade tried to play it cool. He wasn't quite ready to let go of Darcy even if it was only for a night. "It has a nice shower and an iron if you want me to get some wrinkles out of whatever clothes Harper gave you."

"You had me at shower." Darcy laughed. "You don't mind me spending the night? I don't mind showering and then heading back to the boat."

"No need for that. I'm sure after such a day we'll crash as soon as we get back."

Wade began to walk her toward his house when she stopped him. "Should we get my clothes?"

"I'll drive down and get them when you're in the shower," Wade said as he laced his fingers with hers. He noticed she had already been holding out her hand for his. In just a day, they were already naturally reaching for each other. He liked it. He liked it a lot. It felt natural and comfortable and sexy. All these little touches and brushes of their bodies were driving him wild. As much as he wanted nothing more than to act on those wild thoughts going through his head, he was a gentleman, and he'd wait until Darcy gave him a sign that she was ready for more.

They walked hand in hand down the street and away from the marina as Wade pointed out the antique store, the courthouse, sheriff's office, and the town diner named Stomping Grounds. "Then on the corner of Main Street and South Cypress is Lowcountry Smokehouse. Earl Taylor runs it and smokes all the meat with wood. Down by the marina end of Main Street is the Pink Pig. Darius Foster owns that and uses charcoal. It's an ongoing debate in town. In fact, every Sunday they both make a batch of barbecue, and it's served in church. You don't know which is which. You take communion and then barbecue. Then place your donation to the church in either the A or B box. The winner is announced at the end, then it's a race to get to the barbecue place of your choice."

Darcy was laughing as they turned up South Cypress and headed the two more blocks to his house. "You're making that up."

"Nope. We take our barbecue very seriously in Shadows Landing. My family will go to both places, but some are so diehard they will only go to one and never to the other."

"I feel transported here," Darcy admitted.

"How do you mean?" Wade asked as they strolled past a law office and the beauty salon.

"This town is so close to Charleston, yet it seems as if you've stepped back in time when you come here. You all seem to know everyone."

"We do know everyone. It's a really small town," Wade said with a laugh.

"With a pirate pastor and hidden tunnels and brawling barbecue," Darcy said as she laughed harder.

"All true." Wade smiled at her and then pointed. "That's me."

His cottage house was a light blue with white shutters and a small wooden front porch. On it were two rocking chairs and a plant that had died a year ago. He wasn't the best at keeping plants alive. He could rescue a person in thirty-foot waves, but remembering to water a fern was beyond him.

Wade unlocked the door to his house. Small cottages lined the street until South Cypress turned into North Cypress. Bell Plantation's land claimed one side of the road. The other side was lined with houses in the more rural part of Shadows Landing. His brother, Trent, and his cousin, Tinsley, lived in that direction. Trent made beautiful furniture and Tinsley painted. They both said the quiet nature of their surroundings inspired them. For Wade, it was a little too far from the community. When Tinsley and their family friend, Edie Greene Wecker, were attacked in her home, there was no one around to hear and come to their aid. Tinsley's brother, Ridge, had begged her to move into town, but she had refused. On the other hand, Edie lived just a couple houses down from Wade now.

"There's a guest bedroom upstairs, and at the end of the hall is a small guest bath," Wade said as he closed the door.

He was nervous as he wondered what Darcy thought of his house. He knew she appreciated his boat, but his house was something he was even prouder of. He and Ridge had fixed it up. Trent had made most of the furniture from Wade's own designs. Then Ridge had come in and built anything Wade and Trent hadn't been able to do themselves. The result was what he called *historical contemporary*. He used historical designs and modernized them.

Darcy slowly turned as she looked around the house. "The lines are so clean, but you used old materials. It's so beautiful."

Wade let out the breath he'd been holding. "I'm glad you like it. I want you to feel comfortable here."

"It's great. Thank you for letting me stay."

"Please, treat it like your own home. I'll go grab your clothes and be back in a bit."

Wade closed the door and walked over to his small one-car detached garage. As he drove down to his boat, he whistled to himself as he thought of coming home to Darcy.

Darcy walked around the house, feeling like a snoop. But what was a treasure hunter except for the ultimate snoop? The house was beautiful and not exactly what she expected. Wade was so easy-going she expected a messy kitchen and beer cans on the coffee table. Instead, she found a pristine house that also felt homey.

Darcy walked upstairs and easily found the guest room and bathroom. At the other end of the narrow hall was an open door that had to lead to the master bedroom. She knew that since she'd already opened the other door and found a closet. She paused a couple steps from Wade's room. Should she go in? No . . . well, she did need something to sleep in. Surely Wade wouldn't mind her borrowing a T-shirt.

Darcy pulled her shoulders back and marched into his room and fell in love. The master was way larger than she thought it would be and there was a one-of-a-kind king-sized bed against a wall with a whole wall of windows on the opposite side. Part of those windows were French doors that opened onto a balcony on the back of the house, giving her a view of open yards and plenty of trees. Darcy almost pressed her nose against the window as she saw the overstuffed outdoor furniture that begged to be curled up in with a good book.

She turned her attention back to the bed and found a neatly folded gray Coast Guard T-shirt on it. She probably didn't really need it to sleep in, but when she picked it up it smelled like Wade and that sealed the deal. Darcy grabbed it and dashed down the hall for the bathroom as she clutched the shirt to her chest. She knew she was acting like a teenager, but she couldn't help it. There was something about Wade Faulkner she couldn't get out of her system. Darcy was afraid Wade was like diving. Once she took her first dive, she knew she'd never get enough. One touch of Wade's hand and she knew she needed more. Once she got it, Darcy didn't know if she'd ever be able to give him up. And she'd have to. She had a treasure to discover . . . if someone didn't kill her first. Then, well, then she didn't know. Could Wade be a part of her life then?

WADE CAME into the house through the back door. He placed Darcy's borrowed clothes at the bottom of the stairs and headed into the kitchen to make a quick snack. The guys at work teased him because he loved to eat. He ate all the time since he swam so much.

He was putting the grilled cheese on a plate when he looked up and the grilled cheese plopped off the spatula and luckily, landed on the plate. Darcy stood in the doorway to the kitchen with wet hair, a squeaky clean face, and wearing his T-shirt. He'd never seen anything as sexy before in his life.

"Mmm. I could smell your cooking all the way upstairs. What did you make?"

Wade cleared his throat and sliced the grilled cheese in half. "I'm always hungry at night. I didn't know if you were, too, but I went ahead and made you one anyway. It's a smoked gouda and apple grilled cheese on sourdough bread."

"And you just whipped this up?" Darcy asked as she walked into the kitchen.

Wade held out a plate for her. "Yes, but if you don't like it—"

"No," Darcy said, shaking her head and then grabbing the plate. "I just wondered if you were real. No man has ever cooked for me before."

"Well, I will happily be the first." And the last. "Do you want a beer?"

"Sure."

"We can sit in the living room and eat," Wade told her as he grabbed two beers from the fridge. He had a kitchen table that seated four, but he didn't want a table between them.

"Do you have any movies?" Darcy asked excitedly. "Being out on the boat so much, I don't get to see a lot of television or movies."

Wade followed her into the living room and was happy to see that she took a seat on the couch before patting the seat next to her. Wade set the beers on the coffee table and handed her the remote.

"A movie, the best grilled cheese I've ever had, and a beer." Darcy groaned happily after taking a bite of the sandwich. "This is better than sex."

"Then he didn't know what he was doing," Wade said before he could stop himself. He'd been thinking of nothing more than ways to please her since he met her. "But I'm glad I can please you."

Wade smiled as he bit into the sandwich. Darcy had blushed, but she's also scooted closer to him on the couch. "Thanks for the meal and the movie."

"Anything else I can do for you?" *To you?*

"This is perfect," Darcy said as she rested her hand on his leg and snuggled closer. "Thank you."

Wade set down his empty plate and wrapped his arm around Darcy's shoulders. He smiled over her head when she tucked herself against him. Her head fit perfectly against his chest as she wrapped her arm around his waist and sighed with contentment. He wished he could make her sigh with satisfaction, but for now, this was perfect.

Wade put his feet on the coffee table as Darcy pulled her feet onto the couch and rested more fully against him. He reached behind them and pulled a blanket from the back of the couch and draped it over Darcy as they settled in to watch the movie.

15

THE DOORBELL RINGING had Wade's eyes shooting open. He looked down and saw that he had his arm over Darcy's with his hand cupping a full breast. Darcy was still asleep, but now the side of her head was on his thigh with her face facing his, well, his *very happy to see you in the morning* part. And why was it so happy? One of Darcy's hands was resting on his very hard Mr. Happy.

The bell rang again and Wade cursed under his breath as Darcy grumbled in her sleep. Darcy gripped her hand around his even more swollen erection. It was all sexual torture until it turned into just torture when the bell rang for a third time and Darcy pulled his Mr. Happy toward her mouth, and not in the way he'd hoped.

"Hello?" she mumbled into his penis through his loose athletic shorts as if she were answering a ringing phone.

Wade let out a hiss as he involuntarily squeezed her breast.

"I don't know what kind of phone call this is, but I like it," Darcy muttered, her eyes still closed as she continued to talk to his Mr. Happy.

Well, Wade could put up with a little discomfort if she liked it. He'd do anything to please her, including letting her use Mr. Happy as a phone.

"Yoo-hoo!" an elderly voice called from the other side of the front door.

Damn.

Wade lifted his hand from Darcy's breast.

"Hey, is anyone there?" she asked before blowing into the *phone*.

"Darcy," Wade groaned as he tapped her shoulder. "It's time to get up." Gosh knows he was already up.

"Did you hang up on me? Asshole," she muttered as she dropped her hold on him. Wade let out a breath of relief. He'd didn't mind waking up to her touching him, but he'd bet she'd be embarrassed.

"Darcy!" Wade said loudly as Miss Winnie and now Miss Ruby were calling out at the door.

Darcy shot up. The top of her head hit his chin in the process. And there went Mr. Happy as pain shot up his jaw.

"Ow," Darcy said before realizing what had happened. "Oh my gosh, are you okay?"

"I'm fine," Wade said, rubbing his chin. "Are you hurt?"

"No, just a little embarrassed. Hey, did the phone ring?"

Wade pursed his lips to keep from laughing. "No, it's the doorbell. We have company."

"I should put some clothes on."

Wade heard the key in the lock. "Too late." The front door opened behind them and two old ladies teetered in with handfuls of food.

"Oh! We didn't think anyone was home. We did ring the bell multiple times," Miss Winnie Peel said as if she were surprised. She knew they were home. Wade knew this since her face showed no hint of surprise at all as she walked right in and sat down in the living room along with her best friend, Ruby Lewis. Similarly, Miss Ruby didn't look one bit surprised either, probably because they'd looked in the windows before even ringing the bell.

Miss Winnie resembled a chicken somewhat. Her pale skin was wrinkled and she had a very beak-like nose. She didn't weigh much more than a chicken either. On the other hand, Miss Ruby was her complete opposite. She was the rounded grandmotherly type that always had candy and cookies at the ready. Her reddish brown skin might be wrinkled, but she still had the same mischievous glint to her eye as Wade imagined she had as a child. Darcy was sitting up next to him with crazy hair, wide eyes, and the blanket pulled up to her chin.

"Darcy Delmar, these two charming women are Miss Winnie Peel and Miss Ruby Lewis."

"Nice to meet you both," Darcy said slowly as she clutched at the blanket.

"It's so nice to have another young lady in town. We're the head of the church's women's league and we brought you a Welcome to Shadows Landing basket," Miss Winnie said as she set a basket on the table and opened it.

"And I brought you some treats for later," Miss Ruby said as Wade's stomach rumbled at the smell of freshly baked biscuits, sausage gravy, and brownies. You would think they wouldn't go well together, but Wade was pretty sure he'd eat them all by the time Miss Winnie and Miss Ruby made it to their cars.

"It's nice to meet you both. Thank you for this. It smells so good," Darcy told them, leaning forward to take a whiff of the basket of goodies.

"We heard you met the family yesterday. And Reverend Winston. Moving fast, aren't we?" Miss Winnie asked as her eyes dropped pointedly to Darcy's stomach.

"Miss Winnie," Wade warned as kindly as he could.

"Win, I told you she wasn't pregnant. He just met her. They could have been going at it like rabbits, and they wouldn't have any inkling of a baby when they met with the reverend. Though a weddin' would be lovely. After all, when you meet The One, you just know." Miss Ruby sat back, folded her hands in her lap, and smiled widely at them.

Wade glanced at Darcy who was frozen next to him. Her mouth was partially open, her eyes were wide, and she looked down at her stomach before turning to Miss Winnie. "I look pregnant?"

"Told you," Miss Winnie smirked to Miss Ruby.

"I'm not pregnant. It would be impossible. Literally, impossible," Darcy said with a huff as she dropped back against the couch pillows. "But now I don't think I'll be able to enjoy the biscuits and gravy." Wade was about to defend her when Darcy shrugged. "Screw it. It would be a sin not to eat them." Darcy leaned forward again and grabbed the plate of biscuits from the basket.

Miss Ruby chuckled. "You got yourself a good one, Wade. Even if she is a treasure hunter."

"What does that mean?" Wade asked.

"Do you know how many people have been looking for Black Law's treasure over the decades?" Miss Ruby asked as she shook her head. "They get treasure fever. They can't think of anything else. I sure hope you give her something else to focus on so she'll stay around. Everyone in town has been sayin' how much they enjoy having you here, dear," Miss Ruby said, turning to Darcy.

"Thanks?" After that Darcy bypassed breakfast and went straight for the brownies.

"It's not some willy-nilly hunt, ladies," Wade said, feeling the need to defend her. "She found a three-hundred-year-old rowboat belonging to Timothy Longworth."

"Really? How do you know it belonged to Timothy?" Miss Winnie asked. It was clear they were now just as interested as Skeeter and the others had been.

Darcy suddenly went still mid-bite.

"Does it have anything to do with what you're going into the archives to search for?" Miss Winnie asked, zeroing in on Darcy as if she were a toddler telling tales.

"Yes," Darcy said slowly. "Which I really need to get ready for. We have to get to court, and then I have to meet Skeeter." Darcy stuffed the brownie in her mouth and shot up from the couch. She kept the blanket wrapped around her as she practically fell over Wade in her attempt to get out of the living room.

"Thank you so much for the food. I don't want to be late. Excuse me."

They sat and watched as Darcy ran up the stairs.

"Does she know it's only seven in the morning?" Miss Winnie asked.

"You scared her, the poor girl. You went straight for the juicy stuff. You need to learn some tact," Miss Ruby told Miss Winnie with a cluck of her tongue.

"When you're as old as we are, we don't have time for tact. Besides, it was fun."

"Miss Winnie!" Wade shook his head at her but she just winked back at him.

"Let us know if we can help in any way. We know every story, where every hunter has gone wrong, and probably forgotten some too. But we're happy to help," Miss Winnie said as she got up.

"Thank you, I'll remember that."

Wade helped the ladies to their car and returned inside to find Darcy eating biscuits and gravy. "Hurry, we have to leave for court in just a minute. Or I do. Are you coming? I didn't even ask."

"Wouldn't miss it."

THE DRIVE to Charleston seemed to take forever. Darcy was nervous, even though she shouldn't have been. She knew the drill. The state would take over the wreck. She was just nervous about being asked if she'd found anything else. She was going to lie, and she really didn't like that.

When they pulled up to the courthouse, Kord was flirting with Olivia as they both stood waiting on the front steps.

"Bless his heart, I don't know if Olivia would go for a younger man. Well, on second thought," she said as Gerald passed them and shot daggers at Kord.

"I think she's amusing Kord. I also think Kord is just having fun. He isn't exactly known for being in relationships," Wade said as he parked the car.

"Right on time," Olivia said as she walked over to them.

Kord hung back, and when Darcy looked at him, he gave her a thumbs-up. Phew, a little of the pressure was off. The jacket had been returned to the site.

"It's okay," Wade whispered to her as Olivia and Kord took off up the stairs.

"I'm really nervous," she admitted to Wade.

"Do you want something else to think about?" he asked.

"Yes." Anything would be better than potentially perjuring herself.

Wade pulled on her hand to stop her from walking up the steps. When she turned to ask him what was going on, his lips met hers and everything vanished. His mouth was sure, confident, and felt so good on hers. His hands held her neck and her back in such a way she wanted to climb into his arms and never be put down. And then they were gone. His hands dropped, his tongue went back into his own mouth, and she felt empty.

"You're up," Wade said as Darcy looked around as if seeing the world for the first time. Olivia was waving frantically from the door, and Wade held her hand as they walked into the courtroom.

The hearing went by in a blur. Darcy was acknowledged as the finder of the wreck and entitled to a small finder's fee, the right to assist with the excavation, and her name on a plaque if it ever went on display. She was never questioned. Olivia handled it all, and since Gerald had been on scene, they never asked if she took anything from it. Even though what she did was wrong, she was relieved they didn't ask her about it.

"Are you ready to go meet Skeeter?" Wade asked after they were back in the car.

"I'm ready for another kiss." Darcy stopped in the middle of buckling her seatbelt. Had she said that out loud? She hadn't meant to. She looked over to Wade who was unbuckling his seatbelt. She wasn't sure if he had heard her slip.

Suddenly, Wade slipped his hand behind her head as he leaned over the console and kissed her. Oh, he'd heard. And it was like he'd read every X-rated thought that was going through her head because one hand controlled the kiss as the other pulled her top from her skirt. This kiss was way more demanding and *hot*. Darcy was panting and her eyes practically rolled back in her head as he pushed her back against the seat. Wade's tongue took control of her mouth as he used his body to block anyone from seeing his hand roll her nipple between his fingers. When Darcy gasped in pleasure, he deepened the kiss.

His fingers played magic upon her breast as his kiss made her see stars. She reached for him and wrapped her fingers around the erection in his black slacks. Wade's hips surged forward into her hand, and she felt the power she had over him. And then there was a knock on the window.

Darcy screamed in surprise into Wade's mouth as he pulled away quickly. Detective Chambers stood there with red cheeks as he looked down the street. Wade took a deep breath as he rolled down his window.

"Detective. Can we help you?"

"You two are coming very close to breaking the law. But other than that, I wanted to let you know the South Carolina archaeologists are heading to the site. They have asked for your contact information and will want to speak to you. Also, here are the things you asked for."

"Thank you, detective," Darcy said as she avoided looking him in the eye. She'd just been caught making out in a car like a teenager, and now she felt like one after being busted.

"Any leads on the attacks?" Wade asked and all embarrassment fled. This was way more important than being caught making out in the car.

"Turns out there are a lot of treasure hunters in town. Working off the list of names Darcy gave me, I found out that Jules Chasseur, Cash Olweck, and Hugo Lopez are all in town and have all been crossed by Leon Snife at some point. So, no solid leads, just plenty of suspects."

Darcy pulled out her phone from her freshly retrieved purse and pulled up the private social media page for professional treasure hunters. "Cash is putting on a tribute to Leon tonight at Hunters Bay Bar."

"We need someone in there," the detective said more to himself than to her as Wade put the metal detector into the back of the car.

"No offense, but you'd stick out like a sore thumb," Darcy told him. "Wait," she said turning to Wade. "Put Granger in some kind of surfboard T-shirt, a pair of cargo shorts, and flip-flops and he'll fit in perfectly."

"Who?" the detective asked.

"I don't know if I've ever seen him in flip-flops," Wade chuckled before turning to Detective Chambers. "Granger Fox, sheriff of Shadows Landing. I think it's a great idea to send him. He's not local, he's from somewhere with a rich history of piracy, and if we can get him to dress the part, he will blend right in. And he doesn't need to be briefed as we've already filled him in."

"I don't like not having one of my guys there, but I'll look him up. Having a person who knows about it and who can talk the lingo is more important than a jurisdictional pissing contest."

"Couldn't have said it better," Darcy said, trying not to laugh. Plus, she'd feel much better having someone she already trusted with her.

"Plus, we'll both be there, too," Wade said as he got back behind the well.

Darcy smiled. He had read her mind, again. Her mind then went right back to that hot kiss. Wade winked at her, and she really did wonder if he could read minds.

"I'll be in touch before then. Call me if you hear anything else."

"If I speed, I can get home twenty minutes before you need to meet Skeeter." Darcy didn't need to be a mind reader to know what to do for those twenty minutes.

"What are you waiting for?"

16

OH MY STARS. Darcy was breathing hard as her eyes slowly uncrossed. Wade had gotten them to his house with twenty-*three* minutes to spare, and he'd used every single one of those minutes pleasuring her. It was as if he was on a personal mission to see how many orgasms he could give her before they had to leave. She looked down to where he was crawling up her naked body and sighed in complete ecstasy.

"I wish you were naked too," Darcy said as he pulled her into his arms.

"We didn't have enough time for that. And now you have five minutes to get dressed and meet Skeeter."

"Five minutes!" Darcy tried to scramble from the bed but her legs were like jelly.

"I wanted to make every minute count. Plus, there is nothing sweeter than hearing you yelling my name over and over again." Wade grinned and looked every inch a cocky man right now. But he deserved it. The things that man could do with his fingers and tongue made her really want to skip meeting Skeeter to find out what he could do with another part of his anatomy. A part she missed out on since he stayed clothed. A part she had dreamt about and a part she really wanted to see up close and personal.

Wade got out of bed and playfully swatted her bare bottom. "Hurry up. I'll drop you off there before I meet with Granger. I want to fill him in on tonight."

"Set up a fake profile, and I can add him to the group so he can monitor it and get a feel for who he'll see there," Darcy told him as she turned her back and had him clip her bra in place.

"It's much more fun taking this off," he told her as his hands came around front to squeeze her breasts quickly before he let her finish getting dressed.

Wade had her out the door and down the street while she was still a pile of sexually satisfied mush. That was until she saw a man entering Harper's bar.

"What is it?" Wade asked when she shot up from her seat.

"I would have sworn I saw Jules enter Harper's bar just now."

"The French treasure hunter?" Wade asked as he pulled to a stop across from the bar.

"Yes. What is he doing here?"

"There's Skeeter. You meet with him and don't worry about it. I'll find out what he's doing here. The bar just opened. It won't be busy. I'll have Harper question him."

"Text me as soon as you find out something."

Wade was already typing on his phone as she got out and met Skeeter. Darcy felt as if she were breaking into the historical society as she practically ran into the old building with Skeeter trailing behind her, confused as to why she darted past him so quickly.

"Is everything all right?" Skeeter asked in his country twang.

"No, I think I saw a rival walk into Harper's bar. I can't let him know I'm onto something here."

"You betcha. No one will find us where we'll be."

"And just where will you be?" Darcy looked up to see a stuffy man in his thirties standing there, looking and sounding completely out of place. Darcy wasn't from Shadows Landing, but she fit in better than this man did. He was in a tan seersucker suit with a green bowtie. His brown leather loafers were so polished the room was reflected in them. And there was an obvious stick up his ass.

"I'm sorry, who are you?" Darcy asked, instantly disliking the man.

"I'm *Dr.* Stephen Adkins. I run the historical society."

"Oh, how did you end up here? It sounds as if you're from New York."

Skeeter snickered next to her, and *Stef-awn*, that's how he said his name, turned red.

"I'm from Shadows Landing. I got my *doctorate* up north. I must have lost my accent when I was around my intellectual equals."

"Okay then," Darcy said as she looked at Skeeter and rolled her eyes. "It was nice meeting you. If you'll excuse us, we have some research to do."

"I can assist you far better than *this* man can. What do you need help with?"

"Thank you for the offer, but we're good. We'll call you if we need anything." Darcy grabbed Skeeter's hand and dragged him across the large open lobby filled with statues, paintings, and bookshelves. "Am I going in the right direction?" she whispered to Skeeter.

"Yup. Take the stairs to the basement. That was right

funny back there." Skeeter opened the stairwell door and held it open for her.

"I don't like him."

"Most of us don't. He always thought he was steppin' in high cotton. Then he went away for college, and we didn't see hide nor hair of him for years. Then he comes waltzin' back to town as if he owned it."

"Will he tell anyone we're here?" Darcy asked, worried about Jules as Skeeter pushed open the door to the basement archives.

"Darn tootin' he will."

"Then I don't have much time. Jules will come here after he gets as much local gossip as possible. If I tell you something, can you swear upon your life you won't tell a soul?"

"Cross my heart and hope to die." Skeeter used his finger to draw an X over his heart before turning back around and pushing through another door. He fumbled for the light switch as it was black as night in the room. When he turned it on, they saw old microfilm machines and what looked to be a large pressurized vault taking up a wide section of the far wall of the smaller room. Skeeter closed and locked the door behind them.

"What is this place?"

"This is the pirate archives. The vault holds original diaries and such. The old newspapers and records are on microfilm. While Mr. Fancypants up there was off doing his learnin', the historical society was still running. I spent a lot of time down here just readin'. Plus, my ma volunteered here when I was growing up. I helped put many of these documents on microfilm after school. It's also how I know the combination to the vault. Something Stephen is spittin' mad about."

"Why would he be mad about that?"

"'Cause I won't tell him what it is." Skeeter grinned his crooked grin and Darcy broke out in laughter.

"So, what did you want to tell me?"

Darcy pulled up her pictures that Wade had texted her and showed the clue to Skeeter. "I'm guessin' you figured out the Rattlesnake Shoal part, right?"

"Yes, it's the last couple of lines we can't get."

"I don't rightly know either. Let's see if we have anything in the books about a dancing master and someone loving someone so. I'll work the microfilm if you want to look at the original books."

Darcy's heart pounded with excitement. "You bet I do."

Skeeter opened the vault and Darcy stared with wonder. If she hadn't orgasmed so many times that morning she would do so now. In front of her were rows and rows of original books. Black Law, Anne Bonny, and every famous pirate ever to set foot in Shadows Landing each had their own section. All worry about Jules vanished as she threw herself into the books.

"I JUST *LOVE* YOUR ACCENT," Harper said with more of a southern belle accent than Wade had ever heard her use sober. When Harper got drunk, her accent got thicker. "It's so cosmopolitan."

Wade wanted to laugh. Harper was laying it on thick.

"Keep talkin'," she said in such a way it sounding like she said *tawk-en* instead of talking.

Wade took a seat near the bar so he could listen.

"What does the *mademoiselle* wish for me to converse about?"

Harper gave a little shiver and sighed. Wade had to bite his lip to keep from laughing.

"Tell me what you're doing here in an itty-bitty little place like Shadows Landing. I bet it's something real interestin' like."

"I'm looking for a treasure like you," Jules purred in his French accent. Wade probably drew blood from biting his lip to stop the laughter on that line.

"Aren't you a sweet talker? There's a lot of treasure in Shadows Landing. It's said Anne Bonny even hid some here."

"I didn't know the history of this place. I'm in Charleston looking for the lost treasure of Black Law. I believe he was known to hide out here."

"Sugar, *everyone* hid out here." Harper laughed. "But I've never heard of a lost treasure before. Tell me more." Harper leaned over the bar and rested her head on her hands. Her elbows on the bar top helped plump up her cleavage as she batted her eyelashes at him.

"It's said that Black Law had a ship heavy with gold when it went down somewhere off the coast. And I am going to find it. Maybe I'll even give you a piece of gold."

"Wow, ain't that somethin'?" Something sounded more like *sump-thin* and Wade had to hide a laugh under a cough.

Both of them turned to him. "Hey, can I get a beer?"

"Here," Harper snapped as she shoved a bottle of beer at him. Wade got up and grabbed the bottle.

"Thanks," he said as he headed back to his table and pulled out his phone.

"How do you even go about finding treasure in that great big ocean?" Harper asked, her accent suddenly back.

"I got a lead and that's all I can say. You have to know who you can trust when you're hunting treasure. It's very dangerous. A man died because he was hunting Black Law's treasure the other day. I'm sure you heard about it."

Wade wasn't laughing anymore and neither was Harper.

"Yes, I did hear that. I didn't know he was hunting Black Law's treasure like you are."

"*Oui.*" Jules puffed himself up. "But I am not afraid. I will find the treasure and become even more famous than I already am."

"How did Leon know about Black Law?" Harper asked, her voice suddenly serious.

"Why do you care? How did you know his name was Leon?" Jules asked, now suspicious.

Harper rolled her eyes and Wade knew the niceties were over. For once he wasn't going to stop her. Harper's arm shot out across the bar, grabbed Jules's hair at the top of his head, and slammed his head down onto the bar.

"*Putain!*" Jules cursed.

"I don't know what that means, but I'm guessing it's not nice," Harper said, not the least bit upset by the bleeding man cussing at her. "Now, how did you and Leon find out about Black Law?"

"Why do you care?" Jules spat.

"Do you want your head smashed again?"

"*Non*," Jules said as he stuffed a bar napkin up his bleeding nose.

"Then answer the damn question or I'll break a bottle over your head next."

"Leon is scum. Was scum. A bottom feeder. He stole from everyone. So, we stole from him. We followed him, and one night when he was out, we raided his office. We found the reports he had on Black Law and decided we'd one-up him and find it first."

"Who is we?"

"Me and my associates. Why do you want to know? Are you a hunter, too?"

Harper shook her head. "If Leon was a bottom feeder who stole, then where do you think he found out about Black Law?"

"Stole it from someone."

"So, aren't you stealing from the person who originally found all the information out?"

Jules shrugged. "It's worth it to stick it to Leon."

"But Leon is dead so you and your associates can back off. Understand?" Harper threatened.

"No way. This could be worth hundreds of millions of dollars." Jules tried to struggle from her grasp, but Harper wasn't done with him. She pulled her hand back and slammed a punch into his face that sent Jules falling off the back of his stool.

"Who's the thieving scum now? Get out of my bar."

Jules scrambled up and ran to the door before turning around. "I'll have you arrested!"

Harper shrugged. "Won't be the first time or the last."

Jules flung the door open and ran.

17

"HOT DIGGITY! IT'S A SONG."

Darcy's head shot up from Black Law's diary they had found hidden in his home. "What's a song?"

"*He Loves Me So.*

Skeeter was practically bursting with excitement. "I found an article in the paper from a year before Timothy died that said a Jonathan White asked a Catherine Marsden to marry him at the Shadows Landing Harvest Festival while the band played "He Loves Me So."

"*If I shall perish, it was Black Law who captured Samuel, William, and me. His ship rides low and lower shall it ride.*" Darcy repeated the clue. "We know that means the ship had treasure on it.

"*No amount of gold, silver or gems will save me.* We know this is telling the family what kind of treasure was on the ship. *To my family, I shall miss thee, but I leave one last gift.* The last gift is his clue to the ship's location. *As the snake's tail sounds,* which is Rattlesnake Shoal offshore. *You spin me like a dancing master.* I don't know what this means yet,"

Darcy sighed with frustration. "But, we now know 'He Loves Me So' is a song. Why is that important?"

"We need to find the lyrics," Skeeter said as he headed straight to the vault. "There's a music book in here from the 1700s."

Darcy's phone pinged with an incoming text from Wade: *Jules just left. He and his associates know about the treasure. They found out by breaking into Leon's office and stealing info. Leon was killed because he was hunting the treasure. Are you safe?*

Darcy looked to Skeeter who was carefully turning some very old pages in a book. "Are we safe here?"

Skeeter didn't answer. He just pulled up his overly baggy untucked shirt to reveal a very large hunting knife strapped to his waist.

Yes, we're safe. Who were his associates? Darcy typed.

We think Jules's team. Wade replied.

"Our time is running out. Other hunters know about Black Law's treasure."

"No worries," Skeeter said with a sigh. "The lyrics are meaningless to the hunt. See for yourself."

Darcy looked over his shoulder to read the song. It was meaningless. There were no lyrics. It was an instrumental piece; just sheet music. She felt her whole body deflate. "I don't understand."

"I don't either. But it has to be it. This song is the only thing that makes sense."

"Can you play the piano?" Skeeter asked.

"Not really."

"Gator can, well, he used to be able. Then he lost a finger or two, and it just doesn't sound right now. The timing is all off."

"What are you doing?" Darcy asked as Skeeter gently placed the book in a flannel shirt.

"If people are after this, I ain't gonna make it easy to find. Besides, we need someone to play it on the piano to see if the clue is in the notes or the timing." Darcy stared as Skeeter placed the book in the waistband of his pants at the small of his back and dropped his baggy shirt over it.

"Did you find anything?" Skeeter asked.

"I'm reading Black Law's diary. I think I have an idea where he hid the emerald he brought back with him from the sunken ship. He also talked about a nearby shoal, so the treasure has to be in that area. But that's a really big area. If worse comes to worst, I can start a grid search of the area, but that will tip everyone off real fast, and soon I'll be just another boat in the middle of twenty other hunters."

"Here ya go," Skeeter said, peeling off another flannel shirt he was wearing over his baggy T-shirt. "I brought extras."

Well, what the hell. She'd already stolen one clue so why not steal another? Especially when Jules and probably Cash and Hugo were hot on her tail after Leon somehow stole her research. She was dealing with a den of thieves trying to find a pirate's treasure. The irony wasn't lost on her.

Darcy stuffed the carefully wrapped book down the front of her waistband and pulled her shirt out and over it. "Let's go and find someone who can play the piano."

"Do you play the piano?" Darcy asked Wade as he and Granger met her back at his house to get ready for Leon's memorial service at Hunters Bay Bar.

"No, do you, Grange?"

"Sorry," Granger replied. "But Miss Ruby does."

"That's right. She used to teach piano. I forgot about that," Wade said over his shoulder as he headed into the kitchen for some beers.

"Do you have any questions about tonight?" Darcy asked as Granger messed with the buttons on his short-sleeved button-up shirt. Darcy smacked his hand away as he tried to button up more. "I'm telling you the younger hunters, especially ones who look like you, wear their shirts half unbuttoned."

"It's ridiculous," Granger complained.

"Your chest and abs are ridiculous. Ridiculously hot. Trust me. Leave the shirt open and flirt with the hordes of women who will be drooling at your chest. If you don't, it will be suspicious."

Granger grimaced and Wade laughed.

"Did I miss something?" Darcy asked before gasping. "Oh my gosh, you're gay?"

"No, I'm not gay," Granger mumbled. "I just can't stand women who throw themselves at me."

Wade was laughing hard now, and Darcy thought it was strange. She'd never heard a guy say that before. At least the hunters she hung out with didn't.

"See," Wade said as he handed them all beers, "Granger is rather popular, but in college, he gave in to the fawning a lot."

"And learned my lesson," Granger grumbled.

"What lesson?" Darcy asked as Granger's jaw tighten, and she was really curious, but also felt bad for prying.

"After a fun night with a girl I didn't expect to see again, six weeks later she told me she was pregnant. Turns out she was lying, but I didn't find out until I was in a car accident that made playing football impossible. I told her I wasn't going to go pro, not that I ever was. But in her mind, I was going places, and she wanted a free ride along the way. That's when she told me she wasn't really pregnant."

"Oh my gosh, that's awful. I'm so sorry." Darcy wished she could prove to Granger that not all women were like that.

"Don't feel too sorry for him," Wade said with a shake of his head. "The cold, standoffish jerk bit works for a lot of women. He just makes sure they know there will never be a future with him."

"Can arrogance be added into that?" Darcy asked, and Granger crossed his arms and lifted an eyebrow. "Perfect! You will be a smashing success tonight. You just have to brag a little and pretend to enjoy the fawning and you'll fit right in."

"I got the background story you sent. Thank you," Granger said and grabbed his mirrored shades and slipped them on. "Let's go."

WADE AND DARCY walked into the bar first. It was on the water with two stories of large back decks with fans suspended from the beams and drinks flowing. They made their way through the front door and straight to the deck Cash Olweck reserved for hunters.

Wade smiled to himself. Jules was telling people he got the broken nose fighting off a shark. And while the Frenchman was more skin than muscle, his shirt was open halfway to his waist. So were many others for that matter, so Granger would fit in perfectly.

"Darcy! I'm surprised to see you here," a handsome man in his late thirties said with a smile and beer in hand. "Here, take this. Goodness knows you need it."

"And why would I need it, Cash?" Darcy asked with annoyance.

"To loosen that treasure between your legs. It probably has cobwebs at this point. I can give it good stretching if you'd finally let me."

Wade saw red. Cash completely cut him out as he looped an arm around Darcy and pulled her against his mostly open shirt. If you're only going to button the two bottom buttons, what's the point of even buttoning it?

"I'd rather have sex with a porcupine, but luckily I have something way better. Cash, meet Wade. Wade, this dickhead is Cash Olweck."

"At least you're talking about my dick." Cash winked at her before holding out his hand for Wade. "So you finally thawed the ice queen. What's your secret?"

"I'm not an asshole," Wade said between gritted teeth. "And you'll take your hand off Darcy, or I'll remove it myself."

"Is that so?" Cash asked, straightening up. He realized he fell several inches shorter and a good thirty pounds of muscle lighter than Wade and dropped the tough guy attitude. "Well, it must be what I thought—one hell of a treasure."

Cash sauntered off and Wade let out a long breath. "These are your friends?"

"No." Darcy shook her head. "These are all colleagues and rivals. No one is a friend here. They're all out to one-up each other, but part of that is pretending to be friends so they can brag. Nobody else is willing to listen to their crap for very long."

That would be horrible. Wade's colleagues were like brothers to him. They made their way to the bar, and he ordered a beer as Granger walked in. People eyed him and Wade saw a dark-haired, muscular man walk up to him.

"That's Hugo Lopez. He runs Tesoro, Inc. It's his own company and not corporate-sponsored like Cash and Jules are. He found a boat with Mexican gold on it about five years ago so he's able to be completely self-financed," Darcy told him as she sipped her beer.

"Don't I know you?" Wade heard a French-accented voice ask from behind him.

"I don't think so. I would remember a Frenchman with a black eye and cracked nose," Wade said, before holding out his hand. "I'm Wade. I'm here with Darcy. Do you know her?"

Jules would have snorted elegantly, but his damaged nose made it sound more like a wheezing pig snorting. "Darcy and I go way back, don't we?"

"Sure do. What happened to you, Jules?" Darcy asked as she touched his nose gently.

"I was diving and a darn shark got curious. Rammed my mask only to discover I wasn't edible. I scared him off."

"Goodness. I swim these waters every day and always worry about sharks. I've had some close calls myself. Where were you diving?" Wade asked, trying to put him at ease so he wouldn't remember seeing him in Shadows Landing.

"A mile or so from the shore," Jules said vaguely.

"Hope you found what you were looking for."

"Not yet, but I will soon. What are you doing in town, Darcy? The guys were all surprised you came. After all, we read in the paper the police think you murdered Leon."

Darcy laughed and smiled. "As if everyone here didn't want to kill Leon." Then she let her smile slip. "But I am being investigated."

"I heard you made a claim in court this morning, too."

Jules looked around and then called out to Hugo who joined them with Granger. Hugo was built like Wade, but more compactly. "I was telling Darcy you told me she made a claim this morning. Pretty hardcore for someone being investigated by the police," Jules told the group.

"Hugo, this is my friend, Wade," Darcy said, introducing them. The hunters all reminded Wade of sharks circling. Cash was closing back in and Jules was leaning forward as several others took noticeable steps toward her.

"And this is Granger. I just met him. He's an amateur but knew Leon."

"Sorry," Cash said as if joking as he gave up the pretense of talking nearby and joined the group. "So you made a claim?"

"Yes, I found an old rowboat in the river. Nothing major, just neat."

"That's not all you found," Hugo said softly. "Are you okay?"

"Why wouldn't she be okay?" Jules asked.

"Someone dropped explosives out there while she was diving. I'm glad you're okay."

"Thank you, Hugo. I didn't know anyone knew," Darcy said. Wade could hear the slight suspicion in Darcy's voice and wondered if Hugo did, too.

"Small community. I hear *lots* of things."

"What have you heard about Leon's murder?" Darcy asked with a smirk. "Think I killed him like the police do?"

Hugo, Cash, and Jules laughed.

"No," Hugo said.

"I don't know about that. I could see it," Cash said a little more seriously that Wade had hoped for.

Darcy didn't seem upset, though. She just rolled her eyes.

"I know I'm not a pro, but even I've heard about you," Granger said to Jules, "threatening to cut off Leon's head. And Hugo grabbing him by the neck and threatening him." Granger chuckled as he turned to Cash. "And we all know it was probably Leon who pulled that fake relic trick on you."

"Your point?" Hugo asked, no longer sounding nice.

"My point is from what I'm hearing everyone had a reason to kill him. The question is who had the balls to actually do it?"

18

DARCY HELD HER BREATH. Granger had said it jokingly, but no one was laughing. Wade slipped a hand around her waist and gently squeezed the top of her hip, letting her know he had her back. Darcy leaned into him as everyone suddenly got thirsty and took a drink.

Jules held out his glass of wine. "Leon was a son of a whore, but he was one of us. To Leon."

The others all lifted their glasses and toasted the man they all had motives to kill.

"Well, this has been fun," Cash said as his film crew arrived. "But, I must comfort those poor women who lost a valued member of our community."

Darcy looked over to where two women in their early twenties sat in short shorts and barely-there bikini tops downing shots at the bar. Darcy rolled her eyes as Cash sauntered away.

"Come on," she said softly to Wade as Granger, Hugo, and Jules began to talk. "I'll introduce you to some of the amateurs I know."

Darcy and Wade made the rounds, talked about Leon's

death, and heard more conspiracy theories than she could ever remember. Including one about alien abduction from a hunter who swore he'd found an underwater UFO landing site. She was sure Detective Chambers would love that one.

"I don't think we're any closer to finding out who did this," Darcy said as Wade led her to a quiet corner at the end of the long bar.

"I don't think so either. I was hoping it would be clear who did it. And, the truth is, we don't know if it was one of them. I wouldn't mind punching a couple of them myself. Harper already beat me to it."

Darcy felt her mood lighten as she laughed. "And he's telling everyone he battled a shark." Darcy was laughing so hard, tears rolled down her face. "I think Harper has a new nickname."

"We'll tell her tomorrow. It's getting late. Is there anyone else you want to talk to?"

Darcy looked around. Granger fit right in as he and Cash hung out with a gaggle of bikini-clad girls. Darcy had watched from the corner of her eye as Granger made his way around the room talking to nearly everyone there. He'd even chatted up the bartender before bringing Cash a beer.

"No. I think I've talked to everyone I need to. And Granger seems to be talking to a lot of people as well. I was really hoping it would be clear who the murderer was. I hate being the butt of these jokes about being at the wake for the man I killed."

Darcy had tough skin. She was used to spending long stretches of time by herself, and she'd grown up surrounded by members of the military. She was used to keeping her feelings under wraps and under control, but it hurt to have people mock her.

"Then let's get home," Wade said, taking her drink and placing it on the bar.

She liked the way he said *home*. She'd moved around so much as a kid before they finally settled in Key West. And then she moved around constantly with her research and diving. Home was a luxury she didn't have. And when he said *home,* it did something to her. She suddenly longed to do nothing but hold his hand and stroll into a house they shared together. A place that wasn't constantly moving and wasn't always empty. *Home* was more than a place to her. It was a feeling—a feeling of love and support, and she wanted it more than she ever knew.

"I'd like that," Darcy said as she reached for his hand.

Feeling the warmth, strength, and support from Wade made her feel as if she could do anything. All night he'd kept a hand on her arm or back. He'd been the silent strength she had needed. Darcy was also realizing it was getting harder and harder to think about moving on and leaving Wade. In a short amount of time, he'd found a place in her heart.

WADE HAD KEPT her hand in his for the drive home. He'd asked more personal questions about some of the hunters and asked about her experiences, hopes, and dreams. By the time they'd made it back to his house, she felt as if she had a true partner in her search for Black Law's treasure. It felt incredible to share her feelings and excitement with someone who shared them.

"But what about you? Why did you join the Coast Guard?" Darcy asked him as they walked up the porch steps.

"There was a hurricane that hit Charleston when I was seven. I thought I was big and tough, and I snuck out of the house and onto the family boat to really experience the storm. Well, the wind broke the dock, and I floated away with the boat and part of the dock. I tried to be brave, but I was scared out of my mind. I called in a Mayday, and they came even through the howling winds and vicious waves. They swooped in like guardian angels and rescued me."

"I bet your parents were scared to death."

Wade chuckled as he opened the front door. "They never knew I was gone until the Coast Guard brought me home."

Darcy laughed as she could imagine a little Wade showing up at the front door when he should have been in bed. "I bet you got in trouble for that."

"Yes and no. My parents were so thrilled to have me home after hearing how I was rescued they didn't yell at me. They simply told me I would have to go with them to haul the boat back and would then have to clean it—top to bottom."

Wade looked around his house and then to the basket on the table.

"Why don't you go upstairs, get comfy, and meet me on the balcony. I'll bring up the brownies and some wine."

Darcy almost cheered. That sounded perfect. Suddenly the treasure, the hunt, and life on the water began to fade. Not that she wanted to stop, but she felt centered with Wade. "That sounds lovely."

Darcy sent him a smile before hurrying upstairs. She dumped the bag of clothes on the bed, trying to find something cute to wear, but her eyes kept going back to Wade's T-shirt. He did say comfy.

By the time Wade made it upstairs, Darcy was in his shirt and curled up on the loveseat on the balcony. She'd run a brush through her hair, her loose curls bouncing into place the second she hit the humidity outside.

"Here you go," Wade said, handing her a glass of red wine. He placed the plate of brownies on the side table and took the seat next to her. "Here," he said, patting his legs as he leaned back.

Darcy pulled her feet out from where she'd tucked them under her and stretched them out and over Wade's lap. His hand came to rest on her shins as he reached for the plate of brownies.

"How do you want to proceed?" Wade asked as she took a bite and moaned.

"First I want to hug Miss Ruby, then I want to ask if she can look over that song."

Wade quietly chuckled as he moved his hand up her leg. "I meant about us. You feel it too, right?"

Darcy set the brownie down. "I think I made it clear when I was screaming your name that I felt it." She took a deep breath. She was a grown woman, but it was still scary to tell someone how you felt. "I feel such a connection to you. It's like my whole body screams for you when you're not touching me. How is this possible in such a short time?"

Wade's fingers brushed back and forth over her thigh. "I don't know. How was it possible for a teenager to sink a pirate ship and then three hundred years later you find it? Sometimes I think it's just meant to be."

Darcy leaned forward, and Wade slipped his arm around her shoulder and the other under her legs. In one quick move, he had her in his lap. "I'm glad I hauled you out of the water two nights ago."

"I'm glad you didn't think I murdered Leon," Darcy joked as she leaned her head against Wade's shoulder. "Wade?"

"Yes?"

"I'm scared," Darcy admitted.

"You aren't going to jail, and I swear I will protect you from whoever is behind this."

"Not that," Darcy said, taking a deep breath. Admitting her fears was even scarier than admitting she liked him. "I'm scared there will be no treasure, and I'll have to leave again."

Wade was still for a second before he used his finger to lift her chin from where she had it buried against his chest. "If this is truly something more than lust, which I think we both know it is, we will work it out. For now, I have you in my arms and in my life. I intend to enjoy every moment of it."

Wade tilted her lips to his and kissed her with a slow, aching madness. His fingers fluttered down her spine and across her thigh. Darcy shivered in his arms and it wasn't from the cold. She was as hot as the summer night. She clutched at his shirt, pulling herself closer to him, and wondered if she'd ever be able to get close enough.

When Wade pulled back from the kiss, Darcy made a noise of protest.

"I want more, but I'm just as happy sitting here kissing you all night."

"I've wanted more from the first time you touched me. Touch me now, Wade. All night."

Darcy gasped and then laughed as Wade easily lifted her in his arms and practically raced into his bedroom. The curtains fluttered in the moonlight of the open door and the summer air caressed her as Wade pulled his T-shirt from her body. There was no embarrassment or nervousness. It was as if her body knew its match. Darcy rested on her elbows, looking up at Wade as he undressed. It was worth the wait. He was tanned from all the time on the water and his body was that of an elite athlete. And when she finally got to see all of him, she would have sworn her body screamed with joy.

Wade reached for the nightstand and grabbed a condom. Darcy reached for him, but he pinned her hands above her head. "There was one more thing I wanted to try this morning but didn't have time."

Oh. My. God. Darcy's eyes rolled back into her head, but she felt him hanging on for control.

"Let go and take me with you," Darcy said between pants. Wade looked down at her and kissed her.

"I'll always take you with me."

And he did. She was an adventurer, and Wade took her on a trip of her life. Darcy knew that tonight she'd embarked on the beginning of her most important adventure yet—one with her heart.

19

Ding-dong.

Dammit, not again.

Wade groaned as he kept his arm around Darcy. That night had been, well, a treasure. He'd been with enough women to know that last night was something special, and he planned on doing whatever it took to hang onto her.

Bang, bang, bang!

"Who's at the door?" Darcy grumbled.

"Go away! Miss Ruby *and* Miss Winnie!" Wade shouted.

"Police!"

Darcy and Wade shot up.

"That wasn't Miss Ruby," Darcy said, her eyes wide in fear.

"It's also not Kord or Granger. Get dressed. I'll see what's going on."

Wade slipped on a pair of shorts and grabbed a T-shirt as he yelled that he was coming. He padded down the stairs, unlocked the door, and opened it to find Detective Chambers and two Charleston uniforms at his door.

"Detective, what's the big hurry? You could have called. I thought Granger would have filled you in on last night."

"This is official business. Can we come in?"

"Of course." Wade opened the door for them, but the detective turned to one of the uniforms.

"Take the back door. You stay here and guard the front."

"Is this really necessary?" Wade asked, suddenly worried. This wasn't a visit to see how last night went.

"Where's Miss Delmar?"

"I'm right here. What's going on?"

Wade looked up the stairs to see Darcy walking down with her hair pulled back into a messy ponytail that had curls sticking out around her face and wearing a sundress he recognized as Harper's.

Wade held out his hand, and Darcy reached for it the second she stepped off the stairs. "Let's have a seat," he said to the detective as he gestured to the living room.

Darcy and he took a seat on the couch, but the detective stayed standing. "Where were you last night?"

Wade gave a dry laugh. "You're joking. You know where we were. We were at Hunters Bay Bar."

"When did you leave?"

"Ten o'clock," Wade answered.

"What's going on, detective?" Darcy asked.

"Where did you go after you left?" Detective Chambers asked, ignoring Darcy's question.

"We came back here and were here all night," Wade answered. He squeezed Darcy's hand to indicate he'd answer the questions.

"Can anyone verify that?"

"I don't know. You can ask my neighbors if they saw us pull in."

"Ma'am, you can't come in here," the uniform said from out on the porch.

"That look won't scare me. I was married to a SEAL." Wade and Darcy turned to see his neighbor, Edie Greene Wecker, pushing her way past the uniform. Her brown hair was in a ponytail and her electric blue eyes were flashing. "What's going on? Are you okay, Wade?"

· "Ma'am, I must ask you to leave," the detective said, coming to stand between Edie and Wade. They had been friends his whole life, practically family.

"Why don't you ask Edie if she saw us last night?" Wade suggested. "She lives two houses down."

"Why does Wade need an alibi?" Edie demanded. She'd been such a quiet, subdued woman after the death of her husband. He'd been killed by a traitor in his team and Edie's brother, who was on the same SEAL team, was the only one to get out alive. Walker Green had made his way on a containership from Africa to Charleston and then had snuck into his childhood town to seek help from Gavin. After the man responsible was caught, Edie had bought their old family home and moved from the naval base in Virginia back to Shadows Landing. Lately, it seemed she was coming out of her shell.

"Ma'am," the detective started to say.

"Don't you 'ma'am' me. I don't know what time they got home, but I know they were here after eleven," Edie said as she placed her hands on her hips.

"And how do you know that?" the detective asked.

"Because I heard them. I think the whole street did," Edie leaned around the detective. "I'm Edie, by the way. It's a pleasure to put a face with the enthusiastic voice."

Wade saw Darcy turn bright red as the detective shifted

his feet and cleared his throat. "Not to be indelicate, but how do you know it was them?"

"Well, the cries of *Wade, Wade, oh my god, yes, Wade!* along with the *Oh Darcy, You feel so good* groans that came from the house as I walked my dog kind of gave it away."

Darcy buried her face in his shoulder and even Wade felt himself turning pink. It was then he realized he hadn't closed the bedroom door leading to the balcony. Sure enough, the whole street probably had heard them.

Everyone was quiet for a moment until Darcy stood up and held out a hand. "Well, Edie, I'm Darcy, and it's a pleasure to meet you."

"Although not quite the pleasure as last night," Edie said with a wink.

Wade tossed back his head and laughed. It was the only thing he could do after learning people had heard him having sex with Darcy, and that's the only thing that provided an alibi. Speaking of which . . . "So, what is this about?"

The detective took a seat then and put away his notepad. "I got a full report from Granger. He called me when he drove home last night. Basically, it's as you said, Miss Delmar. Everyone hated Leon."

"So, you were going to arrest me because we couldn't find a better suspect?"

The detective shook his head. "Granger left at midnight. Cash, Hugo, and Jules were still there along with some young women and a couple of amateur hunters. At five this morning, I got a call from a fisherman. When I arrived, I found a body with its head cut off. The fisherman's golden retriever was nice enough to bring back the head from the ocean. It was Jules Chasseur."

"Someone cut off Jules's head?" Darcy whispered in

horror as her face drained of all blood. "And you thought *I* did it?"

"With immunity in hand, it wouldn't be unheard of for you to get rid of your competition. Obviously, immunity wouldn't reach to Jules's murder."

Wade was furious, but he took a steadying breath. Showing any tendency toward anger right now would only hurt their situation. "What do you know?"

The detective looked weary as he leaned back in his chair and looked over at Edie. "Well, go ahead and take a seat unless you'll leave and let me talk to them alone."

"I'll get y'all some coffee," Edie said kindly as she patted the detective's wrinkled shoulder."

"Thank you, miss."

"Mrs.," she corrected. "Mrs. Wecker."

"Yes, ma'am."

When Edie went into the kitchen, the detective ran a hand over his face. "I got nothing. Divers are searching the area of the bay where the body washed up, but I'm not holding out much hope. I have no evidence of any kind leading to anyone except you and even that evidence is only circumstantial at best. I had hoped we'd discover something last night, but like I said, nothing there either. Only more suspects with no evidence."

"What can I do to help?" Darcy offered, even though Wade wanted to do nothing more than pull her back and lock her in his house where no one could touch her.

"Here y'all go," Edie said, carrying out a tray with coffee on it. "And if I may make a suggestion, when Walker and Shane had a mission, they would set traps if they didn't know where the enemy was. Better to be ready for them than be surprised by them."

The detective perked up and leaned forward. "That's a good idea. Who are Walker and Shane? Can they help us?"

"Walker is my brother, but he lives in Kentucky with his wife now. And Shane is my—was my husband. He was killed in action."

"I'm very sorry, Mrs. Wecker. But you gave me an idea. A good one." The detective turned to Darcy, and Wade took her hand in his as if that would protect her. "I want you to be visible. And I want you to continue hunting the treasure. Only this time we'll find it."

"Find it?" Darcy squeaked out. Wade was sure she wasn't going to let the police in on her hunt.

"Well, the treasure we leave planted for them."

Wade's tight lips relaxed into a smile, and he felt Darcy breathe a sigh of relief next to him.

"Do you think your friend Granger will help? It would be good to keep him undercover with you so you have law enforcement with you to keep you safe."

Wade nodded. "I'm sure he will."

The detective stood up and tossed back the coffee as if it were a shot of liquor. "Good. I'll go see him now. I'll call when we get the details figured out. Thanks for doing this. I know you're putting yourself in further danger. We'll keep you safe."

Wade wasn't entirely sure of that, but he knew he would do anything to keep Darcy safe. And if it meant drawing out a murderer, so be it.

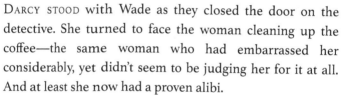

20

DARCY STOOD with Wade as they closed the door on the detective. She turned to face the woman cleaning up the coffee—the same woman who had embarrassed her considerably, yet didn't seem to be judging her for it at all. And at least she now had a proven alibi.

"I'm so sorry we disturbed you last night. But thank you for coming forward to help."

Edie picked up the tray and smiled kindly at her. "Wade and I have been friends since he was born. I grew up here and my brother, Walker, is best friends with Wade's cousin Gavin. The Faulkners are like family. And family sticks together." Then Edie winked at her. "And I'm glad someone on this street is having fun."

Darcy turned to Wade when Edie went into the kitchen. "When did her husband pass away?"

"Almost two years ago now. She hasn't so much as looked at another man, even if they are doing plenty of looking themselves," Wade whispered back.

"She's so young, though."

"Doesn't mean her heart wasn't already taken. Maybe

someday she'll be ready for a second love, but not right now."

Darcy and Wade walked back into the kitchen. Edie was washing the mugs in the sink and Darcy went to join her. She picked up a towel and began to dry them.

"I've been thinking," Edie said as she rinsed soap off a mug. "Shane has some weapons and some SEAL gear packed away. If you'd like to use it, I know he'd approve."

"Thank you. I'll come over later this morning and have a look at it."

"I'll be heading to Keeneston next month to visit Walker and his wife, Layne. It's a great place to hide out if you need it." Edie winked at Darcy and picked up a towel to dry her hands. "It was great meeting you, Darcy. Let me know if I can help in any way."

"I will. Thank you. You're a very kind woman."

Edie smiled and Darcy felt her heart break. While it was a kind smile, it was a haunted one. Darcy could tell Edie was still mourning the death of her husband. Darcy was overcome with compassion and wrapped her arms around a surprised Edie. "Anytime you want to hang out, just come get me. If I ever get my boat back, I can take you diving."

Edie hugged her back. "I'd like that. Thank you." Edie pulled back and turned to Wade. "See you later." With a little smile, Edie left.

WADE CLOSED the front door after telling Edie he'd be over after lunch and turned to find Darcy standing behind him. She was chewing her lip and looking down at the ground.

"Is everything okay?"

Darcy's head shot up as if she were surprised to see him. "Sorry. My mind can go off in so many directions at once. I was thinking about a clue I found in Black Law's diary about the emerald that was stolen from the dowry. At the same time, I was thinking of Edie and her husband's love. I was also thinking of us. Of last night."

"You were thinking about all that at once?" Wade asked as he raised an eyebrow in surprise.

"Yeah. I was also thinking of a good way to set up the murderer, and I was thinking of how I could secretly continue with the real treasure hunt."

Wade shook his head. He'd heard women could do this, but he'd always thought it was a joke. "I'm amazed you could think about all that at once. Let's take it one at a time. Tell me about the diary and the emerald."

Darcy turned and ran upstairs before hurrying back down with an old book wrapped in what looked to be a flannel shirt. "I found this passage talking about the heart of his home. That home has now been turned into Harper's bar. Anyway, I think if I can break down the passage after looking around her bar, I'll be able to piece together his paragraph about it. But, more importantly, if the emerald *is* there, then it's further proof that the treasure is real and I'm not just chasing ghost stories."

"Okay," Wade said, pulling out his phone and sending a text. A second later, he got one back. "Harper will meet us at the bar in an hour. That way we can look all through it before people start showing up. Next?"

"Edie and her husband's love. I hope to find that someday. We—" Darcy stopped and bit her lip again.

"We had something last night that made you think we might have a chance at something as powerful as what Edie and Shane had," Wade finished for her.

Darcy nodded her head.

"I don't know what our future holds, but I want the chance

to explore it. I'll always be honest with you, Darcy. If I don't feel the same, I'll tell you. But right now everything inside of me is telling me to reach for you. I've had crushes before. Infatuations too. Nothing compares to the feelings I have right now. I feel ... centered. So, if you're willing, I'd like to see where this goes."

"I feel the same way, Wade. I want the chance to see where this goes." Darcy took a deep breath and let it out and Wade saw her relax a little.

"So, next is a way to set up the real murderer. I have some ideas on that, too."

"I was thinking of being very public, yet not. Like flashing your cards to one player in a game of poker, but then hiding them from the other player."

Wade nodded. "We let it slip to one person that you've found something. We could use Granger for that. I don't like it, but we can let people know you're in Shadows Landing with your boyfriend. Granger can say he overheard you talking about it."

"I like that idea," Darcy said, nodding as if she were running the scenario through her mind. "But for the actual treasure hunt, I want to take photos of all the documents and then get them safely hidden. I'm so nervous holding on to them."

"Let's get Miss Ruby over to play the music and then we can have Reverend Winston show us another secret hiding place in the church. The whole town could burn and they'd still be safe there."

Wade pulled out his phone and sent the first text. "Reverend Winston said to come any time before four this afternoon, and he'll help us."

Wade sent another text and waited. And waited. "I guess she's doing something. But I've asked her if she has time to come over. So, want to grab breakfast at Stomping Grounds Diner before we tear apart my cousin's bar?"

"I'd like that. I'll jump in the shower real quick, then we can head out."

Wade followed her upstairs but didn't push it when Darcy went into her own room. He'd been feeling as if time was running out, but now he knew they had time to find out if what they were feeling was love. It was certainly possible. He'd been in love before, and while there were some similarities, this all felt new to him. Either way, he was excited to see where they ended up.

Darcy looked around the diner and blinked. Kids were hanging from the rafters. Literally. A young woman around Darcy's age stood in the middle of the diner with her hands on her hips as she looked up at the three large wooden beams that ran across the diner. The ceiling was almost eighteen feet high and the wooden beams were about ten feet up. Lights and fans hung from them, keeping the diner cool.

When Darcy followed the woman's glare, she saw two boys standing on one of the beams about eight feet apart and holding wooden swords. "Levi!" the woman shouted. "You get your little butt down here right now."

The older of the boys on the beam shrugged and didn't seem the least bit concerned that his mother looked ready to kill him. "We're playing gladiator and Lyle said he could beat me."

"Your brother is five. What does he know?" the mother asked impatiently.

"Boys are so stupid," a girl sitting at a large round table said with a roll of her eyes.

"The mom is Lydia. Her husband, Landry, is deployed right now. Every time he comes home they have a baby," Wade whispered. "Landry Jr. is the oldest at ten. Then there's a kid every year. So, the girl who just called boys stupid is Lacy. She's nine. The girl in pigtails nodding her head in agreement is her sister, Leah. She's seven."

"And the boys up there?"

"The older one is Levi. He's eight. The younger one is Lyle. Then the little girl coloring and not paying attention is Lindsey. She's six. And the littlest, Leo, is four."

Darcy looked over to where Leo was smashing his hands in his pancakes.

"How do you feel about children?" Darcy asked almost in horror at the scene.

Wade smiled, and it made her insides do a little flip. "Love them. Even these guys. You know the saying, it takes a village? Well, Shadows Landing is the village helping Lydia out. She's making the best of a tough situation."

"How often is Landry home?"

"Not very often. He's career military and is stationed in the Middle East. He comes home for a couple of months every year."

"How can she manage?" Darcy asked. Her heart was breaking for the young wife who was left at home to run everything while worrying for her husband's life.

"She has us." Wade grinned before he headed over to Lydia. Two men went to join him. They were around the same age, late fifties, and both smelled of barbecue.

"Darius. What's cooking at the Pink Pig?" Darcy heard Wade ask the tall and muscular man with dark brown skin and a shaved head.

"Just smoking up a nice-looking hog. Come on over for lunch, Wade."

"He'll be coming to Lowcountry Smokehouse today for lunch, Darius," said a man of equal age to Darius, except he looked like Santa Claus with a farmer's tan.

"Earl," Darius grumbled.

"How ya doing, Earl?" Wade asked as he pulled a chair from a nearby table.

"Good. My pig is smoking up nicely under the *wood* smoke."

Darius rolled his eyes. "The *charcoal* is making mine nice and tender."

"I've used an electric smoker before," Darcy said, trying to participate in the conversation instead of just standing there.

Darius and Earl gasped.

"Dear Lord, child. You never use an electric smoker," Darius said, shaking his head.

"That's right. You gotta get some real smoke on it. That's why it's called a smoker," Earl said as suddenly the two men became buddies. "Isn't that right, D?"

"Sure is, E. Don't worry, young lady. We'll teach you everything you need to know about smoking meat."

"We can take you around this afternoon. Are you free then, D?" Earl asked Darius.

"Sure am. This little lady needs an education in meat."

There was snorting laughter that came from behind her, and she turned to see Edie trying to smother a laugh by the front door. "Oh, I think she can handle meat."

Darcy surprised herself by bursting out laughing.

"You're telling me, hon," the waitress said, wiping Leo's face and hands for Lydia. "I let Pearl out last night to go potty and the noise scared her something fierce. She came running back inside with her tail tucked."

Okay, now the embarrassment was in overdrive.

"You ready guys?" Wade asked Darius and Earl as he climbed onto the chair and distracted the waitress from commenting further on Darcy's enthusiastic night.

"Do we have a challenger?" Levi asked as he raised his wooden sword.

"I got a better game. Let's play pirate. I'll make you walk the plank," Wade said as he climbed onto a table, jumped up, and wrapped his arms around the beam.

Darcy was pretty sure every woman in there sighed as his shirt rose up to expose his abs and that sexy little line of hair that disappeared down his pants. And then Wade flexed his arms, kicked out his legs, and swung up onto the beam.

Men clapped, woman ooh-ed, and Lacy rolled her eyes again.

Darcy and Edie smiled at each other as Wade stood up on the beam. "Ready?" he asked Darius and Earl. They nodded and moved to lock their arms together. Wade turned to Lyle first. "Ready to walk the plank?"

Lyle squealed with excitement as Wade grabbed him up by the forearms and dangled him over the side of the beam. He squatted down so Lyle was closer to Darius and Earl.

"You've robbed from Black Law and now must pay the price," Wade called out as the diners used their forks and knives to begin banging out a walk-the-plank beat.

Wade nodded to the men who widened their stance. Wade let go of Lyle and the boy fell into Darius and Earl's arms like a cheerleader coming down from the top of the cheer pyramid.

"Again! Again!" Lyle called out as Lydia swooped in to grab him.

"No. No more playing on the beam. I don't know how you got up there," she said as she kept a death grip on this shirt.

"A pirate never reveals his secrets. Argh!" Lyle said before trying to charge his little brother with his sword—a sword that was quickly confiscated by his mother.

"There's no quarter for you, scallywag. It's time to walk the plank," Wade growled out theatrically as he handed a very serious Levi overboard.

"I swear on my life that vengeance will be mine!" Levi called out before dropping into Darius and Earl's arms. The diners cheered as Levi bounded out of his human net and took a bow.

Wade lowered himself off the beam, dangled for just a second, and then dropped the remaining four feet. "Thanks for your help," he told the barbecuers who had suddenly gone back to giving each other grief over their cooking style.

"Thank you, Wade. I have no idea how they got up there," Lydia said, gripping a son in each hand. "I'm counting down the days until Landry gets home. I told him I'd go on his next deployment for him. A war zone sounds like a vacation."

Lydia turned to Edie and Darcy and smiled. "Hi, Edie. And hi, you must be Darcy. I've heard all about you."

Edie tried to cover her laugh up with a cough, and Darcy jokingly smacked her arm. "Apparently everyone heard me."

Lydia joined in the laughter and Darcy felt something she hadn't really felt before—camaraderie. They weren't judging her or making her feel bad. They were teasing her as if she were one of them, and she found that she rather liked it.

"With Wade, who can blame you? It's a good thing I got my tubes tied. Those Faulkner men could get a girl pregnant just by looking at them," Lydia giggled.

Edie and Darcy joined in and then laughed even harder when Wade asked them what was so funny. By the time she and Wade finished breakfast, Darcy felt as if she were home. She had friends. She had inside jokes. And she had Wade.

21

WADE PAID the bill as Granger walked into the diner. Two kids playing gladiator on the beams ten feet up earlier and no one blinked an eye. Granger walking in wearing board shorts, a T-shirt, and flip-flops caused a hush to fall over the diner.

"Well, I'm glad I have your attention," Granger said out loud. "If anyone asks, I'm an amateur treasure hunter and not the sheriff."

"Then what's your job?" Darius asked.

"Maybe I should work for you."

"You don't wear flip-flops when you're working at my place."

"Darn straight," Earl added.

Granger probably rolled his eyes behind his mirrored shades. "I'm helping Darcy out by being undercover. So, let's say I'm an insurance agent. Now, don't anyone tell anyone I'm the sheriff, and if anyone is asking, let me know who they are."

"Sure thing, *dude*," Earl called out as everyone laughed. Granger's jaw tightened, but he ignored them as he headed over to join Wade and Darcy. "I heard you had an interesting wake-up call."

"I'm guessing by your getup that Chambers has talked to you?" Wade asked as Granger took a seat.

"Yup. It's why I look ridiculous. I refuse to put on another barely buttoned shirt. Hope this will do."

"You're fine. And actually, we were about to drop off a special gift with Reverend Winston before going to see Harper," Darcy told him. "Since you're my new hunting buddy, you should probably join us. It'll give us time to come up with what I want you to tell Cash or Hugo. Which one did you buddy up to the most?"

"Hugo. He's not as insufferable of an asshole as Cash is."

"Then we'll have you drop some tidbits to Hugo, and I'm sure he'll pass them along. It's what they all do. They all say they are rivals, but they gossip more than a knitting group."

"Then let's go," Wade said as he stood up. Granger stood, too, and they waited for Darcy, who was staring at Granger.

"What?" he asked.

"Why don't you like to dress in beachwear?" Darcy asked. "It seems strange, given where you live."

"Remember I told you I was in a car accident?" Granger said as they left the diner. "I had to have emergency surgery to set both a broken femur and to fix some internal bleeding. I have some scarring I've been told is not as pretty as my face."

Wade, his brother, and his cousins had been there when Granger had come home from college that summer after the accident. It had been bad. Granger was lucky to be alive. The driver of the car that hit him was drunk and died at the scene. It took a toll on Granger both mentally and physically.

"Well, whoever told you that was ugly on the inside and

not worth a second thought. Let me see your scars." Darcy stopped on the sidewalk and placed her hands on her hips.

"Thank you, but I'd rather not."

"This isn't up for debate. I'm used to hauling things out of the water, and I will pin you down and pull up your shirt one way or another. You need the opinion of someone who is not trying to sleep with you for purely lustful reasons."

Granger looked to Wade, who just shrugged. Darcy seemed determined and he thought it was good. Granger had hidden behind jeans and a polo shirt for too long. With a sigh, Granger lifted his shirt.

"And your leg?"

Granger lifted the loose-fitting swim trunks and then dropped them a second later.

"I've come to a conclusion," Darcy said as they headed for the church.

"That I was right?" Granger asked dryly.

"No. That you pick the absolute worst women to sleep with. Stop looking at their chest size and start looking at their brain size. Any smart woman wanting something more than a one-night stand will have zero issues with those scars."

Granger began to argue, but Darcy cut him off.

"I'm serious. Do you have scarring? Yes. Is it repulsive? No. The only women that would think so are superficial losers. I'd take off your shirt more and more if I were you. Trust me when I tell you, you have a great body and those scars don't detract from it."

Granger was quiet as they walked up the steps to the church. "Thank you," he said quietly before opening the door for Darcy.

Wade wanted to hug her, but he knew if he made a big deal about it, Granger would get embarrassed. Granger always came across as so confident, and he was in his ability to do police work. But Wade knew the scarring had made him self-conscious. Maybe with Ellery, Darcy, Tinsley, and Harper's help, Granger might break out of the cycle he was in. He was afraid to get attached to someone because of the scars, so he went for short-term, which resulted in being with women who wouldn't look past the one-foot-long scar on his side and the eight-inch jagged scar on this thigh where metal had been embedded. It was a cycle that needed to be broken if his friend ever wanted to find love.

"Hello!" Reverend Winston called out as he came into the chapel. "What can I do for y'all? Do you have more clues for me?"

"We have Black Law's diary," Darcy said as she pulled the flannel-wrapped leather-bound book from her purse. "I have something else I also want hidden, but it won't be ready until tonight, if that's okay."

"That's fine. It just needs to be after six. We have the ladies' prayer group tonight at seven. It will be easy for you to slip in with all the other ladies. Have you figured out any more of the clues?" He motioned for them to follow him. He went three rows up and then went down on his hands and knees and began to crawl along the stone floor.

"Yes. We know 'He Loves Me So' is a song," Wade told him as the reverend wedged himself under the pew and began to grunt.

"Do the lyrics help?" the reverend asked, his voice strained with exertion.

"No," Darcy sighed. "It's an instrumental piece, no lyrics. I'm going to ask Miss Ruby to play it for me later. Maybe she'll see some clue in it that we can't."

There was the sound of stone sliding along stone. It echoed in the old building, and then it went quiet. *That's* where I left it," Reverend Winston muttered from under the pew. He held out his hand for the book and Darcy handed it over. There was more stone-on-stone scraping and then the reverend was scooting back, holding a credit card. "I put this *someplace safe* five years ago. Couldn't find it again," he said, shaking his head.

"Thank you for hiding my books. Do you have room for one more? I really don't want anyone to get their hands on it before I've figured it out."

"Sure thing, Miss Darcy."

"Thank you," she said, wrapping her arms around him for an impromptu hug. Reverend Winston chuckled and patted her back.

WADE TOOK her hand in his. She was relieved to have the book safely tucked away in the church. She still had the music book in her purse. She'd taken pictures with her phone just in case she lost the originals.

Granger led them from the church and across the street to Harper's bar. The front door was open and Harper was watering her plants. "Hey y'all!" she called out and waved.

"Are you excited to go on a treasure hunt?" Wade asked as he playfully nudged his cousin.

"Do you really think there's some fist-sized emerald in my bar?" Harper asked as she turned off the water.

Darcy shrugged as they headed inside. "I don't know, but I really hope so. If there is, then the treasure I'm looking for is real."

"Well then, let's see the clue."

Darcy pulled out her phone and showed Harper the paragraph about the heart of the home. "Does this mean anything to you?"

Harper shook her head. "No, sorry. Do you want to look around?"

"I need to know which room was the original kitchen."

Harper looked at the back of the bar. "It was in the back and slightly to the left, if I remember correctly. From what my builders told me, it was a large kitchen. Over time it was divided into a smaller kitchen and a bathroom. Now some of it is my kitchen and the restrooms. Why the kitchen?"

Darcy's heart sped up. She could feel the blood racing through her body. "There's an old saying that the heart of a home is the kitchen. And in your body, the heart is slightly left of center. I think Black Law hid the emerald in the former kitchen."

"How do we know if it's in the section that still's standing or the part that's now the restrooms?" Harper asked as she led them into the kitchens.

She pushed open a swinging door and everyone looked at the modern kitchen. Darcy looked back at the notes and frowned. "It talked about the glow of the heart of the home. I thought that meant a fireplace, but I don't see one."

"You wouldn't," Wade said as he snapped his fingers. "You're thinking of fireplaces like they are now. But when Black Law was here, they weren't like that. Some of them were very large."

"That's right," Granger said, picking up on the train of thought. "Mrs. B's history class. We toured an old house with re-enactors for fourth grade history class."

"So, what were they if not fireplaces?" Harper asked impatiently.

"They were so large you could walk into them," Wade said with a smile as if he knew something.

"And in the south, they were against the back wall so

they wouldn't overwhelm the house during the already warm summers," Granger added.

All eyes turned to the back wall. Darcy saw a large enclave where beautiful natural wood was used as shelving on the top half and on the bottom half were cabinets with a butcher-block countertop. A painting by Tinsley hung above the enclave where the wall resumed normal shape and size.

"I don't see—" Harper began to say when it hit her. "*That* was a fireplace? It's huge."

Darcy was already moving forward. "It's white-painted brick." She turned to see Wade on the phone.

"Trent, I need you and Ridge at Harper's bar right away. Bring your tools." Wade hung up on his younger brother, not giving him a chance to say no. "Let's get all the stuff off the walls and out of the cabinets."

Granger, Harper, Wade, and Darcy attacked the shelves, drawers, and cabinets. By the time Trent and Ridge had arrived, the contents had been completely removed. Darcy was pacing with nervous energy. This was it. Finding the emerald alone would be a huge discovery, but even more important, it would be a sign of the truth of the story about the sunken treasure.

"What's going on?" Trent asked as he set his toolbox on the ground and shoved back his hair from his face. "I was on a job."

"I know, but Darcy thinks there's a huge emerald in this old fireplace," Wade said, pointing to the cabinets and shelves.

Darcy was fully prepared to be called crazy. Why wouldn't they think that?

"Okay. Wade, get the drills from the back of my truck.

Let's get the shelving and cabinets out of the way and see what's next."

"You don't think I'm crazy?" Darcy asked.

"I like crazy women. Heck, I'm used to crazy women. You know my cousin, right?"

Harper flicked him off as the guys got to work. Darcy didn't know what to expect as the brackets holding the shelves in place were slowly taken down and then the cabinets were pulled away. Nothing. She knew better than to expect a giant X marking the spot. But when everything was cleared, she was left with a lot of nothing.

22

WADE LOOKED AT THE WALL. "What now?"

"I don't know. I guess just look around." Darcy stepped forward and began feeling on the wall. She pushed on every brick as Harper joined her. Trent stood back and took in the wall. He and Ridge whispered with their heads together. Granger began to feel along the side of the wall that was even with the room. Wade didn't know what else to do so he began on the wall on the other side of the fireplace.

It felt like hours. Every brick was pushed on. Every joint examined and nothing.

"*In my home where the warm glow is cast is the path to my heart. The heart of my home is forever a keepsake of what I have had and what I will never have,*" Darcy said as she repeated the clue left in the diary.

Wade looked at the fireplace and then across the room. "Where the glow of the fireplace is cast . . ."

Darcy snapped her fingers. "It won't be against the back wall. He's talking about it casting out of the fireplace. Can someone turn off the lights?"

Wade hurried to turn off the light and close the wooden

plantation shutters. It was too bright to turn the room into darkness, but it was enough to cast the area in shadows. He just wondered what she was up to.

DARCY TURNED on the flashlight from her phone. She walked into the center of the fireplace and set it down. The light showed straight up the sealed-off chimney, lighting the whole area. She felt around, but nothing. No loose bricks, no secret buttons, nothing.

"Wait," she said as she stepped back from the fireplace. "He wouldn't want it so near the fire. I know it wouldn't burn, but he would need to be able to easily access it. So where else does the fire glow?"

She saw everyone take a step back and then saw Wade's face change. He was onto something. He grabbed a stool and placed it in the fireplace before setting the phone on it. "There would be a fire grate. It would keep the logs off the ground and cast a wider glow."

The light now shone in more angles, the newest being the glow that was on the floor a foot from where the main fire would be. It was on the edge of the brick fireplace where it met the hardwood floor.

"Trent," Darcy said excitedly.

"Already ahead of you," he said as he got to work with a crowbar. "Don't worry, Harp. I can fix all of this."

"I'm not worried," she said as Trent asked for his hammer and chisel after prying up a few hardwood boards and looking inside the floor.

Darcy cringed. She was worried. This was a historic house that they were tearing up. She held her breath as Trent looked under the floorboards.

"Nothing," he said. "I'm going to tear up the first couple rows of the brick. Is that okay, Harp?"

Harper grabbed Darcy's hand as together they looked over Trent's shoulder while he knelt on the ground. "Stop talking about it and do it already."

Darcy's heart plunged further and further toward the torn-up floor with every brick that was removed. The entire first row—all ten feet of it—was torn out. Nothing. Ridge grabbed his tools and went to work on the opposite side of the fireplace. Brick after brick was removed. Trent moved faster than Ridge, and soon there were only a few bricks remaining.

No one talked as the room echoed with hammering. Suddenly Trent stopped and set down his tools. Darcy felt a glimmer of hope as she and Harper leaned closer. "What is it?" Darcy asked.

"It's a little piece of metal attached to the brick with a spring. The mortar covered it, but it's also painted white to blend in with the mortar so it's hard to see." Trent bent down and squinted. "There's a wire running under the brick here.

"Well, don't just look at it! Push the lever!" Harper said as she tightened her grip on Darcy's hand. Though it was Darcy who was probably breaking Harper's hand at that point.

Wade moved closer and Darcy looked at him. In that moment they had an entire conversation without saying a word. He knew all of her hopes and dreams rested on one little brick.

"Well, here it goes," Trent said as he pushed the little lever back.

Darcy held her breath and stared at the brick. Nothing. But then there was the faintest *click* sound followed by the sound of a gear trying to turn. Everyone held their breath as they looked around.

"It's coming from the wall," Ridge said, looking up from where he was kneeling next to Trent.

"The paint!" Trent cried scrambling forward and running his hands over the side of the fireplace closest to where everyone was standing. "It's stopping it from opening."

Ridge quickly followed Trent's lead and the two of them tapped along the side of the fireplace looking for a weak spot.

Darcy held her breath and clamped her hand down on Harper's as the men worked together. Ridge had his ear to the brick and was directing Trent on where to tap.

"Lower," Ridge said as he knelt back down. "Lower still." He moved to lie on the ground.

Trent joined him as everyone was quiet. "I hear it."

Trent went to work on the paint and mortar and then suddenly there was a pop as the sound of the gear cranking stopped. Darcy struggled to see but Ridge and Trent's shoulders were in the way. "What is it?"

Ridge sat back and tapped Trent to do the same. When they parted, Darcy could finally see. Four bricks, two along the bottom and the two directly above them, were popped a quarter inch from the wall.

"Here, use this," Wade said as he handed Darcy the flathead and moved out of the way.

Darcy looked over her shoulder to Harper. "It's your house. Let's do this together."

Trent and Ridge got up and moved to allow Harper to kneel next to Darcy. "What do you want me to do?"

"Catch anything that falls out," Darcy said with a

quirked smile. This was it. It was time to find out if the treasure was real.

Harper put her hands together and placed them on the floor. Darcy took a deep breath to steady herself and then pried the bricks open. They appeared to fit in the wall like a drawer with no handle. She worked the flathead into the narrow space—a space that was the perfect size for a knife blade—and with a scraping sound, the four bricks popped loose like a drawer opening after being stuck.

Darcy's heart beat fast as she dropped the flathead and used her fingers to pull the bricks the rest of the way out. Her heart stopped when Harper sat up and looked inside. Darcy just stared as Harper looked at her. With a little nod from Harper, Darcy reached inside.

"Is anything in there?" Wade asked.

Instead of answering Darcy held up her cupped hands as if cradling a baby bird. Except this was larger than a baby bird. And much heavier. The cool smooth object was the size of a pear and it was gleaming. The deep jungle greens reflected the light of the phone and sparkled in the light.

"It's real," Darcy gasped as tears of joy, relief, and cheers of excitement broke free all at once. She laughed as tears rolled down her face and Harper flung her arms around Darcy. "It's real. *The treasure is real!*"

"Holy crap," Granger muttered as Darcy stood on wobbly legs and showed them the emerald. "That has to be worth millions."

"It is," Darcy said as she laughed again. She turned and held it out to Harper. "And it's yours."

"You found it," Harper protested.

"In lieu of a finder's fee, you can put my name as the discoverer. This means more to me than the million dollars. This means Black Law's sunken treasure *is* real. I'm *not* on a wild goose chase, but getting closer to potentially the biggest find ever made, and you all helped. Thank you for letting me follow the clues and tear up your kitchen."

"Screw the kitchen. I can build a state-of-the-art one with a full-time cook now. But, what do I do with this?" Harper asked as she turned it over in her hands.

"I'd take some pictures and then hide it in the church," Trent suggested.

"Sounds like a plan to me," Granger added. "I'd be worried having anything that valuable in the sheriff's office. And I also don't want you to have it at your house and become a target for theft."

Darcy turned to Granger. "Are you thinking what I am?"

Granger nodded. "We found our trap for the murderer."

WADE WRAPPED his arm around Darcy. She was shaking with excitement and adrenaline at the discovery. "You did it," he whispered to her before he kissed the side of her head and hugged her tight to his side.

"Not yet, but this was a major step forward. I have to meet with Miss Ruby. If we can figure out that clue, I can narrow down the search for Black Law's sunken ship."

"Quiet, it's ringing," Granger said, and everyone immediately stopped talking. He put the call on speakerphone and Darcy heard Hugo answer. "Hugo, it's Granger. I wanted to ask you a favor."

"Granger, what a surprise," Hugo's smooth voice said. By the crackling sound coming from the phone Darcy knew Hugo was on the ocean. She could hear the waves, the motor of a boat, and the wind hitting the phone. "How are you after all that drinking? I barely made it out this morning."

Hugo laughed and Granger kept his focus on the phone. Darcy could see him getting into character as his whole demeanor changed. "It was rough. I was surprised to see Darcy up so early. I was grabbing coffee before work when I ran into her. That's actually why I called."

"Because of coffee with Darcy?" Hugo asked, but Darcy could already hear the interest in his voice.

"Yes and no," Granger said with a laugh. Harper rolled her eyes at it. Anyone who actually knew Granger knew that wasn't his laugh. "I ran into her here in Shadows Landing. I thought she was in Charleston. But she said she had a big lead, and she told me she was sorry but she couldn't mentor me right now. So, I thought of you. You know way more than her anyway, and I was really hoping you'd answer some newbie questions for me. I'd buy you dinner," Granger said hopefully.

"You know I've heard a lot about Shadows Landing. You could show me around and fill me in on the local stories about the pirates there."

"Sure thing. We have tons of legends. Dinner tonight? Say at seven o'clock at the Lowcountry Smokehouse?"

"See you there, Granger. I'm looking forward to talking to you."

Granger said his goodbyes and hung up. For a full two seconds, no one talked and then everyone spoke at once.

"What will you do?"

"We need to hide the emerald."

"What should Darcy be doing?"

"Does she need protection?"

"I'm her protection."

Granger held up his hands and quieted the crowd. "First, we're going to get this emerald someplace safe. Second, Darcy is going to give me a series of questions to ask Hugo that will hold my cover. Third, at seven-thirty, Darcy will walk past Lowcountry's windows so I can point her out. Kord will be close by at all times. Any questions?"

"Sounds like a plan," Darcy said, feeling pretty good about the trap they were setting. Right now she could see Hugo calling his cronies to tell them she'd found something in Shadows Landing. They'd all be speculating on whether it was something of value or not, and the only way to find out would be to find out in person. And the only person who would care that much would be the murderer who was afraid she'd find the treasure first.

Harper took some pictures of the emerald and put it in the front pocket of her jeans. It bulged out, but she strode across the room and picked up an apron and wrapped it around her waist to hide it. "I'm off to see Reverend Winston. Darcy, when this is all over, you'll have to tell me what to do with this thing."

Darcy hugged her tightly. "Of course. I'll give you plenty of ideas. Thank you so much for trusting me and allowing me to find out if this emerald existed. Can you imagine? The last time this emerald was seen was three hundred years ago."

"I still don't believe it," Harper said, shaking her head.

"I'll go with you," Granger told her as he moved to open the kitchen door for her.

"I'll get your kitchen put back the best I can," Ridge called out as Harper headed out of the kitchen with Granger.

"I'll help and we'll get it done in no time."

"Thanks, Ridge. Thanks, Trent!" Harper called over her shoulder.

"Now what?" Wade asked.

"Now we ask Miss Ruby to come over."

23

WADE WATCHED as Darcy paced along the front of his house. She kept her eyes out the windows the whole time. Miss Ruby and Miss Winnie were headed their way as soon as they finished with their ladies' meeting at church.

"How much longer?" Darcy asked him for the third time in two minutes.

"Probably ten more minutes," Wade said, patting his lap. He sat in a comfortable leather chair facing her. "Sit for a minute."

Darcy stopped pacing and walked over to him. She moved to sit gingerly but Wade grabbed her and pulled her down. She gave a little squeak of surprise and then laughed as Wade sat her on his lap. Her legs dangled over the side of the chair as he rested with one hand around her back and on her hip and the other on her knee.

"Now," Wade said as he smiled, "you've talked about all the things to do, but you need to take a minute to pat yourself on the back. You just found part of Black Law's treasure right here in Shadows Landing. You made my cousin financially secure and changed her life. Plus you've brought a lot of excitement to our lives. Thank you for all of that. How are you feeling?"

"I'm so excited I'm about to burst. It's why I can't sit still. All I can think about is finding the location of Black Law's ship. I've always thought it was real. I've always had faith in my research. But the second I saw that emerald, I knew all the sacrifices and the years spent searching were worth it. I have to know—what happened to that ship? How did Timothy escape? How did the ship sink? As I get closer to finding out, I have more and more questions. I can barely contain myself," she said at a rapid pace.

Wade knew of only one way to get her to focus on something else, so he kissed her. Darcy's lips were still moving as she was running through a thousand questions and scenarios, but when he gently nipped her bottom lip, she stopped talking.

"You did it and I'm proud of you. You need to breathe or you'll pass out. We'll work together and find all the answers to your questions. But right now you need to bask in the accomplishment, even if it's only for ten minutes."

Darcy smiled at him as she looped her arms around his neck. "There's no one I'd rather celebrate with. Thank you for believing in me." Darcy leaned forward and kissed him. Wade groaned into her mouth as she wiggled on his lap. He probably had ten minutes. It wouldn't be as long as he wanted, but when Darcy dropped a hand to slide down his chest, he figured he could do a lot with ten minutes.

Wade used his hands on Darcy's waist to lift her slightly upward. She got the hint and moved to straddle him. He felt her pressing against him as she moved her hips and groaned again. He felt her legs on each side of his as he let her take the lead. There was a connection, a chemistry, a magic, between them. They seemed to be able to read each other's every reaction. Darcy moved against him as she rose above him and deepened the kiss.

Wade was running his hands under Darcy's shirt when he heard something. He froze and pulled his lips from Darcy's, who proceeded to kiss her way down his neck.

"Young love," Miss Ruby sighed.

Darcy yelped in surprise and would have fallen off his lap if Wade hadn't pinned her to him.

"Do you suddenly have a craving for apple pie?" Miss Winnie asked Miss Ruby. Neither of the old women seemed apologetic for interrupting or for entering without knocking.

Miss Ruby sighed. "I need some good apple pie. It always hits the spot."

"I'm glad you're here," Wade said, carefully untangling his body and Darcy's. "But you could have knocked."

"Honey child, we knocked *and* rang the bell. Lord knows you were too busy to hear it," Miss Ruby said as she looked pointedly at him. Wade no longer felt like a grown man, but a little boy who was now in trouble for not paying attention in class.

"Sorry, ma'am."

"I'm just happy to see you with someone as wonderful as Miss Darcy here. I heard about what you did for Harper today. That was a beaut of an emerald!"

"You saw it?" Darcy asked as she stood up and turned to Miss Ruby and Miss Winnie.

"Harper even let us hold it," Miss Winnie said with a nod of her head.

"Where is it now?" Wade asked exactly what Darcy wanted to know.

"We don't know," Miss Ruby said. "Harper and the

reverend were still talking when we left. But now we're here, so what was this about me playing the piano?"

"I was hoping you could play this piece for me," Darcy said sweetly. Wade got up as Darcy pulled out the old leather book from her purse. She unwrapped the flannel and carefully opened it to "He Loves Me So."

"That looks very old," Miss Ruby said, moving forward to look at it. "Where did you get this?"

"Skeeter," Darcy tried to answer innocently enough. Miss Ruby looked up at her with an expression that set Darcy to immediately start rambling as if she were trying to talk herself out of getting caught with her hand in the cookie jar. "Skeeter and I were in the archives and found it. I thought it sounded lovely, but I can't play the piano."

"No one likes a fibber, dear," Miss Winnie clucked.

Darcy looked to Wade for help and he took pity on her. Everyone else knew they might as well tell Miss Ruby and Miss Winnie. They'd been around long enough that maybe they'd heard stories that weren't in the archives or common knowledge.

"It's part of a clue to help us find Black Law's treasure," Wade said as Darcy shot him an exasperated glare. He knew she didn't like telling people about it, and she had told more people in the past three days than she had her whole life.

"I'm good at riddles," Miss Winnie said as she rubbed her wrinkled hands together. "Ruby, you play it and let me see the clue."

"Miss Winnie, people have died over this," Darcy tried to warn as she pulled out her phone. "Are you sure?"

"Oh, honey, you don't reach my age without taking risks. It's the only way to achieve what others say is unachievable." Miss Winnie patted Darcy's arm and took the phone from her.

"If I shall perish, it was Black Law who captured Samuel, William, and me. His ship rides low and lower shall it ride. No amount of gold, silver, or gems will save me. To my family, I shall miss thee, but I leave one last gift. As the snake's tail sounds, you spin me like a dancing master. He Loves Me So. As I love you. Goodbye and Godspeed. Timothy Longworth," Miss Winnie read out loud as Ruby sat at Wade's mother's piano in the corner of the living room and looked over the music.

"We know it's referencing the boat filled with something and that it's sunk. We also know he's talking about Rattlesnake Shoal and 'He Loves Me So' is the song we'd like Miss Ruby to play," Wade said as he filled Miss Winnie in on the clues they'd figured out so far.

"Play away, Ruby, and let me think," Miss Winnie said as she set the phone down and pulled out an old #2 pencil and pad of paper from her purse.

Wade went and slid his arm around Darcy as Miss Ruby began to play. Darcy closed her eyes and listened to the music. It was what she'd describe as a fun upbeat tune.

"Well, child, that's it," Miss Ruby said a couple of minutes later. "This mark here at the end of the song indicates that the whole song should be repeated. Do you want me to play it again?"

Darcy looked at him and Wade could see the failure in her eyes. The song didn't mean anything to them. They were somehow missing the clue or there was none.

"Does anything strike you about the song? Do the notes spell something out?" Darcy asked as hope faded from her voice.

"I'm sorry, child, but it doesn't spell anything out. I'll play it again, though. Maybe we'll catch something."

They didn't. There was nothing there. It was just a toe-tapping song from three hundred years ago.

"Anything?" Miss Ruby asked as she turned toward them on the piano bench.

Wade shook his head. Darcy sat deflated next to him. Her head hung and her shoulders slumped. They'd had such a high today, finding the emerald, to then be crushed with the song not yielding any clue. She was emotionally exhausted.

"It's okay," Wade said as he pulled her in for a comforting hug. "We won't give up. We'll figure it out."

"Ruby, do you remember in tenth-grade English class when we read Jane Austen?" Miss Winnie asked out of the blue.

Miss Ruby motioned with her eyes to Wade and Darcy and then back to Winnie. "Not now, Win."

"Yes, now. Don't you remember the class project when we finished *Pride and Prejudice*?"

Miss Ruby looked annoyed but answered. "Yes. We all made historic British food and learned a couple of the dances they talked about in the book. Can we get back to Wade and Darcy's problem?"

"Do you remember how we learned the steps?" Miss Winnie asked, ignoring Ruby's request to drop it.

Darcy looked up at him and gave a weak smile. "I'm going to get some iced tea. Do you want any?"

"Bring some for everyone if you don't mind," Wade said, kissing her forehead as Winnie and Ruby bickered.

"Just say it, Ruby," Miss Winnie snapped. "How did we learn the steps?"

Darcy froze in surprise as did Wade. Miss Winnie never raised her voice.

Miss Ruby looked annoyed at her old friend. She crossed her arms over her ample bosom and narrowed her eyes. "We used that book with the steps drawn in it. Now, why do you have your panties in a bunch about something we did in high school?"

"*As the snake's tail sounds, you spin me like a dancing master. He Loves Me So,*" Miss Winnie said excitedly.

Wade looked at Darcy who shrugged.

"The name of the book was *The English Dancing Master* and it not only had the music printed in it but also the steps for the dance," Miss Winnie said triumphantly.

Wade saw Darcy suck in a breath. She suddenly began to bounce side to side on the balls of her feet. "*Spin me like a dancing master. He Loves Me So.* We need to find that book!"

"Wait, explain this to me," Miss Ruby said as Wade began to grin. Miss Winnie had solved the last clue.

Darcy was bouncing all around now as she put all the pieces together. "*As the snake's tail sounds* means the starting point is Rattlesnake Shoal. *You spin me like a dancing master. He Loves Me So.* It means starting at the shoal, you follow the steps for the song in the book *The English Dancing Master* to lead to the sunken ship!"

Darcy bounced over to Miss Winnie and Wade was afraid she'd break the old woman as she hugged her. "You did it, Miss Winnie!"

"Now we just have to find that book," Miss Winnie said as she blushed. Darcy was kissing her cheek and hugging her again.

"Let's get this music safely hidden, then I can take you to the Historical Society," Wade said as he carefully wrapped the music book back in Skeeter's flannel shirt.

"Call Skeeter!" Darcy yelled as she bounced over to Miss Ruby to hug her, too.

"And you better not think about leaving us behind," Miss Winnie called out over Darcy's excitement.

"Let's go!" Wade laughed as Darcy ran to the door, turned, and smiled broadly at him.

"We have a sunken ship to find. Are you ready, ladies?"

Wade held out an arm for both Miss Winnie and Miss Ruby.

"This is just as exciting as the shootout at the church. Do you think we should grab a cutlass while we're there?" Miss Winnie asked Miss Ruby.

"Yes, and I'll grab a boarding pike so I can leave my cane in the car."

Darcy looked back at Wade with wide eyes, and all Wade could do was shrug. This was Shadows Landing after all.

24

Darcy felt a shiver race down her spine as she climbed the steps to the church. She turned and Wade looked up at her questioningly as he helped Miss Ruby and Miss Winnie up the steps.

"Something's wrong," she said quietly. Darcy slowly scanned the streets. She couldn't put it into words. It was just her body telling her something was different.

Wade looked around but shrugged his shoulders. "I don't see anything. What did you see?"

"I didn't see anything. It's a feeling." Darcy took a step down and took hold of Miss Ruby's arm. "Let's get inside . . . fast."

"You never question a gut feeling," Miss Ruby said as she moved faster up the steps.

Darcy took hold of the women as Wade hurried ahead and opened the door. She felt crazy. There was nothing out of place, but something had the hair on the back of her neck standing up.

"Thank you for not thinking I'm crazy," Darcy said once safely behind the thick church doors.

Miss Ruby patted her hand as Winnie teetered off toward the front of the church. "Honey child, in the South we never question crazy. We question when you're not. Everyone has someone in their family tree with special feelings. They know when not to go out on the boat or where to fish or which piece of chicken not to eat. It's a true gift."

"Hello!" Reverend Winston called out as he came from his office. "To what do I owe the pleasure of this meeting? Did you recruit some people to help with the clothing drive, Miss Winnie?"

"We're here on pirate matters," Miss Winnie responded as she pulled at the bottom of a large candlestick only to have a dagger pop out.

"I thought she was joking," Darcy whispered.

"I told you the church was founded by pirates," Wade said with humor in his voice.

"Is the church under attack again?" Reverend Winston asked as he looked to the door.

"No, but we need to protect Darcy from harm so she can go after the treasure. She said it was dangerous." Miss Winnie slashed the blade slowly through the air.

"Miss Ruby! Put that down," Darcy cried, scrambling over to where Miss Ruby was knocking a four-foot floor candlestick down. "You'll break it. What is that?"

Miss Ruby looked up from where she had pulled out a long pike that with a sharp arrow tip and pointy hook at the end of it. "I told you I was getting the boarding pike."

"Ladies," Reverend Winston said calmly as Darcy moved closer to examine the pike. "I think we can put these away. They're only to be used to protect the church and those inside of it."

Darcy's eyes went wide as she verified what she thought

she'd seen. "Can I?" she asked Miss Ruby, who handed over the pike. Darcy held it up to get a better look. "This is a William C. Smith."

"Yeah," Miss Winnie said. "So's this. Why is that important?"

"William C. Smith was a blacksmith who came to the colonies from a small town in England to make a name for himself. He ended up becoming a premier weapons maker in the late 1600s and early 1700s before . . ." Darcy stopped talking and looked up at everyone who didn't seem surprised to hear this story.

"Before he became a privateer to test out some new weapons. He eventually developed what would become the grenade. Yes, we know. He donated that stained-glass window," Reverend Winston said, pointing to one of the windows at the side of the church. "Along with all the weaponry. We have a bunch of his old inventions in the armory."

"The church has an armory?" Darcy asked, blinking her eyes as if she needed to wake up from a weird dream.

"Well, it's where I do marriage counseling . . ." Reverend Winston paused as he tapped a finger to his chin. "Maybe I should move marriage counseling to the Bible study room."

"This pike is probably worth more than fifteen thousand dollars," Darcy said, bringing his attention back to the pike. "And you're telling me you have tons of his stuff?"

"Yes, but William is a part of the church family, so we'd never sell it. Anyway, is there anything else I can help you with?"

Darcy shook her head as if to clear it before reaching into her purse and pulling out the songbook. "We need to put this someplace safe. Miss Winnie figured out the last clue."

"Praise the Lord!" Reverend Winston said as he took the book. "Do you have all you need then?"

"Not yet. We need to find one more thing, then we'll be all set." Wade took her hand and smiled down at her as she told Reverend Winston about the latest clue.

"Well, then, let's go." Reverend Winston counted out the pews and suddenly disappeared. A second later he was back up but without the book in hand.

"Is he coming with us?" Darcy whispered to Wade, who just chuckled under his breath. She was glad he was finding this amusing. They were starting to gain numbers and would look like an invading force heading into the archives.

Wade took her hand in his and gave it a gentle squeeze. "Don't worry. I just saw Miss Winnie put the dagger in her purse. We'll be protected."

Darcy couldn't help but laugh. She tried to smother it so it came out as a snort. Wade knew instantly how to drop her stress level. "Then let's get this show on the road."

"IT's NOT HERE," Darcy said as she flopped back in her chair. Dr. Adkins had once again been shut out from the room and had thrown a hissy until Miss Winnie had grabbed his ear and scolded him.

"I'm sorry, but I'm not finding any dancing books either," Miss Ruby called out from where she was going through a shelf of old books.

"Me neither," Miss Winnie said. "And I refuse to ask Mr. Snooty where it would be."

"I'll go ask," Reverend Winston said as Darcy heard him say a prayer for patience.

"I'm right sorry, Darcy," Skeeter said, closing up the vault.

There had been so many fascinating books and diaries that Darcy itched to study. After she found the treasure, she could write a book about Shadows Landing during the height of piracy. She would let Wade read every chapter after he got home from work. She pictured them snuggled up on the couch, him telling her of his day and her telling him of her research.

Darcy paused in closing the book she'd been looking through. After the treasure? She'd never allowed herself to think that before. She'd never thought about life after the hunt. She'd only thought about finding the treasure and curating it. But the idea of staying in Shadows Landing, the idea of a life with Wade, a home here, it felt . . . right.

What if she didn't find the treasure? Darcy looked around at the people helping her and at the room full of books over three hundred years old. Well, if she didn't know before, she now knew what to do with herself. She'd tell the history of Shadows Landing. The vise that had been squeezing her since she started her hunt loosened. She had Wade, whom she cared about, and she had people she could honestly call her friends. It hit her like a lightning bolt. *This* was where she was supposed to be, and Wade was the one she was supposed to be with. The feeling settled over her like a warm blanket on a cold night. The chill left her, and Darcy was filled with warmth and love.

"It's too late now, but we'll go to the Daughters of Shadow Landing tomorrow to see if they have anything in their records," Miss Winnie suggested.

"They have records?" Darcy asked as she was drawn from her thoughts.

"Oh yes. They've been organizing festivals and hosting committees since they were a group of pirate wives filling time while their husbands were out plundering," Miss Winnie told her.

"That's right," Reverend Winston picked up. "All the women in my family belonged. They are the ones who started the park and ordered the fountain. They also run the yearly festival. That's a really good idea, Miss Winnie."

Skeeter's shoulders slumped. "I don't have access to their vaults. They're members only."

Darcy pulled her hand from Wade's and hugged a surprised Skeeter. "You've been the biggest help. I can't thank you enough."

"Shucks, Darcy," Skeeter said as he blushed.

"I know someone with access to the vaults," Wade said suddenly.

"Who?" Darcy turned back to him.

"The Bell family. Maggie Bell is a friend of mine, and her mother, Suze, is the current president of the DOSL"

"DOSL?"

"Daughters of Shadows Landing," Wade told Darcy.

Darcy sighed. That's more people who would know what she was doing. Darcy looked around. No one was trying to steal the treasure from her. They all wanted to see her succeed. "What's two more people?" She sighed.

"I can ask at the Sunday service if we can't find it by then," Reverend Winston offered.

"Let's take it a day at a time," Darcy told him. She was starting to admit the people of Shadows Landing just wanted to help, but she wasn't ready to let the whole town in on it. She could imagine hundreds of people following her from building to building to look at historic papers.

WADE COULD SEE the tension appear back in Darcy's body.

She'd never told anyone what she was working on before, and in three days his whole family, the sheriff's department, Skeeter, Gator, Reverend Winston, Miss Ruby, and Winnie knew about it. After what he'd seen of the other hunters, he understood why Darcy was nervous. But his friends would only want to help, not claim it as their own.

"I'll call Maggie and see if she can meet us at Harper's," Wade said as he tried to sound encouraging.

Darcy nodded, and he called Maggie as they locked up everything. The group exited the room to find a glaring Stephen Adkins.

"Skeeter, for the last time, what it the code to the vault? And you have to stop locking me out! I'm the director, and you're nothing but a ghost-chasing hack."

Miss Ruby's hand flew up to Stephen's ear before Wade could blink. Miss Ruby had Stephen's ear between her fingers and bent him down to her level, and she lectured him. "Those schools up north must have made you lose your manners. You don't talk to people like that. I'm going to call your momma if you don't shape up."

"Yes, ma'am," Stephen whimpered. Miss Ruby let him up and he adjusted his bow tie. "Sorry." He spun on the heel of his loafer and stormed out.

Wade looked at Skeeter and knew he was trying to hide the hurt the words caused. "Well, um, I guess just let me know how it goes tomorrow," Skeeter mumbled.

"You'll know since you'll be with me," Darcy said as if nothing had happened.

"You want me to go with you?"

"Of course. I wouldn't have gotten this far without your help. You're invaluable to me and my search," Darcy said, turning to Wade.

"Will Maggie meet us?"

"Yes." Wade saw that Darcy no longer seemed tense. Now she seemed determined.

"Great," Miss Ruby said. "You just text us when you go over, and we'll meet you all there."

"You might need to change the name of your hunting operation to Delmar and Friends," Wade said with a laugh.

"I just might," Darcy said, smiling back at him, and he hoped above all else that she would stay in Shadows Landing with her new friends. And with him. But right then, Wade made up his mind. If she didn't, they would make it work one way or another because he didn't want to let her go.

25

Now.

Wade looked at the text from Granger as they walked out of the church. He looked to the end of Main Street where smoke from the fire pit at Lowcountry Smokehouse danced up into the sky.

Skeeter thanked Darcy and hurried across the street as soon as he saw Gator's beat up pickup parking in front of Harper's bar.

"I wanted to hurt that asshole so badly for making Skeeter feel bad about himself," Darcy said through gritted teeth.

Wade held her hand in his as he took her down the alley between the church and the courthouse. It was a narrow alley designed for horse-drawn carriages, but one car at a time could now squeeze through it and find a small parking lot behind the courthouse.

"You're loyal to your friends and protective of them. It's a good trait to have. Rumor has it Stephen is thinking of running for mayor. Right now we're so small we don't have one. We're going to be voting on a measure in the fall on whether we want one or not."

"Well, I'd vote for Bubba the gator over Stephen," Darcy said staunchly before she stopped walking and looked around. A slope of grass ran down to an offshoot of Shadows River.

"This is where the pirates would hide their boats. As you can see, it's high tide. It's deep enough for them to come in and be hidden from Shadows River by the swamp over there. That's where your friend Bubba lives."

"Wow. This is where they hid their ships and offloaded them," she said as she turned back to look at the church. "I wonder where the tunnel is that heads into the church."

"I wanted to see if I could see it, too. I didn't know it existed until the other day. But that exploration might have to wait. Granger texted. He said to walk by now. I wanted to pop out this way so we walk past Lowcountry as if we're on the way to the bar. It won't draw attention that way."

Darcy nodded as he threaded his fingers with hers again. "It would look strange if we walked up to it and then turned around and walked away. I'm kind of nervous."

"I'm right here with you."

Darcy rested her head on his shoulder for a moment as they watched the water flow gently by. "I know. You give me strength."

"I don't do that. You were strong way before you met me."

"Maybe *courage* is a better word. I'm not afraid to fall because I know you'll catch me."

"Always."

They walked hand in hand behind the courthouse and out onto South Cypress Lane. The library was across the street from them, and they crossed to stand in front of it. The next building up was Lowcountry Smokehouse.

"Interesting-looking library," Darcy said as he looked up at the building. "It looks like a fancy old house better suited to Europe."

"It probably was. It was built in the early 1700s by a French madam and served as a brothel. Once people started actually enforcing prostitution laws, the madam turned the first floor into the library and swore up and down the women who worked there were librarians."

Darcy laughed as they continued to walk down the street, but she stopped laughing when Hugo called out her name. And it wasn't just Hugo. Wade and Darcy were surprised as they saw Granger, Hugo, and Cash sitting at one of the outdoor tables, drinking beer.

"Darcy! What are you doing here?" Hugo asked in faux innocence. He knew she was here. She'd heard Granger tell him so.

"I think she's doing her assistant. I'm so proud! It's like my little bird has left the nest," Cash said sarcastically before tipping back his beer.

"What are you guys doing here?" Darcy asked instead of answering. She looked pointedly at Granger as if she were upset.

"We're offering our professional insight to our friend here. It's always good to have a mentor. We all did. Well, you didn't, but we did, and it's invaluable to learn the trade from someone who has done it as long as we have. In fact, we tried to get Jules to come, too, but he never called us back," Cash said as he set down his beer. "You didn't answer what brought you to this little slice of pirate heaven."

Wade felt Darcy tense beside him. "Jules won't be calling you back."

Hugo shook his head and looked at Darcy as if she knew nothing. "Jules always calls us back."

"Not when a dog carried his severed head out of the ocean this morning."

"You don't have to make up such a ridiculous story. That's just wrong," Cash spat. "If you and Jules think you're going to work together to beat us, you are badly mistaken."

"You think she'd make that up?" Wade asked incredulously. "We were notified of his death this morning. Someone cut off Jules's head. Sounds familiar, doesn't it?"

"No," Hugo said, shaking his head. "Are you serious?"

Darcy nodded next to him. "Yes. Someone murdered him last night after the party—just the way he threatened to harm Leon."

The men were all quiet as they looked at each other, then back up to Darcy. "Why did the police come to you?" Hugo finally asked.

"Because they thought I did it. Luckily, I had an alibi. Do either of you?"

"You think one of us killed him?" Cash almost yelled. "You're the one who closest to all the murders. You better run, lover boy. You're probably next."

Wade shrugged his shoulders. "I'm not too worried. Are you? Did it occur to you that you could be next?" Wade paused, then wrapped his arm around Darcy's shoulder. "We have someplace to be. See y'all later."

Wade clasped Darcy's hand. They didn't talk again until they were in front of Stomping Grounds. "I think that went well."

"Gossip about me will be flying," Darcy said, letting out a breath. "I guess it shouldn't matter."

Darcy paused, and Wade stopped walking. She was looking in the antique-store window. "They're selling?"

"Yes. The family wants to retire. Why?"

"If the treasure business doesn't work, I can sell antiques. I can become an antique hunter and maybe get a reality show like Cash."

"You can do that for fun after you find the greatest treasure ever lost," Wade said reassuringly.

DARCY LEANED her head against Wade's shoulder as she looked into the store. Like most of Main Street, it had once been a very large old house, and she instantly wondered about the history.

"Come on. You'll love Maggie. Her family owns the large plantation at the edge of town. It's been in the family forever. In fact, Maggie's great-great-great-grandmother Ethel still haunts the place."

Darcy laughed at his joke and appreciated him helping to cast aside her doubt.

"No, really. Ethel still haunts the place."

"You believe in ghosts?" she asked incredulously.

"Hard not to when you're from around here. Ask Skeeter about Eddie."

"Who's Eddie?"

"The pirate ghost who lives in his old house. Around here there are a lot of very old houses with history in them. Sometimes history doesn't want to leave," Wade told her as they passed a clothing boutique called Bless Your Scarf.

"Is Maggie quirky?" Darcy asked, picturing a female version of Skeeter.

"Quirky, yes. Crazy, no. Her mother, Suze Bell, is the current head of the Daughters of Shadow Landing. Her father, Clark, runs their family business and her brother, Gage, just moved back to start working with his dad."

"What's the family business?" Darcy asked as they approached Harper's bar.

"Making money. While they're society types, they're not your New York socialites. Maggie and Gage are named after guns. Gage, the oldest, is twenty-six and is named after a twelve-gauge shotgun. Maggie's real name is Magnum, and she's an Olympic medalist as a sharpshooter."

Darcy blinked with surprise. "And they all live with a ghost?"

"Yup. And Timmins."

"Is Timmins another ghost?" Darcy asked slowly.

"No. That's Timmins," Wade said as he smiled at the man walking toward them. "He's the house manager at Bell Landing Plantation."

Darcy cocked her head as she watched a man in board shorts, flip-flops, and a mostly unbuttoned Hawaiian shirt walking toward them. "I should have asked him to help instead of Granger. How did he get that bun so, well, *messy*? It's perfect. I can never get my hair to purposely look so . . ."

"Messy?" Wade asked with a laugh.

"Wade! I am thirsty AF and need to chill. I was helping Mags with this fundraiser thing and I was, like, Ethel you need to swerve. She was all over the place today. I mean, my hair product is gone. Gone! I can't even right now," Timmins complained.

"The ghost took your hair product?" Darcy asked, completely fascinated with Timmins. It was like deciphering a new language, and she loved cracking codes.

"For real. Who does that? I'm Timmins, by the way," he said, holding out his hand.

"Darcy." She shook it and then looked down. "How do you get your hands that soft? Mine are always cracking because I'm out in the water all the time."

"Me too!" Timmins cried as if they're long-lost siblings. "Living my best life on the waves."

"Scuba diving for me."

"OMG, that's my life goal. I want to scuba, but you have to like, take lessons." Timmins paused as he looked happily between them. "You want to join my friends and me? It's going to be lit."

"Thanks, Timmins, but we're meeting Maggie," Darcy said with a smile.

"That's cool, though. See you around. I might hit you up for some lessons. YOLO, right?"

"Right," Darcy said as Timmins bounded through the open door to the bar.

"You understood that?" Wade asked.

"He's sweet," she replied.

"Well, yeah, I just can't understand half of what he says," Wade mumbled as he ushered her inside.

Darcy looked around the packed bar, trying to figure out which one was Maggie Bell. The girl in a pink camo T-shirt, jean shorts, and monogrammed flip-flops wasn't who she'd guessed. Darcy also felt a little twinge of jealousy when the strawberry-blonde goddess leaped up to hug Wade.

"I am so glad you called," Maggie said with wide happy eyes and perfect smiling lips. She turned her green eyes to Darcy, dropped her arms from around Wade's neck, and flung them around hers. "And you must be Darcy! I have a huge favor to ask you." Maggie unlaced her arms and sat down at the table. There were three beers already waiting for them. "What's going on in the kitchen? Ridge interrupted his work on the old Hurston property because of some emergency with Harper's kitchen. And I don't know if you saw it or not, but there's also a help-wanted sign in the window."

"The floor was damaged this morning in the kitchen, so I'm sure my cousin is trying to get that repaired. I didn't see the sign, but I know Harper has said she needs an extra bartender on weekends. I guess she's finally going to look for one."

"So, I'm trying to figure out how best to ask this . . ." Maggie started as she looked back and forth between them. Darcy wanted her to hurry up and ask so she could get what she needed from the Daughters of Shadow Landing archives.

"I'll just spit it out. Do you think you'll be married by September?"

Darcy blinked in surprise and just stared.

"What are you talking about?" Wade finally asked.

Maggie let out a sigh. "I need you, Wade. Oh, that doesn't sound good. I mean, you know every year I host a fundraiser for my charity, right?"

Wade nodded before turning to Darcy. "Maggie and her mother raise money for a charity that provides grants for people to attend a Paralympic training camp."

"Oh, that's great. And you need Wade's help?" Darcy asked.

Maggie nodded and her strawberry-blonde ponytail bobbed. "This year I'm doing a bachelor auction, so I want both of you to agree to it. I know you're together so I wouldn't want to upset a new relationship."

Darcy was quiet as Maggie continued with the details. Were they in a relationship? Darcy realized that while they may never have talked about it, Wade was very much a large part of her life and had been since he entered it only a couple days earlier. In that short time, he'd become her other half. They were a couple even if they hadn't specifically discussed it.

"It would be in September," Maggie was saying.

"I think it would be great. I'm happy to help, too, if I can," Darcy said before Wade could answer. Wade looked her over and smiled as he reached across the round table and took her hand in his. Again, they hadn't said anything to each other, but it was clear they both wanted a future together.

"Great! And please wear your uniform. You know the women love that. And you can totally bid on him," Maggie said as she smiled at Darcy. "Now, you asked about the Daughters of Shadow Landing archives. What are you looking for?"

"An old dancing instruction book," Darcy told her.

Maggie's nose wrinkled cutely. "I think we have those. But I don't have the key to get into the center. Only my mom does, and she's out of town until tomorrow morning. She said she'd be home by ten at the latest."

"Can she let us in as soon as she gets home? It's important," Wade said when Darcy lost her voice to disappointment. She was ready to go now. She didn't want to wait until the next morning. Not when both Hugo and Cash were in town, and either one of them could be on to her and her hunt.

"Of course!"

"Thanks. We'll meet you there then. Text if something comes up," Wade said as Maggie waved to a group of women.

"Is there anything else I can help you with?" Maggie asked.

"No, we just need that book," Darcy answered.

"Easy-peasy. We'll get it tomorrow. Now, I have to go get some more victims . . . I mean *bachelors*. And those women have some hot brothers. Excuse me."

"How come I don't get asked to be in the auction?" Gator asked while sitting down on the seat Maggie had just vacated.

"You were once, remember?" a scrawny little man answered as he took the last seat at the table.

"Oh yeah." Gator laughed. "I guess they learned their lesson. Darcy, this is my cousin, Turtle."

Darcy shook Turtle's hand. "Is anyone in your family not named after a reptile?"

Both Turtle and Gator looked up to the ceiling as they thought.

"Snake, Toad, Lizard," Turtle said, ticking them off on his finger. "Dino!"

Gator shook his head. "Dino is short for dinosaur and they were reptiles, too, so I guess not. I never noticed that before."

"Me neither," Turtle said.

"Well, we were just heading out," Wade said, standing up. "I'm picking up dinner at the Pink Pig and treating Darcy to a picnic."

"That's real romantic." Turtle bobbed his head and now Darcy understood where his nickname came from. At least she hoped it was just a nickname.

"So is fresh alligator. I've been told it's an aphrodisiac. I got some for you in my freezer."

Darcy watched as Wade's face lit up, and she would have sworn his stomach rumbled. "Save it for me. I have a great recipe for deep-frying it that I want to try."

"You got it. Have a good night, you two, and don't forget to holler if you need any help on your hunt. I am pretty good at hunting things. Just ask your dinner next week."

Darcy shook her head at the bad joke as Wade pulled out her chair for her.

"Thanks, guys," Darcy said as they began to leave. She and Wade waved to a very busy Harper and left.

26

"A PICNIC?" Darcy asked once they were outside.

"Well, on my balcony," Wade said sheepishly. "I was hoping we'd be researching tonight, but I'll take advantage of some downtime with you."

"Yoo-hoo! Wade, I have your order."

Darcy looked up from where they were crossing the street to see a beautiful, dark-skinned girl in a flowing mid-thigh sundress with a small apron tied around her waist. Her curly black hair was natural and regal-looking. She was stunning and looked as if she should be on a magazine cover rather than a waitress for a barbecue joint.

"Thanks, Tamika," Wade called out as they finished crossing the street. "Tamika, this is Darcy. Tamika is Darius's granddaughter and helps out at the restaurant."

"Gotta pay for college somehow," she said pointedly as Wade added another five to the tip. "Thanks, Wade. Y'all have a good night, and I'd be much appreciative if you close your doors and windows tonight. I need to study for the ACT, and the loud noises coming from the house are right distracting."

stripped bare. His heart was pounding and from more than just excitement. When he was with Darcy, he was complete.

REVEREND FLOYD WINSTON whistled a song the choir had been practicing the night before as his freshly shined loafers tapped along the stone sidewalk. The pre-dawn time was his favorite. It was the moment he had to himself as he walked to his church and opened its doors to its flock.

Floyd was a lifelong resident of Shadows Landing, and once upon a time, he'd made this walk with his father, God rest his soul. Now this was his time to pray and his time to speak to his loved ones who had passed before him. He still gained wisdom from the talks he had with this father during these early morning walks.

Floyd straightened his tie as he walked past the courthouse. Only the overnight deputy would be in the sheriff's office. Granger and Kord wouldn't come in for another two hours. Harper's bar was closed up tight and the pits at both Lowcountry and Pink Pig would fire up in about an hour.

This morning was beautiful. It was warm, but the summer heat hadn't set in yet, and there was a breeze that made you want to open your arms wide. He decided then he'd do just that. He'd prop all the doors open as he practiced his sermon for Sunday before the morning prayer group arrived.

Floyd looked up at his church and the smile slid from his face. There was a man leaning against the door. His head was lowered as if he were asleep. A hood from a zippered sweatshirt jacket covered his head and face as he rested.

"My friend," Floyd called out as he walked up the steps. "How about some coffee and you tell me how I can help?"

The man slowly unfolded his legs and stood. "That would be nice. Thank you."

Floyd unlocked the church as the stranger kept his head down and his hands in his pockets. His shoulders were hunched, and he smelled of alcohol.

"How can I assist you this morning?" Floyd asked, already holding the door open for the man. He walked into the church but stopped. Of course he would, it was still dark inside. "I'll just get the light. It's right over here."

He never reached the light. As soon as the door was closed, the man had Floyd by the suit lapels and he felt himself being picked up slightly off the ground. His toes scraped the floor as the man shoved him hard against the wall.

"You can help me by telling me what Darcy Delmar was doing in here so often."

"Darcy is a member of the church. She's welcome anytime. Unlike you. Put me down at once and leave this holy place."

"Or what?" The man laughed as he slammed Floyd against the wall again. Only this time his head smashed into the wall, too. Pain shot through Floyd's head as sudden bursts of light flashed in his eyes from the hit. "Will God strike me down?"

"No," Floyd gasped after being punched hard in the stomach. He doubled over as he tried to drag in a breath. "But the ghosts of those who built this place might drag your soul to hell."

Another hit. This one was to the chin. Floyd would have dropped to the ground if it hadn't been for the man holding tight to his jacket with one hand. "What was Darcy doing in here?"

"Praying." Floyd gasped out as he was flung to the ground.

"Then let's pray for a better answer to that." The man grabbed Floyd by the back of the collar and marched him up the aisle to the church's altar. Floyd was flung to the ground beneath the cross suspended from the old wooden beams of the church.

"No ghosts, gods, or fallen angels will save you. You will tell me what I want to know or you'll meet them right now. Darcy Delmar. What has she told you about Black Law? And don't you dare lie or I'll start with cutting off your fingers."

Floyd looked up to pray. The sun broke the horizon and shone through the stained-glass window. A ray of red light landed directly in front of him, highlighting the candlestick on the altar—the candlestick that hid a pirate's dagger inside.

Floyd held up his hands to the cross. "Lord Jesus," he called out as he struggled to his feet. "Forgive me for breaking the sacred trust and privilege that holds a parishioner's secrets confidential."

Floyd lowered his hands and "accidentally" knocked the candlestick over. He caught it as if he were trying to prevent it from falling and spun around. The face of the man was covered in a full-face wetsuit with only his eyes visible. Floyd saw them for only a split second before the hood was pulled down.

"Are you really going to attack me with a candlestick?" The man didn't seem to be worried and Floyd thought twice when the man pulled a knife from his pocket. "I'll take my knife over a candlestick. Stop wasting time and tell me about Darcy. I can tell you know something."

Floyd grabbed the base of the candlestick and pulled. The dagger sprung free and gleamed in the multicolor sunlight streaming through the stained glass. "I think I'll take my knife over yours."

The man froze as he looked at the long, thick dagger and down at his short and stubby knife. "What kind of man of God keeps a dagger at the altar?"

"The kind who will do anything to protect his people. Now, get out or we'll settle the question of whether or not size matters." Floyd spun the knife in his hand expertly to show the man he was adept at handling the weapon.

"I'll be back," the man threatened as he darted through the pews and out the back door of the church.

Floyd let out a deep breath and dropped to the ground. Keeping a hand on the dagger, he pulled out his phone and called the sheriff's department.

27

"WHAT?" Wade yelled into the phone.

Darcy bolted upright in Wade's bed when she heard the anger in his voice. Something had happened. Something bad. And with a sickening feeling, she knew it was her fault.

"We'll be right there," Wade said as he grabbed a pair of shorts and a T-shirt from the chest of drawers. "No, I won't say anything to anyone. Be there in five."

"What is it?" Darcy asked as soon as Wade hung up.

"Reverend Winston was attacked inside the church this morning."

Darcy went dizzy as the blood drained from her face. "Is he hurt?"

"Yes, but we don't know how badly. He's asking for you."

"The clues. They were after the clues, and he's hurt because of me."

"We don't know that."

Darcy sucked in a trembling breath as she got up and grabbed the clothes from yesterday. She didn't even bother brushing her hair. Instead, she yanked it up into a messy bun that even Timmins would envy.

"Let's go." Darcy was already racing down the stairs as Wade sprinted to catch up.

"We'll take the car."

Darcy had wanted to run there, but the car would be faster. In less than two minutes, they parked in front of the church behind Kord's cruiser. Darcy didn't wait for Wade. She shoved her door open and sprinted up the steps. She didn't even remember if she closed the car door as she flung open the church door.

"Oh no," she gasped as a woman in scrubs was cleaning blood off the back of Reverend Winston's head. "This is all my fault."

"Don't you be saying that." The young woman was around twenty-five and had sun-kissed blonde hair. The scrubs had a low V-neck that showed off her tanned skin and a hint of a pretty bra. "This is the work of a bad man, not you."

"She's right," Reverend Winston said, holding out his hand for Darcy to take. "Darcy, this is Gavin's nurse, Sadie. She said it's just some bumps and bruises."

The door was flung open again as Miss Winnie and Miss Ruby hurriedly wobbled in. Their eyes landed on Reverend Winston, and they made the sign of the cross. "Lord help me if I get my hands on the scoundrel who did this."

"You'd be proud of me," Reverend Winston said with a smile. "I used the dagger to scare him off."

Kord sat next to him as the old ladies clucked about. Kord tried to ask what happened, but the door was opened again as practically the whole town rushed in. Edie and Tinsley raced in first. Trent and Ridge were next. Even Ryker showed up. And that wasn't counting Gator, Turtle, and Skeeter who came armed to the teeth.

"I told you not to tell anyone," Kord said to Wade as he

shook his head. "Not even five minutes and all y'all are here."

"I didn't tell anyone," Wade swore.

"Oopsie," Sadie said, looking up from the bandage she was putting on. "My bad."

"What happened?" an elegant woman with a rather large rifle asked as she and a similarly elegant man with a similarly large rifle burst in. Right behind them were Maggie and a handsome man, both armed.

Kord groaned. "Someone lock the door. Now, Rev, what happened?"

"I was opening the church when it looked like a drunk was asleep against the door. I offered him coffee and opened the church to him. Then he attacked me. He wanted to know what Darcy had told me about Black Law, and why she was here so much." Rev squeezed her hand hard. "I didn't tell him anything."

"And you used the dagger you handed me to scare him off?" Kord asked as Darcy felt tears of anger and sadness for Rev, fighting for his life.

"Yes. And he ran out the back door."

Everyone began talking at once. Reverend Winston dropped Darcy's hand as Sadie moved to the front to clean up his face. Wade was engrossed in a conversation with his family when Darcy stood up. Everyone was in such a tizzy they didn't notice her grabbing the tall candlestick by the back door and walking outside.

She turned it upside down and wasn't surprised to see a boarding pike inside it. She pulled the pike out and looked around. There were footsteps dug into the freshly mulched garden. Darcy followed them at a run. They disappeared in the cemetery.

The cemetery overlooked the branch of the Shadows

River and was filled with Spanish moss hanging from the large Southern live oaks and bald cypress trees that stood all around her. Tombstones of all shapes, sizes, and ages were in perfect rows. A few mausoleums were scattered throughout the cemetery.

"You want me? Here I am!" Darcy yelled.

Darcy heard a footfall on the grass behind her. She spun but saw nothing. Slowly she crept further into the cemetery. A man laughed behind her and she spun once again ready to attack with her pike.

"Ask for me again," a deep voice sang. This time she didn't jump. She found the most open spot in the cemetery and crept toward it.

"Tell me you want me." The voice was closer now.

Darcy held her ground and tightened her hands on the pike. "You wanted me. Here I am."

Darcy was expecting a knife. She was expecting a cat and mouse game. She wasn't expecting the man to rush from behind a tombstone and crash into her. The pike went flying from her hands as she hit the ground hard. Breath was forced from her body as the man straddled her waist. As she lay struggling to breathe, he grabbed a knife and held it to her neck.

"Here I am. Now, what should I do with you?"

"You can go to hell," she spat.

"I've already been told that once today." He chuckled. Darcy felt the knife press into her throat. "Tell me about Black Law's treasure. Where is it?" he asked in a deep voice she was sure wasn't his real voice.

Hiss . . .

Both Darcy's and the attacker's heads swung to the side to see a massive alligator lumbering toward them. He'd pause, open his mouth and hiss, and then walk toward them a few more steps.

"Bubba?" Darcy asked as her heart thundered. She was way more terrified of the gator than the man who was now barely holding a knife to her. The gator looked at her and then looked up at the man.

Hiss . . .

Well, if that wasn't an order from a gator, she didn't know what was. Darcy flung her hips up and rolled toward the gator at the same time she screamed at the top of her lungs.

"Bubba!" she heard Gator yell from up at the church.

The man went tumbling toward Bubba who was only three feet away with his mouth wide open. Darcy covered her face and prayed. She heard a snap that seemed louder than a lightning strike and then a scream.

Darcy watched through her fingers as the gator held on to the man's forearm. The gator opened his mouth again and the man yanked his arm free and ran. She saw the blood, but it looked like he still had his hand attached.

"Good Bubba, good Bubba," Darcy chanted as she tried to slowly back away on her hands and knees.

Suddenly Gator leaped through the air and landed right on top of Bubba. A smaller, screaming Turtle landed on the tail, wrapping his arms and legs around it and holding on.

The back door of the church opened as Skeeter shot past her. Darcy scrambled back behind a headstone and watched as Skeeter pulled his knife and tried to throw it at the man now climbing into a boat. He wasn't fast enough and the throw wasn't far enough. The knife landed in the mud as the speedboat tore away.

"Are you okay?"

Wade was by her side, holding her tightly as he ran his

hands over her body looking for injuries. The Bell family rested their rifles on tombstones and fired. The sound of glass shattering and bullets ripping into metal had Darcy spinning around. They were hitting the speedboat, but it wasn't enough. The man had ducked down behind the chair and was steering the boat out of sight.

"Call it in!" Suze yelled to Kord. "Speedboat with broken windshield and three bullet holes near the motor.

"Damn. I shouldn't have missed that shot." Maggie's face was set in a tight line as her mother reached up and smacked the back of her head.

"Language."

Maggie rolled her eyes and turned to her. "Sorry."

"You all were wonderful." Darcy felt the tears pricking the back of her eyes and buried her face in Wade's shirt as they broke free.

She took a deep breath, but keeping her face buried, called out, "Can someone help Gator and Turtle? And can someone get me some pork right now?"

"You want to eat?" Trent asked from somewhere behind her.

"I always eat after killing something," Gator said from where he was lying on top of Bubba.

"No, I want to give it to Bubba. He saved me."

"I'll get it!" the peppy voice of Tinsley called out.

When Darcy got herself together, she took a deep breath and looked up into Wade's furious face. "What on earth were you thinking?"

"I didn't want him to hurt any of you. It's my fault the Rev was hurt."

"The hell it is. It's the attacker's fault for killing off the competition instead of just doing a better job. What *is* your fault is putting yourself in danger."

Darcy leaned back as everyone went quiet. Wade was the calmest and laid-back person ever, but right now his face was red, and she could see his carotid artery pulsing. He was pissed. Even Bubba stopped fighting and stared at him.

"Wade," Trent said quietly, trying to calm his brother.

Wade pushed his brother's hand off his shoulder and stood up. He began to pace, and it felt as if they were all at a tennis match. Every head, including Bubba's, turned to watch him going back and forth.

Darcy pushed herself up. Her body was drained from the adrenaline release and her heart was breaking. "I'll go," she said softly as she hung her head.

Wade spun and grabbed her arms, but it didn't hurt like she thought it would. In all his anger, he still held her with gentleness. "No. You're not allowed to leave without me."

Darcy was confused. "Why not? You're mad at me."

"Mad, yes. But I'm mad at you because I love you. I love you, and you put yourself in danger. Do you have any idea what it did to me to hear you scream? I don't think I've started breathing yet. I love you so much it hurts just to think of you down here by yourself. I should have been with you."

Tears streamed down her face as he pulled her against his chest. "I love you, I love you, I love you," she heard him repeating for her ears only.

"What's going on?" Tinsley asked.

"We have the pork," Edie said.

Shhhh!

"What'd we miss?" Edie whispered.

"Wade lost his temper because he loves Darcy, and she was in danger and he wasn't here to protect her," Ridge recapped.

"Well, does she love him?" Tinsley asked with a sweet sigh.

"Of course I love him," Darcy called out before Wade crushed his lips to hers for a quick kiss. "I think I loved you before I even met you. I was yours the second you wrapped your tuxedo jacket around me."

Wade framed her face with his hands as his friends and family cheered. "We do everything together from now on, okay? I can't lose you right after I finally found you."

"You won't get rid of me that easily. I fear you're stuck with me," Darcy laughed. She was euphoric now as she kissed him. Because for once in her life she knew, without a doubt, she was in the right place with the right person at the right time.

28

WADE WANTED to be mad at himself for just blurting out that he loved Darcy. He'd planned a romantic date to tell her, but with her in his arms telling him that she loved him too, he didn't care about perfection anymore. He cared only for her.

His lips met hers, and the kiss they shared held all their emotions: fear, relief, love, and hope. Wade took a deep breath as he pulled away and looked down on Darcy's face. He felt whole. He felt loved. He also understood the stupid little smile Gavin had worn after meeting Ellery because Wade didn't need to see a mirror to know he had the same look on his face right now.

"This is very romantic," Granger said as he joined them. "But we need to get you someplace safe."

"No way," Darcy said as Wade dropped his hands from her face. Darcy walked over to Tinsley and Edie and grabbed the two pulled-pork barbecue sandwiches and headed over to Bubba. "They want the treasure, and we already know they'll kill for it. Now it's an all-out race to who gets to it first."

"And who can keep it," Wade added. The smile Darcy sent him made him feel ten feet tall. They were on the same page. "We need to get to the archives."

"I'm glad I got back early then," the classy lady said. "I'm Suze Bell. This is my husband, Clark. You know Maggie, and this is my son, Gage."

"Thank you for coming home early," Darcy said as she pinched off a bite and threw it toward Bubba. "Good Bubba."

Turtle slowly released the tail and Gator sat up and then climbed off as Darcy pinched another piece and tossed it toward the water. Bubba ran after it and then turned and looked back at her. "Good Bubba," Darcy said, tossing another piece. She followed Bubba toward the water, telling him what a good boy he was until she threw the last bit of sandwich into the water. Bubba gulped it down as Darcy walked back to them.

"You're like a gator whisperer," Gator said reverently.

"He doesn't do that for me, and he loves my apple pie," Miss Ruby complained after finally making it to the cemetery just as everyone was headed back to the church.

"Where y'all going now?" Miss Winnie asked with a huff.

"The DOSL archives," Suze told her. "Let's go, everyone!"

Wade took Darcy's hand as they fell in line behind the Bell family.

"Miss Ruby, would you like a lift?" Ryker asked as Miss Ruby struggled her way back up the small incline.

"Can you get your car down here?" Miss Ruby asked and then squeaked as Ryker scooped her up in his arms. "Oh my."

Wade turned to get Miss Winnie when Ridge picked her up. Miss Winnie gently kicked her dangling feet and smiled so widely it outshone the sun. "Ruby, I think we should make some apple pies for these strong, fine young men."

"You read my mind, Win. They are worthy of apple pie," Miss Ruby called out over Ryker's wide shoulders.

"Are they talking about apple pie or something else?" Darcy asked, and Wade laughed. He held her hand in his as they walked to the DOSL building and they debated if they were really discussing pie.

Wade and Darcy stood silently while Suze unlocked the old doors to the Daughters of Shadows Landing. No one spoke as the heavy lock tumbled and Suze pushed the doors wide.

"What exactly are we looking for?" Suze asked, waiting for everyone, including Reverend Winston and Nurse Sadie, to file in. Once inside, she closed and bolted the doors. Ryker and Ridge put down Miss Ruby and Miss Winnie, who winked at them.

"We need *The English Dancing Master*. I remember we used a copy of it back in high school to learn some old-time dance steps," Miss Winnie answered for Darcy.

"I think we have lots of those," Suze answered as she motioned for everyone to follow them.

Wade felt Darcy's grip tighten on his hand as they headed for the massive library on the second floor.

"The whole top floor is a library. We keep everything that could possibly be considered historically important," Suze told them as she walked up the stairs. "It used to be organized by year, but when I took over the presidency I organized it by author, and Gage was dear enough to help me with a computer program to search for what you need. Now we can use a computer to type in the author, title, or year to find it. Here we go."

. . .

SUZE OPENED two double doors and flipped on a switch. Darcy looked up at fifteen-foot ceilings that had bookshelves from floor to ceiling filled with books. The room took up almost the entire second floor.

Books were on tables covered by large glass boxes. Books on walls, on free-standing bookcases, and there were even fireproof shelves eight feet long by six feet tall that were locked up. This was going to be impossible to find, computer system or not.

"*English Dancing Master . . .*" Suze said slowly as she typed it into a laptop that stood on a podium in the center of the room. "Oh dear."

Darcy's stomach flipped. "What?" She nervously held her breath, afraid of both hearing the news and missing the news.

"There are eighteen editions. Which edition do you need?"

Darcy looked to Wade and back to Miss Winnie. "I don't know. We need to find the steps to a song titled 'He Loves Me So.'"

Darcy heard a chorus of *ohs* as the Faulkners connected the name of the song to the clue they'd all read the first day together under the church.

"Everyone take a volume." Darcy looked over Suze's shoulder. "Where are they?"

"Follow me!" The troop followed behind Suze, talking excitedly about how the clue was deciphered. "Here we go. This whole row."

Darcy stepped forward and looked at them. They were all in protective covers to keep them safe. She pulled the last one out and saw the date. It was after Timothy had died. She hurriedly went through them until she reached the first one dated prior to 1719.

"Okay, all of them up to this one."

People stepped forward and one at a time took an edition.

"There are two big research tables right over here that you all can work at," Suze called out.

"Last one's ours." Wade took the sixteenth edition and carried it to the table.

DARCY AND WADE SAT SHOULDER-TO-SHOULDER, thigh-to-thigh as they slowly and carefully turned the pages of the book published in 1716. The room was quiet until Harper and Tinsley sighed. "Nothing in the first edition."

"Same with the second," said Trent.

"No song by that name in the third," Ridge added.

Darcy tried not to be distracted as edition after edition yielded nothing that would help them.

"Don't worry. We'll find something," Wade said as he turned the next page.

"Stop!" Darcy yelled. The entire library went quiet.

"I'm sorry," Wade said with confusion clear in his voice.

"He loves me . . ."

"And I do love you," Wade said as Darcy began to laugh. "I was trying to be encouraging."

Darcy leaned over, and in a quick and loud *smack*, she kissed his lips. "And I love you. But it's the song! You found it."

Darcy and Wade looked down at the book, and there were the steps to the treasure. "We need a map!" Wade called out as everyone went scattering.

"Maps, maps, maps," Suze muttered as she raced across the library. "Over here!"

En masse, they all followed Suze to a massive drawer.

She pulled it out and thumbed through it. "Here! Charles Town map from 1715."

She pulled out the giant map that was at least four feet by three feet and protected in a plastic sleeve. Wade took it from her as Darcy carried the book with the steps to the nearest table.

"Does anyone have a dry erase pen that we could write on the plastic with?" Darcy asked, and Suze shouted she'd get it.

"Which steps would it be?" Miss Winnie asked.

"What do you mean?" Darcy looked down at the book and then saw it. There were two steps to learn.

"Do you follow the male or female steps?"

"We can mark them both on the map," Wade suggested.

"I think we should do that, but I think it's going to be the male steps. Timothy would have learned those." Darcy wasn't positive, and it was only a gut reaction, but she felt confident in it.

"Here," Suze called out as the crowd parted for her.

"I'll read and you map?" Darcy was very good at reading maps, but Wade did this every day. He knew every inch of the waters in this area.

"Give me the first line."

Darcy began to read and Wade began to mark. They marked O's for girls and X's for boys. The pattern was a simple one. Bow to your partners, promenade, take hands and skip three steps, and so on. One line at a time they marked it out. And then there was the final line. "*Spin your partner one full turn, stopping as you face the far end of the dance floor. Take her right hand in yours, step back, and bow over it.*"

"X marks the spot," Wade whispered as he put the last mark on the map at the same spot as the O." Wade met her eyes and Darcy didn't dare breathe. They had the best lead she'd ever discovered. Now all that was left was . . .

"Well, are we going or not?" Miss Ruby's question broke the silence as everyone let out their collective breaths and started talking at once.

A sharp whistle pierced the air and the room fell quiet.

"Thank you, Ryker." Wade turned to Kord and Granger. "We have a security issue. They're going to be watching us."

"The way I see it is we either all go and keep you safe in numbers or we create a diversion and send you out alone." Granger paused and placed his hand on his hips.

Darcy didn't let him finish. "But if we're all out there, and I don't find anything, it will tell them about where it is. It could take months to grid out the area and find it."

"Diversion it is then." Granger turned to the group. "Raise your hand if you have a boat. "One, two, three . . . eight."

"Okay, good. Here's what we're going to do. Trent, since you look the most like Wade, you and Harper take Wade's boat out with Kord. Harper, wear a hat. I want them to think you're Wade and Darcy. But to confuse them even more, I wish I had the same hats for everyone. Then we all leave at the exact same time and as soon as we get out of the harbor, we each break off in a different direction. It would be eight options for them to choose from and, hopefully, we'll be able to see if anyone is following, and I can cut him off."

"I have plenty of identical hats," Maggie said with a smile.

"Great. Get them," Granger ordered as he went back to studying the map.

"I need something in exchange." Darcy wondered what Maggie was getting at because it looked like she had something up her sleeve.

"I'll pay for them, just get them," Ryker barked.

"It's not money I want, but your body."

"Magnum!" her father said with wide eyes.

"I want every single one of you—" Maggie smiled even wider, "—*bachelors* for my charity auction."

Darcy hid her laughter by coughing, but the rest of the women let loose.

"Honey," Suze said as she fought, and lost, not to smile. "I don't normally condone blackmail, but it is for charity. Gentlemen?"

One by one they agreed, reluctantly. Darcy had to hand it to Maggie. She'd just gotten a month's worth of begging and cajoling done in one minute.

"I'll be right back."

"Will you take Trent's boat?" Granger asked as they waited for Maggie to return.

"I was hoping to take Ryker's since it's the fastest." Darcy thought she'd be a nervous wreck when she found a clue this big, but it was hard to be nervous when they were making her laugh.

Ryker's lips fell into a frown as he crossed his arms over his chest. "It's a brand new boat," he complained.

"But it's the fastest, and we have the farthest to go," Wade pointed out.

Darcy was pretty sure Ryker growled, but he dropped his arms in defeat. "Fine," he said, tossing his keys to Wade. "But no dead people in it this time."

"Here you go," Maggie called out. She was breathing heavily as she carried a box so large that Darcy couldn't see her face from behind it.

Ryker turned and grabbed it from her and set it on the floor. Maggie opened it and pulled out not only identical hats, but identical shirts that all read *BACHELOR* on them.

Ryker turned his glare to Darcy. "You owe me, and I always collect."

"I'll give you a diamond if I find the treasure," Darcy joked.

"I have enough money. I deal in favors."

"I'm pretty sure half the town wants to give you their favors," Miss Winnie said in the quiet. Darcy laughed again as each man and woman put on the matching T-shirts and hats.

Darcy snapped pictures of the map and had Suze put it in the most secure location she could find, which turned out to be a safe in the office. Edie ran over to Wade's house and got Darcy's equipment while they were getting ready. Fifteen minutes after the possible location of the treasure was marked, everyone stood behind the closed doors in the lobby. Everyone had on matching *BACHELOR* shirts and hats and were carrying DOSL tote bags. They had been paired as best they could in teams of one man and one woman. They'd all been assigned boats to take and had keys in hand.

"Thank you," Darcy said loud enough to get everyone's attention. "Before meeting Wade and coming to Shadows Landing, I thought I didn't need a team. I didn't need friends. I thought I could do it all on my own. I realize now, that while I probably could, it's not nearly as meaningful. In a short time, I've found love, friendship, and a place to call home, and it's because of each of you. Thank you."

Wade pulled her against him and kissed the top of her head as her friends rushed to give her hugs. It was an odd yet absolutely right feeling to suddenly belong. Her heart was full, and she was ready to face anything with her friends at her side.

Darcy reached over and laced her hand with Wade's and

faced the group after the last hug was given. "Now, who wants to see if this crazy theory of mine is right?"

29

SUZE AND CLARK opened the locked doors to the street. No one talked as they kept their heads down and walked quickly down the street to the marina or the nearby riverfront houses as one large group. They peeled off, two by two, headed to their assigned boats and prepared to launch. In under ten minutes, they had the Cooper River looking like a highway during rush hour as they sped toward Charleston Harbor side by side, row by row.

As Wade drove he kept his eyes on the people in front of him and glanced behind him as well. A minute behind them, almost out of sight, was Granger. He was keeping his distance in order to see if anyone followed them.

"The equipment looks good," Darcy said from where she sat on the deck of the boat, checking scuba gear. "Actually, it looks better than good. I've got to hand it to your cousin. Ryker sure knows how to get the best of the best. He even has a wireless diver communication system. I just push it to talk and communicate with the boat."

Wade smiled down at Darcy who was so excited she was

practically vibrating with excitement. "Would you check mine, too?"

"I was thinking about that," Darcy called up to him as she grabbed the other diving gear. "If you're diving with me, no one is keeping an eye out for whoever is behind these murders."

"My family will be close."

"Close, yes, but still a good distance away. That was the point—to divide up so whoever is behind this wouldn't know who to follow. Most of your relatives will be out of sight completely." Darcy took a deep breath, and Wade saw the vulnerability but also the trust she was showing him. "And I trust you to keep me safe. I will be able to focus one hundred percent on the treasure when I know you have my back."

Wade hated having her out of sight, but Darcy made an excellent point. And with the communication system, they could talk to each other. Granted, underwater wireless communication wasn't always the best. However, it was still better than nothing.

"I'll always have your back. I'll keep watch and you finish what you started. I have no doubt you'll find it."

Darcy stood up and wrapped her arms around him as he drove. "Thank you so much for believing in me."

"Always." Wade turned his head and kissed her quickly before slowing down as they entered the harbor.

Wade's phone indicated there was a text message, and he looked down at it. "Granger said no one is following us."

"Good. Let's hope it stays that way."

Darcy wrapped her hands around his arm and leaned her cheek against his shoulder. In silence, they made their way out of the harbor and the group split as soon as they were in open water.

"It's crazy to think about," Darcy said, breaking the silence.

"What is?" Wade asked as he headed for Rattlesnake Shoal.

"Thinking that three hundred years ago a teenage kid sank the ship of one of the most notorious pirates of his time. He would have been rowing for his life right through here. It's almost as if I feel Timothy with us here. The tension. The heart-pounding nervousness. Is this how he felt being chased?"

"Hopefully, we aren't being chased, and back then Timothy was just with his two buddies. You have half of Shadows Landing here to back you up. No one will touch you. We'll all make sure of it." Wade looked down into Darcy's upturned face. "But Timothy is here. He's waited three hundred years for someone to find what he left."

Wade looked around at the boats already out on the waters. The number of his friends and family in sight had decreased. There were already some tourists, some fishermen, and some cargo ships out here. Nothing seemed out of the ordinary, though.

"The shoal is another mile out," Wade told Darcy.

"How many miles offshore are we?"

"We're almost three miles out now," Wade confirmed for her. It would be a legal nightmare if the boat were in state waters. The best scenario was to be beyond the state's control of the water, but not so far out that it became international waters. Dealing only with U.S. federal laws would make things easier for salvaging.

"Good. There should be no fighting over the distance then." Darcy stood stiffly as she looked out ahead of them. Wade didn't bother with conversation. Darcy was deep in thought. She was probably running over every clue to verify they were in the right place.

It seemed to take an age, but they finally reached the shoal. "There's Rattlesnake Shoal," Wade said, breaking into Darcy's thoughts.

"Okay, let's do this." Darcy looked at the map with the dancing steps drawn over it and began giving him step-by-step instructions.

DARCY FELT COLD. Her whole body felt as if it were frozen. She was stiff, and while she wanted to move, she couldn't without thinking about it. It was as if her whole body was on overload when Wade stopped the boat. This was it.

This was the moment she found out if she was a failure or if she had achieved her dreams. Twelve years. She was about to discover if twelve years of her life had been wasted hunting for something that didn't exist.

"What's the depth?"

"We're in luck," Wade told her. "The shoal is only eleven feet or so. Then it goes down to thirty feet. We're a mile past the shoal and this spot happens to be only eighteen to twenty feet deep for a couple hundred yards before falling to thirty. A little way out and the ocean floor drops dramatically. Around this area is a different matter, though. It's shallower, but you also need to be careful. This area was used as a mine-dumping site. It's why I'm not anchoring."

"*Mines?*" Darcy asked shocked. Why hadn't he told her this before? "Are you saying I am excavating a freaking minefield?"

"The Navy used the area for sonar-detection practice. The Coast Guard was told about it and the Navy said there were probably some bombs left down there but most likely inert, not armed or anything."

"*Probably*?" Oh great. Now on top of finding a treasure, she had to avoid a murderer *and* not get blown up. "Did they set off explosives in this area?"

"I don't know. It was before my time."

"If they did, they could have damaged the ship or at the very least either exposed it or worse, covered it with debris." Darcy blew out her breath. She was agitated now and snapping at Wade. It wasn't his fault, but her nerves were frayed.

"Take a deep breath." Wade took her by her upper arms and rubbed some heat into them, even though it was ninety degrees outside. "We know X marks the spot, literally. It's right down there, and you're going to find it. You're about to validate your life's work."

Darcy took a deep centering breath and nodded. "I've got this."

"You do." Wade helped her put on her oxygen tank and walked to the steps at the back of the boat with her. "I have faith in you. Be safe and find your treasure."

Darcy leaned forward and kissed him hard and fast. She was afraid he'd be able to taste her fear and her nervousness. She pulled back, and he bent down to strap a knife to her thigh and a second one to her forearm.

"Now, just be careful and go get it. I'll be here, waiting to kiss you as soon as you come back up."

Darcy nodded and pulled her mask on. She pushed the transmitter. "Testing, testing."

She heard it crackle on the transmitter setup on the boat and Wade gave her a thumbs-up. This was it. Darcy took another deep, slow breath with her eyes closed. When she opened them and looked around, she saw her friends way off in the distance on both the right and left. Between them were some fishermen and a party boat filled with young women tanning and sipping on drinks. If this all went well, tonight she'd be toasting with a big bottle of champagne to the greatest treasure ever found.

Darcy looked over her shoulder and winked at Wade before jumping into the Atlantic Ocean.

WADE LET out the breath he was holding, but his body didn't relax. Instead, he was on high alert. He picked up his phone and sent a group text.

Wade: *She's gone under. Does anyone see anything suspicious?*

Granger: *No one followed you that I could tell.*

Ridge: *Nothing here. I'm keeping an eye on the party boat between us.*

Tinsley: *Stop looking at scantily clad women and watch the waters.*

Ridge: *You're no fun, sis.*

Wade smiled as the rest of his friends and family texted that they didn't see anything. If he were anyone else he'd relax, but he knew better than anyone how the ocean could turn dangerous in a split second.

Now all there was to do was to wait and remain vigilant. Wade picked up the transmitter and pushed the button. "How are you doing?"

"All clear so far."

He let out another breath at Darcy's response. "I'll check in every five minutes."

"Okay."

Wade set his watch to beep every five minutes before turning to pick up a pair of binoculars. He slowly scanned the area as if he were conducting a search-and-rescue. Not a single wave was unaccounted for by the time his watch beeped again.

30

Darcy swam almost straight down. She wasn't herself, and she was afraid she'd mess up. She was jumpy and completely on edge. Every fish, every sea creature had her jerking to a stop and reaching for her knife.

"Check in." She knew the first five minutes were past as Wade's voice crackled through. It wasn't loud, and it wasn't clear, but it was good enough.

"I'm at the ocean floor. You were right. It's not that deep here. I am registering eighteen feet." What she didn't tell him was she'd been here for minutes, too scared to see what was below her.

"Begin your grid search and I'll check back in five minutes for an update."

The coms went quiet, and Darcy shifted into action. She spent the next ten minutes marking out a hundred-by-hundred-foot section of the sea floor with bright yellow flags. Every ten feet was marked with a tiny GPS coordinator that had her name on them.

The routine was familiar and relaxed her. When Wade checked in again, she asked him to pull up the GPS trackers to verify they were on. "I've got a large field of active GPS," he told her.

"I'm going to start in the first grid in the lower right. I'll work my way left and then to the second row and work my way back to the right. First grid is one. Second is two. I'll call up when I clear each grid if you don't mind marking it on the app."

Darcy was organized now and ready to get started. She pulled out her metal detector and got to work.

WADE HAD the GPS app up on his phone as he waited for Darcy to clear the first grid. He scanned the waters while he waited. The party boat hadn't moved. Fishing boats were coming and going while some were trolling the area for the best spot.

"Five minutes," Wade said.

"Okay," Darcy said back.

Wade set the communication device down and scanned the area with binoculars again. A second party boat had just come into view way off in the distance. People were still hard to make out, but it was clear this boat was filled with young men. One of the men pointed and Wade followed his direction. They'd seen the girls' party boat. The guys' boat turned almost comically straight for the girls. In fifteen minutes, the boys and girls would meet up. Wade moved on with his scan. He'd let Ridge handle that one.

He was about to check on Darcy again when she reported that grid one was clear. After a moment of pressing buttons, Wade got a check to appear on the outer flag on the first grid.

His phone rang as he was watching the ocean. "Yes," he said when he saw Granger's number.

"I don't see a darn thing. I called Detective Chambers and asked for the location of Hugo and Cash. Their boats are still docked in Charleston. According to the marina owner, they've been there all night and all day."

Finally, Wade felt as if he could breathe. "Thanks for checking on that. Are you going in?"

"No, I'll stay out until Darcy is done diving for the day. I'm at the entrance of the harbor, so I'm a good distance away from you. Kord is the closest to you with Trent and Harper."

"Yeah, Ridge is close too. He's with Edie since she's the second-closest in appearance to Darcy."

"How is Darcy doing?"

"Grid two, clear," Darcy's voice said as if answering Granger.

"Got it," Wade responded back to Darcy before putting the phone on speaker and checking off the second grid. "She's set up a grid and has started a search. I wish I was down there with her."

"It's better that you have eyes above the surface. If we have two boats together, it will clue anyone in that you're the main target. This way Darcy can do her thing and you can watch her back."

"As you watch mine."

"What are friends for?" Granger said, not expecting a response. "I'll check in again in thirty minutes."

"Darcy will come up for air in another hour. She said at this depth she gets almost two hours with her oxygen, but to be on the safe side, she'll surface every ninety minutes."

"Okay. Talk to you soon."

WADE SET down his phone and picked up his binoculars.

Time seemed to creep by slowly, but one by one, he marked off the grids as Darcy searched them. Granger checked in twice again as did the rest of the group via text.

"Darcy, it's time to surface."

"I'm on the last grid of the row. My pressure gauge shows that I have enough time as long as I keep my breathing as steady as I have been."

"Okay, but don't push it."

Wade stepped away from the transmitter to retrieve the next tank of oxygen. Ryker being Ryker meant the boat was beyond stocked. There were enough tanks to dive for an entire week. Wade grabbed a new tank and set it down next to the seat at the back of the boat near the steps where Darcy would be coming up. Hanging off the back of the boat, dangling deep in the water, was a glow stick tied to a string that led straight to the steps to make it easy for her to find.

Wade turned away from the steps and bent down to double-check the pressure in the oxygen tank when suddenly a stabbing pain shot through his calf. Wade yelled out and stumbled forward as he felt the blade of a knife being pulled out of the muscle it had just cut.

Wade had two choices—try to grab the phone and call for help or turn and fight. Knowing help was minutes away and that Darcy would surface at any moment, Wade didn't think twice. He spun around and charged.

The man had climbed up the steps and had the knife in hand and was in the process of dropping his small oxygen tank to the ground. His face was covered with a mask, but that didn't stop Wade from throwing a roundhouse punch that hit the guy right in the side of the head.

Pain exploded across Wade's knuckles, but he kept going. Hook, uppercut, and a solid knee to the stomach had the man dropping the knife and doubling over. Whoever he was, he wasn't used to fighting.

Just as Wade went to deliver a crushing uppercut, the man grabbed him by the shirt and slammed his masked head into Wade's. The mask cracked against Wade's nose, and he felt it break. The head butt had him seeing stars as he fell backward. He landed hard on his ass as the man shook his own head. Unfortunately, he was still standing. With his own nose bleeding, his calf bleeding, and his vision slightly blurry, Wade crab-walked backward until his back was against the steering wheel.

"Son of a bitch, that ~~fucking~~ hurt," the man spat. When he bent to pick up his knife, Wade grabbed his phone.

Mayday!

The text was sent. Help would come, but it might be too late.

"Sure, call for help. Won't do any good."

The man yanked his mask from his face and blinked.

"Cash. I thought it was you."

"Bullshit. You didn't know anything."

"I know you are a prick who would do anything for money, and there's a ton of money out there." Wade kept talking as he reached slowly behind him. He felt the cabinet door and he slowly moved it open. "You just weren't smart enough to figure out how to find it. And so, what? Now you're going to kill me?"

Wade reached behind him, his hand closing over the EPIRB, and turned on the emergency beacon. A signal would be flashing at Coast Guard headquarters and further help would arrive. It would take minutes he didn't have, but maybe they would arrive in time to save Darcy.

"Yeah, I'm going to kill you. Duh." Cash rolled his eyes and pointed the knife at him.

Cash charged and Wade kicked. His foot connected with Cash's balls and Cash went down to his knees, gasping for air. Wade pushed aside the dizziness and shoved against the cabinet behind him to propel himself forward.

Wade wrapped his arms around Cash as they crashed against the deck. Wade scrambled on top of Cash as Cash tried to use both hands to shove the knife into Wade's chest. Wade grabbed Cash's hands as they struggled—each fighting to live.

There was no talking. There was no taunting. There was nothing but the struggle, the burning muscles, and the will to live. But one thing Wade knew without a doubt. He wouldn't go down without a fight, and he had leverage. You couldn't escape physics. Wade sat up tall and used his swimmer's strength to push the blade toward Cash's stomach. As he gained an inch, Wade maneuvered himself to squat over Cash. Using leverage and his body weight, Cash had no chance. Both their arms shook with exertion, but it was done the second Wade was able to get above Cash. With a final grit of his teeth, Wade pushed his whole body downward until Cash's arms gave out and he felt the knife sink into Cash's belly.

Cash moaned and cursed as Wade sat back to expose the knife sticking up from the other man's belly. The sound of boats had Wade looking up to see Trent, Harper, and Kord bearing down on them from one side. Ridge and Edie approached from the other.

Trent was on his phone calling for emergency medical evac from the Coast Guard as Kord leaped from the boat Harper was now driving.

"What happened?" Kord asked as he secured Cash's hands in cuffs and started first aid.

"He swam in with scuba gear. I'm guessing from the

party boat. When I wasn't looking, he stabbed me in the leg. There was a fight and he lost," Wade said, wiping the blood from his face.

"Dammit, Wade, you're hurt. Where's Darcy?" Harper asked as she secured her boat to his.

"She's searching the last grid before coming up. She should be up any minute," Wade told her as Harper squatted down in front of him.

"Now, I'm not gonna lie. This is going to hurt." Harper cupped his face as she examined his nose.

"Not as bad as the head butt." Wade tried to laugh, but his nose hurt badly. "Leave it. The EMTs will . . . Ouch!"

Harper leaned back and rolled her eyes. "Stop being a baby. It wasn't that bad, and I bet it feels a lot better already."

It did. But it also hurt like crazy when she put his nose back into place. She reached into the first aid kit Kord and Trent were using to try to stabilize Cash the best they could. Belly wounds were tricky. He should feel remorseful and maybe he would when it was all over, but right now he was only thinking about protecting Darcy.

Wade hissed again as Harper cleaned the wound on his calf and pulled it together with butterfly stitches before slapping a waterproof bandage on it. "Hold still," she ordered as she packed his nose and taped it on the outside to help stabilize it.

"You're good at this," Wade said, his voice sounding funny with his nose packed.

"You have no idea how many broken noses I have fixed over my lifetime as a bartender. When did you say Darcy was coming up?"

"Any minute," Wade said reaching up for the transmitter. "Hey, Darcy. We've had some action up here."

31

Okay, so she'd told Wade she'd be up after searching the last square, but it was kind of addicting. Darcy looked at her pressure gauge . . . one more. Besides, he hadn't called her to remind her to come up so maybe she was clearing each grid faster than she thought. Darcy looked over at the row of flags. She was almost to the middle of the third row. With each square searched, she felt both closer to the sunken pirate ship and farther away. It was a mix of one step closer, one step back.

Darcy chose to be optimistic so she was thinking it was one step closer. With her metal detector in hand, she started scanning the next grid. Clear. Crap. No, she was going to be positive. Maybe the next one was going to be the one.

"Hey, Darcy." Wade's voice crackled over the transmitter, but it was cutting in and out and mostly she heard just part of her name. Double crap. The rest came out as static as she looked at her pressure gauge. It was time to come up. She was almost out.

Darcy turned and jerked. There was a person swimming right toward her. Since Wade had just talked to her, she knew it wasn't him. Whoever it was, he was swimming full speed and Darcy was at a full stop. She kicked as hard as she could to evade him. It felt like she was slowly pushing through the water to dodge whoever was coming after her and knew chances of escape were little. If she could make it to the surface, she could scream. Instead of continuing to swim away from her pursuer, Darcy tried to swim for the surface.

It wasn't any use, though. The person rammed into her as Darcy was flung back in the water so hard the metal detector slipped from her hand and arm. Sand kicked up as their fins fought against the water and tangled against each other as they fought. Up this close, she could tell her assailant was a man, and he was fighting to hold her near as she fought to get away.

Darcy reached for her knife on her thigh, but it wasn't there. It was in the other person's hands as suddenly her respirator tubing was cut. She was out of time and out of air.

"WHERE IS SHE?" Wade demanded as if his friends and family would know. He stood looking out the back of the boat as he scanned the water. Something wasn't right.

He turned to ask Cash, but the man was unconscious.

"I'm going in."

"Help!"

Darcy's voice crackled over the transmitter, and it was enough to send Wade into action. "Get me a knife!" he yelled to whoever would do it as he pulled fins onto his feet, snapped a weighted belt on, and yanked the gauze from his nose before putting on a mask.

"Here," Harper said, handing him the knife. "I'll get the tanks ready."

"No time." Wade took a deep breath, then exhaled fully before breathing in as deeply as he could manage. He was diving into the water before Harper could even pick up the first tank.

DARCY COULD FEEL her lungs begin to burn. She could hold her breath for four minutes, but she hadn't gotten to prepare as she would for a free drive. She had two minutes tops. The man drove her downward. She fought. She tried to reach his mask, she tried to pull his oxygen, but he was pushing her down from behind and had her right arm pinned behind her.

Darcy couldn't get to the knife hidden up the sleeve of her wetsuit on her left arm. She couldn't beat him physically, but she had one more trick up her sleeve. Darcy closed her eyes and went limp. She pretended to attempt to struggle, but weakly, and after ten seconds, she went deathly still.

He shoved her to the bottom and pushed her face into the sand. Darcy didn't move. She didn't react. And then he did what she'd prayed he'd do. He let go of her arm to hold her head buried in the hard sand and use his other hand to check for a pulse.

Darcy didn't wait. She reached for her knife and pulled it out before he yanked her head back and slammed it into the ground. He didn't let go of her arm as she had hoped. Instead, she felt the knife he'd been holding slice into the back of her upper shoulder.

WADE KICKED hard as he shot through the water like a bullet. He had his arms pinned to his sides with his knife in hand as he dove toward the brightly colored flags. As he drew closer, he watched in horror as he saw the back of a diver drive a knife into Darcy's back.

Bright red blood emanated from her shoulder as it dispersed among the water. While shark attacks weren't the norm in South Carolina, this was a different scenario. They were in open waters with an open wound sending blood all around them. Hammerheads, tiger sharks, and bull sharks were known to be in the area as they dropped off their babies in the safe sounds of the coastal shore.

The diver pulled the knife out and was in the act of swinging again when Wade tightened his grip on the knife and stabbed him in the side. Wade tried to pull the knife out, but the man turned to fight. Wade had to drop his hold on his own weapon and move out of the way of the arcing knife.

DARCY SAW the man swing toward Wade. The knife he'd taken arced through the water as Wade backpedaled. With her vision turning black along the edges, Darcy dug her feet into the sand to help give her something to kick off from. Her foot squished through the sand and hit something hard.

Darcy's eyes shot to the ground. Eighth row, fourth square in. She unclipped her weights and her tank a second before she reached out for the man. The man lunged toward Wade and Darcy sliced his oxygen. She'd wanted to stab him in his neck, but she plunged the knife as hard as she could into his retreating leg as he swam toward Wade.

The man swung toward her, but Darcy used all her force to push off the ocean floor. When she shot up, the weights and tank fell from her body. She clawed at the water as she battled through the water for the surface. She saw the light.

She was closing in on it as the darkness took over. Her sight was reduced to tunnel vision, but she kept her mouth shut. She knew better than to open it until she was fully out of the water. Too many people drowned because they opened their mouths to gasp for air just below the surface.

Her hands broke the surface first and then her nose. Finally, her mouth was free from the water and she dragged in a breath of air. She screamed as she exhaled. She heard shouts and then she heard water splash.

She opened her eyes as she tried to focus. Ridge was by her side. "Help him," she ordered as she dragged in breath after breath. As Harper and Edie leaped into the water to help her, the sound of a helicopter cut through the air. Thankfully, Ridge didn't wait. He took a deep breath and dove.

WADE WAS RUNNING out of time. It had been at least two minutes since he dove down. That was two more minutes of oxygen the attacker had than Wade had. Wade was trained and could hold his breath for a long time, but that was at the bottom of a pool, but not during a physical battle where his body used oxygen at an accelerated pace.

Wade blocked a hit and suddenly the man pulled his arm to his chest and pulled away from Wade. Wade swung toward Darcy but saw her kicking madly toward the surface. It was then he saw she had no oxygen tank. It was also when he saw the knife she'd stuck into the attacker's leg.

The man tried to lunge again, but he was running out of strength. Suddenly behind the man came a diver—a diver in a white shirt that read *BACHELOR* on it. Wade darted past the attacker and straight for Ridge. Ridge held out the handle of the knife and shot back up to the surface. Ridge

could scuba dive, but he wasn't a trained diver and because
of that, he wouldn't be able to hold his breath very long.

Wade turned and saw the man was swimming away
from him as he angled for the surface. Wade made a quick
calculation and swam for the surface at a sharper angle. He
broke free of the water, blinked long enough to see that
Darcy was being pulled aboard and that his Coast Guard
brothers were arriving. He signaled the helicopter that he
was in danger and motioned to where the other diver would
be surfacing. The helicopter took off for the location as the
rescue swimmer on duty, Aaron, got ready to jump. While
he was a couple of years younger than Wade, there was no
one better to be in the water than Aaron, especially in a
combat situation. Aaron was a fighter.

Wade swam as hard as he could to get to the man. His
lungs burned, but he knew he was getting oxygen so he
didn't slow. Up ahead he heard Aaron shout. "Float on your
back with your arms out."

The attacker had surfaced.

"Drop the knife!" Aaron yelled. "Faulkner, he went
under!"

Wade took a deep breath and dove under. The waves
from the helicopter blades disappeared as he saw the man
swimming just under the surface. There was a splash next to
Wade, and he saw Aaron begin to match him stroke for
stroke.

"Get out of the way," Darcy yelled as she pushed Trent
aside and pulled Ridge out of the water. She didn't care if
Cash lived or died at this point. She was surprised to see
him on the boat when she had thought he was underwater
attacking her. What she needed now was to get to Wade.

The boat was getting crowded. As Ridge crawled up the rest of the stairs onto the deck, Darcy moved around an unconscious Cash and her fearless rescuers. She'd hugged them all, especially Harper and Edie, as they helped swim her back to the boat. But she had recovered a bit, and she was pissed off. "Ryker!" she screamed as he came into view on his borrowed boat.

"That man better not be dead!"

"Don't you have a gun on here?"

"Don't you dare kill him on my boat. I will not have death cooties on my boat."

Ugh! Darcy grabbed the emergency box and pulled out the flare gun and flares. "Gun?"

"I don't have one on the boat."

"What do you need a gun for?" Kord asked from where he and Trent were trading turns on trying to slow the bleeding.

"To kill the bastard that stabbed me."

"How are you going to get to him?" Harper asked.

Darcy looked around. This boat was too busy.

"Come on!" she yelled as she grabbed Kord and shoved him toward the boat Ridge had used.

They jumped on it and untied it. Darcy didn't bother gradually easing into her speed. Edie and Harper helped push them off and Darcy went full throttle. Kord had to hold on for dear life as she shot the boat forward.

"What's the plan?" Kord had to scream over the engine and wind.

"I told you. Shoot him."

Darcy went wide around Wade and the other rescue swimmer and pulled an arching circle until she was ahead of her attacker and cut the engine.

"Cash is almost dead and you will be dead if you don't

stop right now!" Darcy yelled. The attacker looked up and then looked behind him to where Wade and the rescue swimmer were gaining ground. "Shoot him."

"As much as I'd like to, I can't shoot him," Kord said to her before turning to the attacker. "Sheriff's deputy. You're under arrest. Surrender now."

"He's going under," Darcy said as soon as she saw him take a deep breath. She didn't wait for Kord. She aimed the flare gun and fired.

WADE REARED BACK when he saw the sparks from a flare gun and then heard the screams.

"I think that woman just shot our suspect with a flare gun," Aaron said after spitting out his snorkel. "Damn, she's hot."

"That's my girlfriend, Assron." Wade used Aaron's nickname before picking up his strokes again. He heard Aaron chuckle, and then he was next to him again.

As they grew closer, he heard Aaron call out for high-low. The man was cursing and trying to swim away as Darcy was reloading and Kord was threatening to let her shoot again.

Aaron tapped Wade's shoulder, and Wade took a breath and dove down deep. He maneuvered until he was behind and under the attacker. Wade made his move when he saw Aaron go vertical in the water five feet in front of the attacker.

Wade swam up and wrapped his arms tightly around the attacker and squeezed as if giving a bear hug. The man began to fight but Wade hung on. He felt the scrape of the blade against the side of his leg, but it was just a scratch. A second later he felt the attacker's head being pulled forward as Aaron ripped his mask off and then his head snapped back and the struggles ended.

The body was pulled up and Wade swam up with it.

"Wade!" Darcy screamed before jumping into the water and swimming straight into his arms as the helicopter hovered above them. "Are you hurt?" Darcy asked as she wrapped her arms around him.

"Just a broken nose and a stab wound. Nothing too bad."

Darcy kissed him on the mouth. "I love you so much. I can't believe it was Hugo and Cash who were trying to kill us!"

Wade watched as Aaron pulled an unconscious Hugo onto a flotation device the helicopter crew had tossed down. Coast Guard boats were speeding in so they'd load Hugo onto one of them. Wade looked up at the helicopter and sent them to Ryker's boat to airlift Cash to a hospital. That is, if he wasn't dead yet.

A minute later that crew was lowering the basket to the speedboat. "Gosh, I hope Cash doesn't die on Ryker's boat," Wade told her as she started to laugh.

"He was still alive when I left."

"Wade's hottie," Aaron called out as a Coast Guard boat approached. "Do you need a lift to the hospital to have that shoulder looked at? It probably needs stitches."

"I'll take her," Wade called out as Aaron worked to hand off Hugo to the boat. "Just offering to help a brother out."

"Aaron, this is Darcy. Darcy, Aaron."

"Thanks for having Wade's back," Darcy called out as Aaron swam over to join them.

"Happy to help. He's had my back more times than I can count. So, what were you doing out here?"

"Sightseeing," Darcy said quickly.

"Date," Wade added. "We were on a sightseeing date."

Aaron looked all around. "With your family and a sheriff and a sheriff's deputy?"

"We're all very close," Darcy said with a bright smile as they bobbed in the water.

Aaron shook his head clearly in disbelief. "Whatever floats your boat."

"Aaron, you need a lift?"

"Yes, sir," Aaron called out to the boat as they helped hoist him up. "Looking forward to seeing you on dry land." Aaron winked at her and Darcy laughed again.

"Let's get you to a hospital. We can get matching stitches," Wade said.

"No. We can't go. Not yet."

"Why not?" Wade asked as he treaded water with her in his arms.

Darcy leaned forward and pressed her lips to his ear. "I found it."

32

"*It, it?*" Wade asked as Darcy practically bounced with excitement.

"I think so. I have to see if it's really the one."

"Okay, then let's do it." Darcy thanked her lucky stars that Wade understood. "Kord, help us up."

Wade hefted Darcy up so Kord could bend over, grab her by the arms, and haul her out of the water. When she was on deck, Kord gave Wade a hand up. "Nearest hospital?"

"Nope," Wade told him. "Get us back to Ryker's boat."

"That was a badass water takedown," Kord said as he drove the boat to join the others.

"We do learn water combat. Something I'm very happy I learned."

Ridge reached out and grabbed the rope Wade tossed and tied them off to Ryker's boat again. Ryker was using buckets of water to wash the blood from his deck.

"I'm getting a new boat," he muttered.

"It's not death cooties," Wade pointed out.

"It's close enough. Are you two okay?"

"I need to fix up Darcy's shoulder," Wade answered as they climbed onto Ryker's boat.

"Here you go," Harper said, handing over the first-aid kit.

Wade cleaned out her wound as the others all formed a circle of boats around them. They left a space for Granger who was dealing with the Coast Guard and actively pointing to Wade who just waved to them and went back to bandaging her wound.

"Yoo-hoo!"

Darcy looked up to see Suze and Clark Bell on a luxury yacht with Reverend Winston, Miss Winnie, and Miss Ruby.

"What happened?" Suze called out as they pulled their yacht into a spot next to Maggie and Gage's speedboat. Granger and his police boat were out of luck now.

"Wade's a badass," Kord called out.

"I believe it was Darcy who shot that man with a flare gun," Harper added as the two of them filled the new arrivals in on what went down.

"All set," Wade whispered into her ear. "Now, how do we get rid of everyone?"

"We don't. They're all a part of this and deserve to be here if what I felt was really Black Law's ship." Darcy had hidden her research and her life's work for twelve years. She was done hiding it. She was done being worried about failing. She had friends who would celebrate with her if it was there and get her drunk enough to forget if it wasn't.

"Y'all, seriously? I had to deal with the Coasties, and you don't save me a spot?" Granger pulled up behind Maggie and Gage who helped him tie off before he jumped onto their boat.

"You snooze you lose," Miss Winnie called out. "Now, are we just gonna sit here? I did bring provisions. I have brownies, pies, and even put a couple of casseroles in Suze's onboard oven to keep warm."

Darcy held Wade's hand as she leaned against him and smiled. This was where she was always meant to belong. "I think I might have found it. I felt it under my feet, but Wade and I need to go down to see if it's actually something and not a rock."

"Then get down there! You can't leave us in suspense like this," Ridge only half-joked as he hefted an oxygen tank and helped Darcy get it on.

"And take this!" Gage called out. He handed it to Maggie who handed it to Gator, who handed it to Trent, who handed it to Ryker, who handed it to Wade. "It's a waterproof video camera with a light attached to goggles. Just in case it is what you're looking for you will want to preserve the find."

"That's a great idea. And if I'm wrong, we can all watch it while I eat all the brownies by myself," Darcy called out as she watched Wade turn on the camera and pull it onto his face.

"Dear Lord," Reverend Winston began as everyone bowed their heads in prayer. "May you guide Darcy and Wade on their quest and keep them safe. And Lord, will you protect the brownies from Turtle's munchies so Darcy may eat them in joyous celebration."

"Amen," everyone said as Darcy battled to keep the laughter from spilling out.

She pulled her mask down and jumped into the water. This time there were no nerves. There was no jumpiness or fear. Wade motioned for her to take the lead as she confidently dove straight to the site. She counted off the flags to the eighth row. Then she turned up the row and counted them off—one, two, three, four.

Darcy turned and found Wade holding her weighted belt, the metal detector, and her bag. They had all been dropped in her fight with Hugo. She gave him the thumbs-up signal and held out her arms. He handed her the bag and metal detector and clipped the weights around her waist to help with the proper weight for the best scuba dive.

Darcy held out her hand and Wade reached over to take it. He gave her an encouraging squeeze and then dropped his hand so she could turn on the metal detector. The current had smoothed over the divot she'd made with her feet, but she knew she was in the right spot. Taking a deep breath, she moved the metal detector over the spot she'd felt something under the sand.

She didn't even need her submersible headphones to hear the detector going off. Her metal detector had gone crazy. Darcy tried to tell herself it could be a beer can. But she didn't have a simple hobby wand. This was a professional, heavy duty, thousands of dollars type metal detector, and she could tell from the tone of the pinging that it wasn't aluminum under them.

She unhooked the detector from her arm and reached into her bag. She grabbed two tools to help dig. He motioned for her to lead and she did. She used her tool, which was a small shovel with blunt edges to prevent harming anything under the sand, to take away layer upon layer of dirt. As soon as Wade saw what she was doing, he took a spot a couple of feet away and began doing the same.

At first, her emotional high fell, and as the mountain of sand she was moving began to pile up, she thought she might have been mistaken all along. Darcy was beginning to seriously doubt herself when her tool hit something solid. She looked up to get Wade's attention, but he was busy digging. She waved and caught his attention and he began to swim toward her.

Okay, Darcy. This is it.

She took a deep breath and began to carefully excavate the area. Finally, with her heart beating wildly, she dropped her tool and used her hands to brush off the sand. A cannon portal. That's what triggered the metal detector. Darcy sat frozen as she stared at the side of the ship lying on the bed of the ocean. She'd found a ship exactly where Timothy Longworth had said it would be. She'd done it. She'd found Black Law's ship!

She looked up as her heart pounded and her head floated with disbelief, joy, and excitement. Wade wrapped her in a hug and she gave in to the feelings. Finally, Wade pulled back, and she had to get into archaeology mode. She needed to flag the site so she'd know where everything was. Then she'd take the video evidence to court, claim the wreck, and begin to truly excavate it.

Wade gave her a thumbs-up and then swam away from her. Every twenty feet or so, he'd stop, dig hard and fast, then swim some more.

Darcy pulled out her bag, wrote on a flag, and planted it. She took a deep breath as she began to mentally map the ship. It was then that she noticed she couldn't see Wade anymore. Darcy picked up her metal detector and bag before following the path she'd seen him take. Her detector went crazy again and she stopped at the first hole he'd dug. Another cannon portal. She marked a second flag and planted it. She looked around and still couldn't see Wade.

Darcy began to worry as she swam after him. But then she saw another exposed portal. The archaeologist in her took control as she quickly tagged it again and then again when she found he'd dug another up.

Ahead the water darkened and she knew the depths were going to increase. Darcy swam forward nervously, wishing she could call out to him. She took a deep breath and told herself not to be scared as she went to dive deeper and froze. It wasn't much deeper, maybe ten feet, and there at the bottom was Wade. And he was frantically shoveling. What? Wait. Darcy turned her head to see how far she'd swum. Around a hundred feet. Pirate ships during that time were one hundred to one hundred and twenty-five feet and around twenty to twenty-five feet wide. Which meant . . . Wade had found one of the ends of the ship.

Darcy dove down and felt her eyes fill with happy tears. The aft of the boat was partially exposed. The current had covered the rest of the ship but flowed over the aft instead of against it, leaving about half of the aft visible. She could see part of the captain's quarters and the rudder. And where Wade was digging frantically into the sand under the rudder was where the cargo hold would be.

Wade looked up and motioned for her to join him. Darcy turned on the metal detector and heard a sound she never dreamed she'd hear. The pulse was different from the cannon. This time there were many different pulses indicating many different metals were beneath the sand.

She looked up at him and dropped the metal detector. Together they dug. She was using more oxygen that she should, but she couldn't help it, but then they both stopped. Boards were missing. It's why the ship had sunk. She and Wade looked at each other and with a nod, they used both hands and shoveled handfuls of sand away. A hole big enough for a teenage boy to swim through opened up. As Wade dug frantically, Darcy reached into her bag for a strong flashlight. She flipped it on and tapped Wade's shoulder, then pointed to his camera. He held her left hand as they both leaned their faces into the small opening they had managed to dig out. At first, they couldn't see anything, but then Darcy wedged the flashlight in.

Her breath caught. Trunks as far as she could see. They had tumbled down during the sinking and were lying on the side of the ship that now served as the bottom. There were so many trunks that they reached past her and she had to look up to see the rest of them.

Wade tapped her on her arm and asked for the flashlight. He slowly scanned the area and then pointed for her to go inside. Darcy couldn't tell if time stopped or time sped up. But with her adrenaline pumping, they cleared a space large enough for her to fit through, but only if she took off her oxygen tank.

Wade removed his mask and handed it to her. Darcy gave him hers and once their new masks were secure she unhooked her tank. Wade held it for her and handed her a knife. In one hand, she held her knife, in the other, the flashlight. Darcy took several calming breaths and then exhaled fully before taking a deep breath, filling her lungs to capacity.

She looked once more at Wade, who gave her a nod of encouragement. Darcy turned toward the small opening and fit her arms through first. She had to maneuver her shoulders carefully and painfully through the opening as the old wood scraped against her wetsuit but finally, almost with a pop, she was through.

Darcy gave Wade a thumbs-up and slowly swam through the cargo hold. She counted all the trunks she could see and headed back to him. He pushed her mouthpiece through and she took some deep breaths as she held up her hands to indicate the number of trunks. Wade clapped in excitement and took back the oxygen as she dove back in.

Darcy headed for the nearest trunk and tried to open it. It still held tight, but she used the knife to hammer at the lock. It gave way and sank to the bottom of the boat. Darcy should go back for another breath, but she was too excited. She had to use both hands to push open the lid and then she just stared.

Darcy wedged the flashlight into her armpit and used one hand to hold open the trunk. The light showed across an entire chest filled with gold coins. Gold coins that matched the one coin Timothy had left with his note. Darcy heard a thumping noise and turned to see Wade's arm sticking through the narrow hole with her bag in hand.

Darcy slowly let the lid close before grabbing the bag, taking a full breath of air, and heading back to the trunk. She pushed it open again and carefully counted out fifty coins. She placed them in her bag and then put one of her GPS chips with her personally marked flag inside the trunk. Darcy then made sure the lid to the trunk was securely closed. She had a claim to make.

Darcy swam back to the opening, took another breath as she handed the bag to Wade, and then crawled her way through the hole. Wade had worked on opening it some more and it wasn't nearly as painful as getting in. He helped her put on the oxygen and then she reached into the bag and showed him a gold coin. He wrapped his arms around her and spun her in the water.

She pointed upward and they swam for the surface hand in hand. The second they surfaced, she screamed and flung her arms around him. They were well outside the ring of boats, but when she screamed with joy they heard the calls from their friends.

"You did it! That was unreal. Absolutely unreal!" Wade tossed his head back and howled with excitement.

"Did you find it?" they heard Harper yell.

"Ryker!" Darcy yelled as she laughed. Wade held her in his arms, and she was glad that he did. Otherwise, she might have floated off to cloud nine.

"Yes?"

"What time is it?" Darcy yelled back.

"Four, why?"

"Call Olivia and have her meet us at the United States District Courthouse with a petition to claim Black Law's sunken ship and treasure!"

There were cheers from the boats as Wade kissed her hard and fast. "We have to get going. The courts close in thirty minutes."

He and Darcy swam to the boats as they started up. Their friends were still cheering as Darcy and Wade climbed aboard. She emptied out the bag and everyone gasped. She took pictures and emailed them to Olivia.

"Give me the camera," Gage told her as he hopped from boat to boat. "I can upload it and email the relevant parts to your lawyer before we even get there and put the whole thing on a flash drive."

"Yes, please." Darcy handed him the camera and he hopped boats until his dad helped him back onto the yacht.

"Talk to Olivia," Ryker said, shoving the phone at her as boats began to untie from each other.

"I found it!" Darcy yelled into the phone.

"What, when, where, and how?" Olivia asked.

Darcy rattled off the answers and even sent the GPS location of the chip inside the trunk.

"How fast can you get here?" Olivia was completely

unfazed by the fact the largest treasure ever found had just been recovered by her client.

"How fast can we get to the courthouse?"

"Fast," Ryker said as he took control of his boat. "And I'm driving!"

Ryker called out to Kord to stay put and guard the site until he got back. "Granger, how about calling in your buddies in Charleston and have them look the other way at a boat speeding through the harbor?"

"You're seriously overestimating my pull," Granger called back. I can try to give you a police escort, but I have a feeling you'll be going faster than I can."

"Damn right. Tell Olivia she'll also need to make sure I'm not arrested." Ryker looked at them as Darcy relayed the message and hung up. "Hold on."

33

RYKER SMILED, and Darcy grabbed the nearest seat as Wade pinned her in with an arm. Ryker shot off and there was no holding back. He went full throttle and shot across the water and waves at well over fifty knots. Darcy heard his laughter being ripped through the air as he pressed his boat to the brink. He covered the miles in minutes and didn't slow down much as he raced through the harbor, weaving in and out of traffic. People were yelling at him, flicking him off, and cursing, but Ryker didn't slow.

Darcy heard sirens and Wade shook his head. "Harbor Patrol!" Wade yelled. Ryker just laughed and whipped around a boat full of tourists heading to Fort Sumter.

"Hang on!" Ryker called back as he sped around Castle Pinckney on Shutes Folly Island and headed straight for shore. He blew by yachts and boats as he practically slid into the closest open slip at the fancy marina. There was a decorative sign that read "Yacht Club."

"Are you a member here?" Darcy asked as a teenager dressed in white slacks and a white polo ran toward them.

Ryker just looked at her.

"Of course you are."

"Mr. Faulkner," the boy called out. "Your slot is over there. I'm happy to move the boat for you."

"Thanks," Ryker said, leaving the engine running as the boy secured the boat enough for them to get off. Ryker pressed a bill into the boy's hand before they sped off on foot. "The courthouse is up Broad Street. It's maybe a half a mile to three quarters of a mile from here."

"What time is it?" Darcy asked again. Her phone was in her bag but Ryker still wore a watch.

"Four ten."

"We have to move then," Darcy said, pulling up her bag and taking off at a run. She was still barefoot and in her wetsuit, but that didn't stop her or Wade, who was similarly dressed.

Ryker took the lead as he effortlessly ran in suit pants, a button-up dress shirt, and leather loafers. He had taken off the bachelor apparel as soon as Hugo and Cash had been caught.

"It's right this way," he called out as shouts began to sound from behind them.

Darcy looked back and saw two police officers chasing after them. "Um, Ryker, police. I don't think they appreciated your driving as much as I did."

"No problem," he said with a grin and no heavy breathing.

Darcy looked up Broad Street. Office workers were sneaking out of work a couple of minutes early, and Olivia was standing there tapping one foot.

"Hurry up!" she yelled down the street.

Darcy dragged in a ragged breath. Her feet hurt and were probably bleeding. And that wasn't counting the sharp pain in her shoulder now. Wade similarly looked in pain as he grimaced with every footfall.

"Officers, call an ambulance!" Olivia ordered in a voice no one should dare refuse. Darcy didn't turn around but heard the officer's radio squawk. The police were closing in on them . . . *they* had shoes.

"Judge!" Olivia called out. "You can't leave yet. Here are my clients. I have an emergency petition."

An older man had a briefcase in hand and was pinned on the bottom step by Olivia. Wade grabbed Darcy's hand and Darcy dug deep to run harder.

The judge had a fluffy gray mustache and bushy eyebrows. As he looked down the street at them, his eyes widened when he saw them in wetsuits and bare feet.

"My clients have been attacked, beaten, and stabbed as rivals tried to murder them just moments ago. This is a discovery of a lifetime, and your honor will want his name on it," Olivia argued as Ryker slid to a stop in front of the judge.

"Your honor, I'm Ryker Faulkner. Please listen to this petition."

Darcy slammed to a stop, her feet throbbing as she leaned on Wade and he leaned on her.

"What is this all about?" the judge demanded before turning to Ryker. "Faulkner Shipping? How are you involved?"

"It started with a guy dying on my boat and only gets more interesting from there," Ryker said. "And the only way you'll get the full story as to why someone tried to kill my cousin and his girlfriend, why police are chasing us, and what's in that bag is if you hear the petition."

An older woman started down the steps as the judge turned to take them all in. "Well, if I'm going to be late for golf I might as well get a good story out of it. Open up the courtroom, Clara. We have an emergency petition to hear."

"She's the clerk," Olivia whispered to them.

"Sir, we need to talk about your boat driving," an officer said, interrupting them.

"Y'all come too. We'll take care of this in one fell swoop," the judge said.

"It's local, your honor," he said a moment before Detective Chambers slid to a stop, sirens sounding.

"Shit on a cracker," Olivia mumbled as Chambers and Gerald Hemmings got out of the cruiser.

"We need to be heard, your honor!" Gerald yelled as they jogged over to the courthouse steps.

"Everyone into my courtroom. We'll get this all sorted out. Clara, call the club and tell them I'm running late."

The whole group filed into the courtroom as Clara turned on all the lights and video recording equipment. The door was flung open as another attorney ran into the room. "I object!"

"Stan, there's nothing to object to yet," the judge said with an eye roll.

"He's the assistant United States attorney," Olivia told her a second before the doors opened and nearly everyone from Shadows Landing rushed in.

Gage handed Darcy the flash drive before taking a seat. "Here's the video evidence," Darcy whispered to Olivia as she handed her the device.

The judge slipped into his robe but didn't bother zipping it before banging his gavel. "The court is in session. We're hearing an emergency petition for . . . Miss Townsend, what are we all here for?"

"My client, Miss Darcy Delmar, is here to petition for the rights to a three hundred year old abandoned shipwreck under the Law of Finds. She asks the court to assert jurisdiction and control of the wreck and to then award her sole rights to said wreck in its entirety."

"I object!" Stan and Gerald both said.

"Stan?"

"It's federal property and the federal government should control all rights to any wrecks found."

"And who are you?" the judge asked Gerald as Darcy held tightly to Wade's hand.

"Gerald Hemmings, attorney for the county. We claim the right to the wreck as it is in state-owned waters."

"Miss Townsend?"

Olivia smiled and Darcy knew right then they'd won. She showed the GPS tracker active inside the ship and cited so many laws and cases Darcy's head was spinning.

"It's clear the wreck is outside the state's jurisdiction," the judge ruled. "Mr. Hemmings, you're dismissed. Is this a war ship or a ship that belonged in any way to the government?"

"No, sir." Olivia smiled again and sent Stan, the U.S. Assistant Attorney, slinking away after systematically dismantling every argument he had or could have before he'd even made them.

"So, what is this ship and how do you know it's abandoned?" the judge asked.

"You're up," Olivia whispered to her.

Darcy reached into her bag and emptied the fifty gold coins onto the table.

"Holy mackerel. This was worth missing my tee time," the judge said as even Stan and Gerald approached wide-eyed to see. Detective Chambers, the police officers, the clerk, and everyone else did, too.

"Your honor, I found the wreck of the ship belonging to

Captain Lawrence Stringer that sunk in 1719. Captain Stringer is better known as the pirate Black Law. Inside was a dowry belonging to a Spanish lord. He was killed three centuries ago and the dowry seized by Black Law. While there may have been some attempt at locating the ship three hundred years ago, there has not been any effort by either the lord's family, Spain, or any of Black Law's family for at least one hundred fifty years. Therefore, the ship should be judged to be abandoned and all rights to the find given to me."

"And there's more of this inside?"

"Yes, which is why I need an order to show my rights to the ship so I may hire full-time guards to enforce those rights."

"Your honor," Stan tried again. "When she's pulling Spanish gold up, you can bet Spain will want it. That's why the rights should belong to the United States."

"Nice try, but I have my ruling. The wrecked ship did not belong to Spain. In fact, the owner of the wrecked ship was domiciled in South Carolina. Shadows Landing, if my pirate history is correct. A private Spanish citizen freely took the gold onboard his private ship and left Spain. Therefore, Spain has no claim to it. Further, while the wreck is outside of state waters, it is still well within the United States' waters." The judge held up his finger to stop Stan from speaking. "But as I ruled earlier, this is not a government ship of any kind, with no U.S. government merchandise onboard. Therefore, I declare salvage rights to Miss Delmar for sixty days. During those sixty days, Miss Townsend, you will run worldwide notices about the find and asking anyone with a documented claim to submit them to the court. I will hear any legitimate claims coming forward sixty days from now in this court. If they prove to have a claim to the ship and its contents, they must prove active salvaging and searching attempts before they would be awarded any claim. If none are found, I will rule the ship abandoned and award all rights to it and its contents to Miss Delmar under the Law of Finds."

The judge rapped his gavel and hurried down from the bench. "Can I take a picture?" Darcy was shaking but she nodded her head. The judge handed his phone to Olivia who took a picture of him with his hands in the gold. "Thanks. I can't wait to rub it in Judge Sylvina's face at golf today. He thinks he gets all the good cases."

"You know we'll appeal," Stan grumbled.

"Go ahead, but you know as well as I do that my ruling followed the law. Congratulations, young lady. I'll see you in sixty days. Good luck."

Darcy shook his hand, and then it was over. She had rights to the ship . . . for now.

34

SIXTY DAYS. It didn't sound like much but it all had been a nonstop whirlwind of activity. Wade and Darcy had been taken to the hospital after the hearing. Ryker paid a fine for speeding through the harbor. Olivia was being flooded by claims, although, according to her, they were all going to be tossed. And for the rest of that week, Wade had helped Darcy excavate the ship.

He had had to go back to work, but thanks to a loan from Darcy's financial backer, one Ryker Faulkner, she was able to hire full-time security for the site and a PR firm to handle the press so she could focus completely on the excavation. She was borrowing a warehouse on Ryker's shipping grounds to store the treasure she brought up. Ryker had offered to hire her a team to help, but she wanted to use only trusted friends.

So, whenever Wade had days off, he and Aaron helped out with Darcy's full-time team of Gator, Skeeter, and Turtle. And after sixty days, all of the trunks had been transported to the warehouse. They'd only gone through a quarter of them. Each item was cleaned, photographed, weighed, measured, and cataloged. As of that moment, it was going to be over a billion dollars' worth of treasure. To help with the cleaning and cataloging, Darcy had invited in students and experts who leaped at a chance to work the discovery of a lifetime.

But every night Darcy came home to Wade. Fifty-nine nights and today was the sixtieth day, and he wouldn't trade a single minute of it. He'd never been happier and with all his being he knew today would be the best yet, hands down.

Wade slipped his hand into Darcy's as they followed Olivia up the stairs to the courthouse. His family and their friends trailed behind them as the press lined both sides of the steps. Olivia had told them she'd reviewed all the claims and none could prove they'd been actively searching or trying to salvage the ship, and she had every reason to believe the judge would assign full rights to Darcy.

It had been a learning curve for sure. It wasn't every day Spanish diplomats were trying to come after your discovery or that the president of the United States came for a visit. President Stratton and his wife, First Lady Tate Stratton, both dove the site and examined the treasure. He also told Spain in the nicest way possible they had no shot at claiming the treasure as theirs. However, he and Darcy had worked out a deal to sell a portion of the treasure to Spain for their museums, but only if she were awarded full rights. Wade shook his head as he remembered a fifty-million-dollar pledge being signed on his kitchen table with the president and the Spanish ambassador. After the ambassador left, Darcy and President Stratton had agreed to set up a traveling exhibit to hit the top museums in the United States free of charge in exchange for President Stratton barring any international claims to the treasure.

Shadows Landing was also getting used to the media

circus. It was great for tourism and the economy. But the locals were getting worn out from the constant attention. They were all ready for a break, but today was not that day.

Wade was glad when he and Darcy entered the courthouse until he heard Gator's booming voice. Wade turned to see Gator, dressed up with a collared shirt under his overalls, pointing at his South Carolina Cocks hat and screaming, "Go Cocks!"

Locals cheered for the University of South Carolina Gamecocks. Others blushed. Darcy laughed.

"Are you nervous?" Wade asked as they entered the packed courtroom.

"Very," Darcy said. "But thank you for last night. I was definitely not thinking about the hearing."

"It was my pleasure," Wade whispered against her ear.

"No, it was all mine." Darcy winked at him and followed Olivia to the defendant's table.

Wade took a seat next to his brother, Trent, and cousin, Ridge. "Are you both ready?" Wade asked them.

"We got this," Trent said as Ridge winked.

The judge came out and took his seat. He was trying to look serious, but Wade could see how excited he was, too.

"There were no claims of merit submitted to this court. I hereby rule that the sunken ship once belonging to the pirate known as Black Law is abandoned. Per the Law of Finds, all rights are hereby granted to Darcy Delmar in full." The judge slammed his gavel down as everyone erupted in cheers, clapping, and excited talking.

Darcy hugged Olivia and all of Wade's family, who over the past couple months had also become her family. Once all the celebratory embraces were done, Darcy leaped into his arms. He swung her around and kissed her. Cameras clicked, but he didn't care. She was his heart.

"They want you to make a statement," Olivia said as she looked over at the crowd of reporters.

"Not yet. Tell them I'll hold a press conference next week. Or, better yet, find one person for me to give an interview."

"Why don't you talk to them?" Wade asked. Olivia perked up.

"That would be great," Darcy said, reaching out to take Olivia's hand in hers. "Would you do that for me?"

"Of course," she said as she straightened her jacket. "What will you be doing?"

"Sneaking out the back," Wade said with a grin. "Come on. Let's go home."

"WHY ARE we going into the backyard?" Darcy asked. "I thought you promised me a quiet afternoon at home. Besides, I have a surprise for you before dinner and I was really hoping we could find a way to *relax* before we leave."

"Well, I guess I wasn't the only one keeping secrets. A surprise for me?"

"Yes," Darcy said. It was really hard not to tell him, but she wanted to show him instead.

"Well, I have a surprise for you, too. Close your eyes."

Darcy closed her eyes and Wade came up behind her and placed his hands over hers to make sure she wasn't peeking. "Do I hear water?"

"Maybe."

She kept walking as Wade steered her. She definitely heard the sound of running water. "Surprise!"

Wade took his hands away and Darcy gasped. There was a small pond lined with rock. A small fountain was in the middle. Behind it was an arbor with a swinging bench under it. Freshly painted white by the smell of it.

"When did you do this?"

"Ridge and Trent put it together when I made us leave early for lunch before the hearing."

"Oh my gosh. It's so beautiful!" Darcy turned and hugged Wade. She relaxed instantly into him. He was her other half.

"Take a closer look." Wade pulled away and led her over to look at the pond.

Darcy laughed so hard she thought she'd double over. Under the water were fake gold coins and pearl necklaces. There was even a sunken ship that the goldfish could swim through. And then from the grasses came a motorized speedboat and Darcy laughed again. She had never known a time when she'd been so happy.

"It's perfect! Wade, I love . . . what's that?" Darcy bent forward. There was something in the boat coming right for her.

Darcy bent as the boat slowed and gasped, "Wade!"

When she turned, she found Wade on one knee. He leaned into the boat and pulled out the diamond ring. "My life started when I pulled you from the water. I love how you can solve riddles faster than anyone I know. I love that we laugh and love with our whole hearts. You are my better half, my one true love, and the only thing that could make me more complete is if you were my wife." Wade looked up at her and held up the ring. "Darcy, will you marry me?"

"Yes!" The word was out so fast she and Wade laughed as he slipped the ring onto her finger. He rose up and captured her lips with his. "I love you, Wade."

"And I love you, Darcy."

"I'm afraid I can't beat your surprise," she said, giggling.

"Why don't you try?" Wade winked and Darcy threw herself into his arms again. "Then come with me."

She led him down the street and onto Main Street. "Well, this isn't the surprise I thought."

"Did you think it was something from that book you saw me looking at the other day?"

"Maybe," Wade said with a grin.

"That's for later tonight. First, I want to show you this."

Wade looked up at the building. "The antique store? You want to go shopping?"

"Look at the door."

They both stepped closer. "Future home of the Shadows Landing Delmar Museum," Wade read.

"You're going to put your museum here?"

"What do you think?" Darcy asked nervously.

"That it's as perfect as you are!" Wade kissed her again as friends walked by calling out their hellos. She was home in his arms and home in Shadows Landing.

EPILOGUE

ONE MONTH LATER ...

"ARE you seriously not going to bid on your very-soon-to-be-groom?" Harper asked her.

"I think it's great. Make sure he knows he's lucky to get you."

"Thank you, Great-Aunt Marcy," Darcy said with a smile. They all turned and looked up at the stage.

Maggie motioned for Wade to turn around. "Bachelor number eighteen is a rescue swimmer with the Coast Guard and is known for not only saving lives but finding a woman's treasure. Bidding starts at one hundred dollars."

Darcy turned bright red. Great-Aunt Marcy snickered. Suze rolled her eyes.

"I'll bid one hundred."

"Ellery," Darcy said, shaking her head. "Do not pity bid my fiancé. He can get his own bids."

"Five hundred!" a voice called out from the crowd.

"Who's that?" Darcy asked as Ellery tried to stop from laughing.

"That's my friend Tibbie. She loves a man in uniform. Don't worry, that's her husband of sixty years next to her."

"Oh, I'm not worried. I think it's great."

Darcy watched as a bidding war broke out between some of the high society of Charleston, and that was before the younger socialites got into it.

"Now I would worry," Ellery whispered. "That girl thinks because Daddy has money she owns everything and everyone."

"Six thousand dollars going once," Maggie called out.

"Fine," Darcy said with a roll of her eyes. "Ten thousand dollars," she called out.

Wade grinned and started unbuttoning his dress uniform shirt.

"Fifteen thousand," the socialite yelled out.

"Look, I have a bachelorette party to go to, so let's end this," Darcy said loudly. "Fifty thousand."

"Sold!" Maggie said, slamming the gavel down. "And I will accept payment in gold."

"Good, 'cause that's all I've got," Darcy laughed as Wade jumped off the stage and kissed her rather deeply in front of everyone.

"What kind of date do you want me to take you on?" he asked.

"How about one to the church tomorrow at say, six o'clock?"

"You got yourself a date. Have fun with the girls tonight. And watch Aunt Annie and Aunt Paige. Don't let them shoot anything. And *don't* let Cousin Greer talk you into wrestling an alligator."

"Hey, your Keeneston family doesn't come to town every

day. I can't deny them the simple pleasures of Shadows Landing. Besides, I'm pretty sure your uncles and cousins have something planned by the way they're literally all standing by the door. Uncle Cy just opened the door and is standing there waiting."

"We have to wait for Ridge. He's up now. Then we're outta here, and I promise to behave."

"Don't promise that because then I'll have to promise to behave."

"Ridge Faulkner is the owner of Ridge Builders Company. He's been featured across the world in architectural magazines for his houses," Maggie said.

"Fine," Wade said, drawing attention back to her. "As long as we don't behave together, we're good."

"Deal."

"Five thousand. Sold!" Maggie called out.

"Hey, who just bought Ridge?" Trent asked as they watched Ridge talk to a redhead dressed to perfection.

"I don't know," Wade responded. But then Ridge nodded and shook the redhead's hand.

"Come on, Ridge!" Gavin called out.

Ridge jogged over to them and kissed Darcy's cheek. "Have fun. Did Wade warn you not to give Aunt Paige or Aunt Annie a gun?"

"Yes, and no gator wrangling either. So basically no fun at all," Darcy said sarcastically.

"Who bought you?" Trent asked as they headed to leave.

"Someone named Savannah Ambrose. She bought me to get me to fix things at her house. Apparently, she just moved here permanently," Ridge said before being swept up by his male relatives.

"I'll see you at the church tomorrow," Wade said before kissing her. "I can't wait to start our forever."

"Me too. I love you."

"I love you, too."

WADE STOOD by his wife's side the next night as she held a large pair of scissors. "We've come a long way since he hauled me from the water thinking I'd murdered someone," Darcy called out to their wedding guests.

The service had been beautiful. His wife had walked down the aisle, her curly hair loose around her shoulders under a veil secured by a tiara she'd found in Black Law's treasure.

To avoid any media, the town had been shut down. The roads had been closed and police from Charleston were making sure no one but residents was able to get in that night. The doors to the church were open wide and the fall breeze swept inside as Reverend Winston had held up the chalice for them to drink from—a chalice that was solid gold and encrusted with emeralds. The chalice had been part of the donation made to the church from Darcy. She'd also donated three new daggers, six cutlasses, and a blunderbuss gun.

"You all were by our side through hunting the treasure, finding it, raising it, logging it, and now you will be the first to see it in its new home here in Shadows Landing. Wade and I can't thank you enough for all you've done for us. Your friendship and kindness will never be forgotten. And, Miss Winnie, we're really sorry we shot the statue in your back garden from Suze's yacht last night. Someone gave my new Aunt Annie a gun, and she thought it was a burglar. But, back to now. My husband and I are proud to welcome you to the new Shadows Landing Delmar-Faulkner Museum."

His wife turned to him and smiled, and Wade knew pure happiness. He placed his hands over hers on the scissors and together they cut the ribbon in front of the museum. The doors were opened, the music began to play, and they celebrated their life-to-come surrounded by everything that had brought them together.

RIDGE WALKED around the museum as couples danced. Rubies, emeralds, and diamonds, each worth a fortune on their own, were on display behind bulletproof glass. Ryker had worked with a specialty company to design the security while Darcy had asked Ridge and Trent to help on the inside.

"I read that you built this display with your cousin."

The soft Southern voice had him turning around. "Yes. You." Smooth, real smooth, he thought. "You bought me last night. Was our date for tonight?"

"Savannah, and no. I'm just here to see the museum and give my best to the newlyweds. I'm hoping to put in my application to work here."

"That's right. You told me you just moved here. Well, would you like this to be our date?" Ridge certainly would. Savannah Ambrose was stunning. She was quiet, composed, and had the smoothest skin that he wanted nothing more than to kiss. Of course, she didn't look like the type to go for men who worked with their hands for a living. Ridge tucked his callused hands behind his back.

"Oh, I wasn't joking about our date being a working date at my house. I know nothing about houses, and now I have one of my own and I need help."

Of course she did. Women like Savannah didn't look at men like him as anything other than help. It didn't matter that he was one of the top builders billionaires hired to build their houses. He was still a man with a hammer.

"But a dance would be nice," she said so softly he almost missed it.

Ridge offered her his arm and escorted her to the dance floor. They didn't talk as they swayed to the music. When it was over, Ridge reluctantly let her go. "How's Monday morning?" Savannah asked, pulling out a card with her address on it.

"I'll see you then."

Ridge watched her head over to introduce herself to Darcy and Wade and almost jumped when Gavin's hand came down onto his shoulder. Ridge turned and saw his Shadows Landing and Keeneston cousins as well as his uncles all grinning at him.

"What?" Ridge asked.

"Well, since we did so well betting on Wade getting married, I'm willing to try it again," Ryker said, pulling out a twenty-dollar bill. "Ridge is next."

"You have to be more specific than that," Walker Greene, Edie's brother who was married to Layne Davies, one of Ridge's Keeneston cousins, said.

"Well, how specific?" Trent asked, pulling out his own twenty.

"To the day gets the biggest payout," Uncle Miles told them.

"Like, I won a bet last night that my wife would shoot something," Uncle Cade said. "But I would have lost if someone else said a statue. So, the more specific the bet, the better the payout."

"Hmm," Ryker said as he crossed his arms and stared at Ridge. "Gavin surprised us by moving so fast. Wade was more in line with what I thought. You're way more like Wade. However, you are Tinsley's brother."

"What does that have to do with it?" Ridge asked, getting annoyed they were all betting on him to be married. Now he knew what it felt like and felt bad for placing a bet against Wade. However, he'd won a hundred dollars off it so he didn't feel *too* bad about it.

"She's an artist," Uncle Cy said. "Good call on thinking about that."

"And he is artsy himself. After all, what is designing but art?" Cousin Ryan Parker said knowingly.

"Again, what does that have to do with anything?" Ridge asked.

"Artists can be more . . . unconventional," Cousin Dylan told him. "Which could mean a shorter courtship."

There were several more discussions, but Ridge just shook his head. "Why do you think it's me next? After all, Edie is . . ."

"Edie is not whatever it is you're about to say," Walker cut in. "She's still mourning her husband's death, and I won't have anyone hurting her heart again. It's already been broken."

"Who's to say love won't heal it?" a new voice asked.

"Seriously, Nash? You kill people for a living, and you're talking about love healing a broken heart," Walker said with a roll of his eyes.

"Whatever, I think it is. Did you see the way that hot redhead looked at Ridge?" Trent jumped in, cutting off the argument over Edie's future love life.

"Twenty on two months," Ryker finally said.

Ridge had enough. He wasn't going to get married, especially to someone who only wanted him for his hammer. And unfortunately that wasn't meant figuratively, but literally.

WADE LOOKED at his wife's face as they danced. They were surrounded by friends and family and couldn't be happier.

"I'm sorry to interrupt. I'm heading home, but I wanted to introduce myself."

Wade and Darcy looked over at the redhead who had won Ridge in the auction the night before.

"I'm Savannah Ambrose. I'm going to submit my application on Monday morning to work here and just wanted to introduce myself first."

Darcy held out her hand. "Darcy Del—Faulkner," she looked at him and smiled. "I like saying that, it's just so strange to say it, though."

"I like hearing you call me husband," he whispered to her.

Savannah blushed and Wade smiled at her as he shook her hand. "Wade."

"Nice to meet you both. Anyway, congratulations. You're such a cute couple."

"I'll look over your application when we get back from the honeymoon in ten days. It's very nice meeting you and thank you for coming," Darcy told her.

"It's such a beautiful exhibit, I'm in awe. Anyway, I won't bother you any longer."

Savannah turned to leave and Wade called out to her. "Savannah, welcome to Shadows Landing."

"As much as I love it here, I'm ready to leave," Darcy told him. "How do you feel about starting our honeymoon?"

"You read my mind. I love you, wife."

"And I love you, husband."

Wade didn't wait to get home before he kissed his wife among cheers from their friends and family. For in his arms he held his present, his future, and his very own happily-ever-after.

THE END

Forever Devoted

Forever Hunted

Forever Guarded

Forever Notorious

Forever Ventured (coming later in 2019)

<u>Shadows Landing Series</u>

Saving Shadows

Sunken Shadows

Lasting Shadows (coming later in 2019)

<u>Women of Power Series</u>

Chosen for Power

Built for Power

Fashioned for Power

Destined for Power

<u>Web of Lies Series</u>

Whispered Lies

Rogue Lies

Shattered Lies

<u>Moonshine Hollow Series</u>

Moonshine & Murder

Moonshine & Malice

Moonshine & Mayhem

ABOUT THE AUTHOR

Kathleen Brooks is a New York Times, Wall Street Journal, and USA Today bestselling author. Kathleen's stories are romantic suspense featuring strong female heroines, humor, and happily-ever-afters. Her Bluegrass Series and follow-up Bluegrass Brothers Series feature small town charm with quirky characters that have captured the hearts of readers around the world.

Kathleen is an animal lover who supports rescue organizations and other non-profit organizations such as Friends and Vets Helping Pets whose goals are to protect and save our four-legged family members.

Email Notice of New Releases

https://kathleen-brooks.com/new-release-notifications

Kathleen's Website
www.kathleen-brooks.com
Facebook Page
www.facebook.com/KathleenBrooksAuthor
Twitter
www.twitter.com/BluegrassBrooks
Goodreads
www.goodreads.com

39403375R00185

Made in the USA
Lexington, KY
17 May 2019